You have a beautiful soul, Rose, a caring, loving attitude toward others and the ability to enjoy God's beauty in nature, even if it is transient. The beauty I cherish in you is eternal...like my feelings for you."

How could she reply to that? No words, no kiss, not even the tears in her eyes seemed adequate. She weakly squeezed his hand, and together they gazed across the white-topped lake. Somewhere birds chirped from their forest perches, and in the bay the wind whipped the whitecaps higher. But all Rose could hear was the even thudding of the faithful heart next to hers. She rested her head over it and listened, hearing in its strong, steady beat the rhythm of the future.

Palisades.
Pure Romance.

FICTION THAT FEATURES CREDIBLE CHARACTERS AND

ENTERTAINING PLOT LINES, WHILE CONTINUING TO UPHOLD

STRONG CHRISTIAN VALUES. FROM HIGH ADVENTURE

TO TENDER STORIES OF THE HEART, EACH PALISADES

ROMANCE IS AN UNDILUTED STORY OF LOVE,

FROM BEGINNING TO END!

A PALISADES CONTEMPORARY ROMANCE

CHERISH

CONSTANCE COLSON

PALISADES

This is a work of fiction. The characters, incidents, and dialogues are products of the author's imagination and are not to be construed as real. Any resemblance to actual events or persons, living or dead, is entirely coincidental.

CHERISH
published by Palisades
a part of the Questar publishing family

© 1995 by Constance Colson
International Standard Book Number: 0-88070-802-6

Cover illustration by George Angelini
Cover designed by David Carlson and Mona Weir-Daly
Edited by Deena Davis

Printed in the United States of America

For information:
QUESTAR PUBLISHERS, INC.
POST OFFICE BOX 1720
SISTERS, OREGON 97759

95 96 97 98 99 00 01 02 — 10 9 8 7 6 5 4 3 2 1

To Him who heals the brokenhearted.

And he himself bore our sins in his body on the cross,
that we might die to sin and
live to righteousness; for
by his wounds you were healed.

1 PETER 2:24

One

❧

Rose Anson let her gaze drift over the wide expanse of fathomless blue. Jet-skiing on Wayzata Bay and sail-boarding on crowded Lake Calhoun hadn't prepared her for the immeasurable stretch of water she now traveled. Lake of the Woods was a sea, an ocean, in comparison to the lakes she'd known in the Minneapolis-St. Paul area.

Rose clung to the *Island Wanderer's* iron deck railing and leaned far over, watching the old freighter's prow split the dark blue border waters, creating a line of silver where sunlight reflected against the spreading wake. The slender thread of water looked like a lifeline to Rose, and she held onto it with her eyes as tightly as she gripped the railing. A lifeline. Maybe that was what she'd come to northern Minnesota to find.

She straightened and watched the sparkling pockets of June sunshine shimmer on the wave's crest as she reached into her pocket to touch a folded letter. Aunt Maddie's invitation to visit her small island resort had seemed the closest answer to a prayer Rose had ever known. Despite protests from her parents and friends, Rose had accepted. A trip to the wilderness would be

11

good for her art. And maybe things would be different when she came back.

Although it had been a year since she had broken her engagement to Dr. Frederick Flaaten, Rose couldn't seem to quit thinking about him. And now, even though she was four hundred miles away from him, and moving farther as fast as the antiquated vessel could go, she still felt as though Frederick might be near, maybe watching her from the *Island Wanderer's* cabin.

Rose turned to catch the cabin boy staring at her through the big glass windshield. His hand was arrested in mid-swipe, but he quickly resumed shining the cabin's chrome when he caught the captain's warning eye.

Rose stifled an unexpected smile and faced the oncoming water, smoothing a lock of her black hair into place and listening to the rumbling rhythm of the *Island Wanderer's* engines. Rose had been on many boats before: ships, yachts, launches, and even a canoe once or twice when she and her friends paddled the shores of Lake Minnetonka, but the *Island Wanderer* was unlike any of them. It was without question the most decrepit water craft she'd ever ridden.

She marveled that the old freighter, a remnant of the fifties, still navigated the waters of Lake of the Woods more than forty years later and was the islands' main source of passenger service from the Warroad mainland. She hoped the *Wanderer* could stand just one more journey and carry her to a particular island among Lake of the Woods's fourteen thousand, an island her aunt and uncle called Singing Pines.

"Like the view?"

Rose turned to see the *Wanderer's* grizzled captain approaching. The wiry old man balanced himself carefully with the aid of the railing, bending away from the moving water as he walked. He wore trousers of sea-gray that matched the color of his vessel's deck and cabin. His long-sleeved flannel shirt was partially covered by an old down vest, and on his head at an angle sat a captain's hat. Wisps of white hair escaped from the hat and trembled with the boat's progress.

"Yes, it's a gorgeous view, Cap," Rose said, addressing him by the name Aunt Maddie used in her letters. "Aunt Maddie was right. The lake is huge! How much farther to Singing Pines?"

"More than an hour. I came to see if you'd be more comfortable in the cabin with the other passengers. It'll be some time before the sun draws enough strength to heat up the air. Maddie'll skin me if I let you catch a chill!"

When Cap finally reached Rose, he stared at her with an intensity even greater than the cabin boy's—an expression nearing disbelief. He appeared to be mulling something over in his mind. Rose was about to question him when he spoke again, gesturing toward the cabin. "It's much warmer inside."

The cold iron railing and the wind coming across the bow had made goose bumps on Rose's bare limbs, though she hadn't felt chilly until the captain's comments. She knew her silk sun dress wasn't warm enough for a dawn cruise, especially standing unprotected on the bow as she was, but she loved being on the open deck. Blue, her favorite color, surrounded her: the faint powdery blue of the sky and the deep, indigo blue of the lake. She wished she had brought her acrylic paints along. She promised herself she'd try to capture the color as soon as she got replacements. No doubt about it, this extended holiday should prove a time of growth for her art, if nothing else.

"Thanks, Cap. I'm fine. I can't tear myself away from the water."

"Yep." Cap turned his gray eyes to the horizon. "I know. I've navigated this lake thousands of times, but I never get tired of it. The deck's my favorite place, too. When my rascally mate gets his chores done, I hand him the wheel and come out here. I love to smell the lake."

He inhaled deeply and wrinkled his nose, adding more lines to an already well-weathered face. "The reeds rimming the shore, the wind on the water stirring up the pines—all smells that mean home to me." A slow smile drew the flesh of his cheeks upward. "Not even the finest perfume can compare!"

Rose agreed with Cap's assessment. A soft aroma, she would have called it, a whiff of weeds and pines, water and moist soil; a rich, earthy scent full of life.

"See that green line starboard?" Cap pointed to a string of color that cleft the blue of sky and water.

"Yes, I think so."

"That's Garden Island. We've almost crossed the open part of the lake. The big lake, we call it. Soon we'll be heading into the sheltered part of Lake of the Woods, by Singing Pines. Beyond is the Canadian section and the islands of Ontario."

Rose nodded. In her letters over the past few years, Aunt Maddie had often claimed that the American and Canadian islands together gave international Lake of the Woods sixty-five thousand miles of shoreline. Rose thought her aunt had exaggerated. But now Rose could see the lake for herself. She wondered if the islands were as fantastic as Aunt Maddie declared, full of pines, grasses, lichened rocks, berries, and wildflowers in season. Rose couldn't wait to see Singing Pines Island and the resort her aunt and uncle had built on it.

She turned to question Cap, but he was already moving away.

"I better take the wheel again," he said over his shoulder as he walked back to the cabin, using the railing to steady himself.

Rose was sorry to see him leave. She would have liked to talk with him more. Maybe he could tell her what to expect from this hinterland. Maybe he would have liked to hear a little about what had driven her here. And maybe, just maybe, he would understand what, so far, no one else had.

Alone again, Rose examined the horizon. The green strip grew wider, closer. She could make out its ragged edges, probably consisting of tall white pines or jack pines, according to what Aunt Maddie had written. The foremost tree in this isolated land was the pine. Some pines grew on the grounds of the Anson estate, lining the drive and the west side of the gardens by the fish pond, but Rose couldn't wait to step onto an entire island filled with them. What a dramatic portrait that would make! Pine green against the celestial blue of the lake!

She leaned over the railing until she could see her reflection skimming across the water, superimposed upon the silver-crested lifeline. Rose smiled at her blurry features and focused on a point of light radiating from her image. At the spot where her hand grasped the railing, a dazzling dot, bright as the sun, glowed.

Since the boat had left the dock at Warroad three hours ago, Rose had forgotten the burden on her right ring finger. She gazed at the solitaire diamond on its thick band of gold. Its facets caught the sun's rays.

Rose raised the diamond and felt the cool, cut edges on her lower lip, thinking of the man who had given it to her. The ring had first been a promise of love to come, then a comfort in the death of that love. After the break-up, Frederick had insisted she keep wearing it as a token of their long friendship. But lately the

15

ring had bothered Rose. She'd seen no evidence of Frederick's friendship for months, and the ring now felt like a mockery.

Slowly Rose slipped it off and held it between her left forefinger and thumb, turning it in the sun. The large diamond scattered light in all directions, scoring the water's surface with electric blue highlights. Rose inhaled deeply, extended her arm, and opened her fingers. When she let the ring drop, she didn't look back to see where it broke the water's surface.

"That's the strangest thing I've ever seen a woman do!"

Rose had been contemplating the water and the sudden lightness of her ring finger when she heard the voice.

She turned to see a young man grinning at her, one of his black eyebrows raised above keen, dark eyes. His face was well-tanned, and below his temples were high, full cheeks that drew in suddenly to create dramatic hollows running diagonally to his shadowed jaw. His fiery features and the white European-cut suit he wore bore the mark of the French, though his accent was clearly North American.

"What?" Rose met his stare with her own.

"Your ring," he said. "I stepped on deck just in time to see you drop it overboard. Sure you don't want Cap to turn around and try for a recovery?"

Rose shook her head and faced back to the blue water.

"Just as well. It would be almost impossible to find it anyway. Wish you'd changed your mind now?"

Her head swiveled no, and the ends of her hair shimmied across her back.

"Amazing!" He laughed, and Rose liked the rich, warm sound of it. She turned to give him a second look.

"I already got your name from Cap, so allow me to introduce myself, Rose. I'm Eric Savon. I've been waiting for you to come back inside the main cabin since we left Warroad. I finally realized you were determined to stay out here, and I decided I'd better come out myself, even if it is freezing."

He took her hand in his. Rose noticed that he wore on his index finger a large gold ring of quite good quality, molded into some kind of design.

Eric took his hand away. "Thinking of throwing my ring into the lake, too?" He smiled, his black eyes bright. "You have me interested, Rose. Most women I've known wear their jewels like trophies, and here you are, tossing yours into the lake. Maybe you'd like to tell me why you did it."

Rose was almost tempted to unburden herself, but she turned back to the horizon. "Explaining that would take more than the hour I have left."

She looked toward the dots of green emerging past Garden Island. The pines on the islands were beginning to lengthen in the distance; the islands themselves beginning to spread. "My destination is just ahead, Singing Pines Island Resort. Do you know it?"

"Yes." He smiled warmly. "Rose, I haven't had a good talk with a beautiful woman since I came to the boondocks. If you don't mind, I'd like to spend the rest of your limited time in conversation. Any topic will do, but you know the one that interests me most. I'm a good listener," he added, bringing his hand to rest next to hers.

And so it was that, with a little more nudging, Rose found herself spilling her story to a stranger whom she supposed she would never see again.

Eric shook his head after Rose finished speaking.

"And after all that you still wore his ring?" he asked. "Now I understand why you threw it in the lake. What amazes me is how long you waited! What a fool your Dr. Fred is! How could he—"

"His name is Frederick," Rose said, still inclined to defend him.

Eric softened his tone. "I'm sorry. It's just that I can't understand...well, you did right to leave ol' Frederick behind."

"Maybe." It had seemed right at the time. Rose had wanted to get away, and Aunt Maddie and Uncle Mark's island retreat seemed as far away from civilization—and Frederick—as possible. The place was so primitive it didn't even have telephones. But the trip had been more difficult than she'd imagined, even with all Aunt Maddie's arrangements. Although the beauty around her whetted Rose's artistic appetite, she wondered if she'd made a mistake in coming.

"You did right," Eric said firmly, crossing his lean arms over his chest. When he unfolded them, one of his hands rested on her own. Rose looked at him warily, but when he continued speaking as if nothing unusual had happened, she relaxed.

Eric's words also comforted her. She had never heard Frederick criticized before, not by her acquaintances, and certainly not by her parents. And Rose's friends were too impressed by Frederick's position and wealth to utter a word against him. Eric's ideas began to revive her own doubts about Frederick. Maybe marrying him wasn't the fairy-tale ending she'd once thought. Maybe...

But Rose still felt a familiar ache in her heart.

Two

L ook at her, Mark! Just look at her!"

Rose had scarcely told Eric good-bye and descended the *Wanderer's* gangplank when Aunt Maddie's strong arms wrapped themselves around her almost tighter than was comfortable. When her aunt finally released her, Rose took a step backwards.

"Hello, Aunt Maddie." Rose recovered her smile and greeted the stocky man beside her aunt. "Hello, Uncle Mark."

"Child, you're the breathing image of—" Aunt Maddie stood holding her hands to her chin. Rose thought she saw tears rimming her eyes but couldn't be sure, for the short woman turned away to squeeze her husband's hand. When she looked back at Rose, her eyes were clear.

"Oh, Rose! Rose, darling, we're so glad you've come! You're a young lady now, but I would have recognized you anywhere. A Nichols through and through, with your dark green eyes and long raven hair—and those black eyelashes and brows. Yes, you favor your mother's side. Maybe a bit of Anson in your cheeks, rosy as your father's ever were. My dear, you're a delight!" Aunt Maddie's arms surrounded Rose once more as five whistle blasts sounded from the freighter.

"Maddie, let the poor girl breathe! You've got months to smother her. Don't ruin her wind the minute she arrives at Singing Pines." Uncle Mark put his hand on his wife's shoulder and gently pried her off her niece. Rose sent him a look of thanks.

"I'll get your baggage from Cap, Rose. He's just given the boarding signal, and he's particular about leaving on time. You two go on to the house. And Maddie," Uncle Mark said, his ruddy cheeks wrinkling in an indulgent smile, "go slowly, eh?"

Rose waved to Cap, who looked even more diminutive standing on the freighter's broad deck. Although Rose didn't expect him to see her, his thin arm moved in a slow arc of farewell. She searched the cabin windows for Eric, but he was nowhere in sight.

"Bye, Cap!" Aunt Maddie hollered. "Thanks for bringing Rose! I'll reward you with fresh rhubarb custard pie on your next trip!"

The old man waved again and walked toward the cabin to greet Mark, who was just climbing on board. Aunt Maddie rested her hand on Rose's wrist. "I'm sorry we couldn't come with the launch to pick you up ourselves, dear, but we're expecting another group of guests this morning. Mark was scheduled to guide them, but they haven't arrived yet. I hope you didn't mind. The *Wanderer* is much safer across the big lake, and I thought you'd enjoy the ride."

"I did, Aunt Maddie. And thanks for arranging everything. It all went according to your letter. I appreciate—"

"No trouble at all. I'm so thrilled you're finally here! Now, please follow me, Rose; I'll show you to your new home. Careful of the rocks. Stick behind me, and you'll be fine."

From the marina where the *Wanderer* had landed, the island rose considerably. Aunt Maddie, however, was surefooted, leaping more than walking up the steep path. She and Rose climbed until they could almost look down on the freighter.

When Rose reached a spot where the path leveled out, she slowed her pace. She thought Eric might have stayed on deck to wave to her, but the boat was moving away and the deck was empty. Eric was probably inside the cabin, Rose decided, talking with the new passengers until the boat was underway.

"Look out, Rose, you'll—"

Rose heard her aunt's words just as she took one more step off the path and met air. Down she slid into a large muddy hole, straight into the work-hardened arms of the young man digging it. His muscled arms did not afford a particularly soft landing. Rose struggled out of his grip, stood proudly, took one staggering step forward, and fell face-first into the mud.

As Aunt Maddie rushed down the path, Rose regained her footing with the man's help. She pushed him away, barely noticing his fine blond hair and pleasing features under his covering of mud. She was completely preoccupied with her own covering.

Mud dripped from her face and neck and fell in globs down her blue dress. She shook her hands, flinging clay in all directions, not caring that some splattered the laughing man next to her. His work uniform, a pair of ragged denim cut-offs, was spotted with gray like his powerful tanned legs and muscled brown chest and arms. Rose turned away and tried to climb out of the pit, but her feet slid down the wall.

"Benjamin Haralson! What have you done to my niece?" Aunt Maddie clucked in amusement. "She was fine a second ago." Maddie bent over and gave Rose an arm up as the young man assisted with a wide, firm hand on Rose's back.

Once she was on the rim of the path, Rose looked down, knowing she should thank him for his help, yet wanting to slap him for his laughter. She chose to remain silent.

He quieted as he stared at her. He seemed at a loss for words—or for wind, Rose thought. Her landing had been hard, but not that hard.

"I'm sorry." Benjamin reached up to put one hand level with the ground. "I could have called out to warn you, but I didn't realize you hadn't seen the hole until it was too late and you were—"

He looked at her so intently that Rose wondered if her landing had stunned him. Either that, or he was as starved for the sight of a young woman as the rest of the men she'd met on the lake. She was used to collecting an occasional admiring glance in the cities, but here the reception was almost overwhelming—and it was beginning to irritate her.

"Now, Benjamin, don't worry," Aunt Maddie said. "No harm done. We'll clean her up fine. You go on digging, and Mark will tell you if the hole's big enough in a few minutes. He's getting Rose's luggage. She just arrived. Cap was a bit early today or you might have had time to make a better impression. You look all right to me, though, even under the mud. Remind me of Mark in his prime, a rugged Adonis. What do you think, Rose?"

Rose averted her eyes. "I can't think of anything but getting this mud off me. Is that your lodge up there, that big log cabin?"

Maddie nodded. "That's our house—yours too, now."

"Excuse me, then. I'd like to get myself cleaned up, if you don't mind. Good-bye...and thank you," she added as an after-thought. Then she began ascending the path, shaking off mud with every step.

Maddie stared after her niece then looked down at Benjamin. "She's had a hard time of it lately, and you didn't make a splash just now, Benjamin. The nearest Rose has probably ever come to mud is when the sprinklers over-water the estate gardens. Well, I suppose we'll just have to give her time. It took me awhile to adjust, too."

Maddie rushed to catch up to her niece, leaving Benjamin to stare after them, his chin resting on the shovel handle.

Even under the mud she looks like Jesse, Benjamin thought, as he tried to stop staring at Rose's retreating figure. *Eyes deep as summer grass. Haven't seen thick, black hair like that since—* Benjamin pushed the painful memories aside, but he didn't stop looking at the graceful girl walking alongside Maddie. He watched her until she stepped delicately up the cabin steps and disappeared behind the screen door.

Rose climbed the loft stairs carefully, her gold flats balancing on the narrow wooden rungs. She felt much better after her shower and change of clothes. Maddie had ended the tour of the Winters's log cabin by inviting Rose to climb to her room.

Realizing that her aunt was not joking, Rose mounted the ladder to which Maddie pointed. The rungs pressed through the thin soles of her shoes and felt hard under her hands as she climbed.

"Sorry about the ladder," Maddie called from the entryway.

"Your Uncle Mark is planning to build a stairway one of these days. I know this all must seem very primitive to you, as everything was to me when I first came, but I hope you'll get used to it, too."

Rose kept climbing until she reached a wooden railing that skirted the small landing. In front of her was a log wall with two lace-curtained windows and a glass door covered with folds of thick white lace.

"Go ahead, open it," Maddie instructed from below.

Rose turned the doorknob and stepped into a large loft apartment with a low ceiling. The beams overhead were stained the same rich honey-brown as the downstairs of the cabin. Logs lined the walls and ceiling.

Rose would have called the room rustic but for its natural beauty. A series of simple woodland sketches hung on the walls, probably her aunt's creations, Rose figured, like the vase of fresh lilacs that cast a lavender scent about the room. Her aunt had made the best of the few materials she had to work with. Rose wondered how her aunt had ever managed the move from mansion to log cabin living.

At the far end of the room, a bay window seat overlooked the lake. Rose crossed the varnished wood floor toward it, passing a brass bedstead that framed a soft-looking white comforter and two large pillows. The lace edges trimming the pillows and comforter matched the snowflake pattern of the window curtains. A nightstand stood near the bed, and next to it a vanity with a brass-rimmed mirror.

On the opposite side of the room was a large open closet. Packing boxes lined the highest shelves, but the rest of the closet was empty, affording ten times the amount of space Rose needed for the few belongings she had brought from home.

Rose approached the bay window at the far end of the room and noticed a small stack of books piled near the seat. The lace curtains were drawn back from the glass, and the sloping grounds of Singing Pines and the blue lake stretched in front of her. She could see the tiny *Wanderer* chugging away, leaving a trail of light on the water.

"Like it?" Aunt Maddie asked through the open door.

"Aunt! I never imagined you'd climb up here!"

"Nonsense, Rose. Humans are made of flesh, not glass. I'm a tough lady yet. But do you like your room? I know it's much smaller than what you're used to," she said, as she entered it and walked toward her niece.

"It is small…" Rose answered truthfully, "but it's a dream, Aunt! Lace and logs!" She laughed. "I've never seen that combination before, but it's fitting somehow, like snow capping the trees."

"Well, you've just paid me for the trouble of getting it ready, my dear, with your pretty smile and apt words. Snow in the forest. Yes, that's it exactly. Jesse…well, your cousin loved it, too. You're so like her.…"

Maddie turned to flick off some microscopic dust on the night stand's polished surface. "Jesse was just starting life, just like you…when we built this room for her." Maddie smoothed the white comforter on the bed, even though no wrinkle disfigured it.

"Starting life like me?" Rose took several paces toward her aunt, who had sunk into the comforter's softness. "Sometimes this past year I felt like my life had ended."

Aunt Maddie leaned near her niece. "A broken engagement or a closed door is the start of something else, my dear. It's the

Lord's way. He always provides a window leading out. When my daughter died, I felt my life had ended. I guess that's one of the reasons I started reaching out to you and your family. I couldn't stand the thought of losing any of you without ever really having known you." Maddie smiled quickly, then lowered her head. "It was difficult...very difficult for me to get over Jesse's death, but the Lord sustained me."

Maddie looked up at Rose. "Showers pass, flowers return. You'll heal, Rose, and learn to bloom again. I promise you that God will not give you more than you can bear. He will sustain you through whatever problems you go through, if you trust in him."

Rose touched her bare ring finger thoughtfully. "I think I took a big step toward healing today."

"That's it! Take one step every day, and soon you'll be running—and the wound will be completely healed." Maddie gave Rose a hug and walked with her to the bay window. "This is where I thought you'd be most happy. Reading here by the window, the lake in front of you. The view is fit for a king—or even an heiress!"

Rose looked out the window, catching sight of a tousled blond head spotted with clay, bobbing up and down as shovelful after shovelful of muck piled on the ground above him.

"What was his name again?" Rose asked, watching the sunlight blaze the young man's bulging shoulders.

"Benjamin. Lilla calls him Ben. So do I, at odd moments."

"Who's Lilla?"

"My cabin helper. I wrote you about her. She's a little firecracker. I think you'll like her. She certainly likes Benjamin." Maddie laughed. "You'll meet her soon. Lunch is in another half hour, and we all eat together."

Rose watched the young laborer's rhythmic shovel. "Does… Benjamin work for you, too?"

"He works, but not for us, not for pay anyway. He likes to give us a hand when he can in exchange for the cabin he stays in. He says the quiet around here is worth diamonds. But he can tell you more about that than I can. And I think he might even like to."

Rose watched as Benjamin vaulted out of the deep hole with the aid of his shovel handle. He stood, wiped his hands on his cut-offs, and surveyed his work. Then he raised his head toward the loft window. Rose moved away, but not before he spotted her and waved his arm in greeting.

"My dear, I think you've made a friend," Aunt Maddie said. "Let's head downstairs and get lunch ready, shall we?"

Rose lingered near the window. "Aunt, do you know *him?*"

Maddie looked where her niece pointed to a young man in white, strolling across the lawn. "Oh, yes. That's Edna and Jack Savon's son, Eric. He's been coming to the resort with his parents every summer since he was a child. But didn't you meet him on *Wanderer?* He just got back from a cruise to town."

"He's staying here at Singing Pines, too?"

"Yes. Didn't you two talk at all on the trip from Warroad?"

Rose's eyes narrowed; she dropped the lace curtain abruptly. "We talked. And I can't *wait* to talk with him again."

Three

❧

Why not?" Maddie regarded Benjamin imperiously from her post at the kitchen sink. Her back was to the window and her attention on him as he sat at the dining room table. "What do you have to do today that could be more important than showing my only niece around her new home?"

Benjamin patiently pushed the book on organic chemistry away and looked across the half partition to where Maddie was drying dishes. "The MCAT is only three months away, Maddie. You know that. If I don't do well, I don't have a chance of getting into medical school next year. I have to study. Hardly a moment's my own anymore." He smiled and leaned back, finishing the crumbs from a homemade biscuit left over from lunch.

Benjamin tried to put the vision of his recent lunching partner out of his head, but he could still see Rose's downcast green eyes fringed by her thick black lashes opposite him. Green eyes, black lashes, just like Jesse's. Too much like Jesse's.

Maddie flapped a dishtowel in his direction. "Nonsense! Benjamin, you were top in your class! A solid 4.0 grade-point average. Scholarships and awards galore. And now you're telling me you can't spare an hour to show Rose the resort? You're a smart boy, Ben, but I'm a smart lady. And I don't buy the excuse—especially since you just spent the morning digging the hole for our septic tank at your own insistence."

Ben shrugged. "Some things are worth sacrifice, Mad." He hid his smile by opening the book again. "I plan to use the rest of the day for studying."

He read a few paragraphs in silence, then looked up as Maddie began grumbling. "Maddie, I'm not as sure as you are that I can get high enough scores to be accepted at the U of M. Undergraduate work is a lot different than studying for the MCAT. That was a breeze. The MCAT's a killer."

"I realize that, Benjamin. But you do have three months. Can't you spare an hour?"

He answered with a negative shake of his blonde head.

Maddie finished wiping the last dish and set it in the cupboard, then she crossed the room and sat in the heavy wooden chair next to Benjamin.

"What is it, Ben? You don't like Rose? Or do you like her too much already? She does look like Jesse, doesn't she? I never dreamed the family resemblance could go so deep until I saw her myself. My sister and her family aren't good at writing, although there's been a big improvement in the past few years. But we never did exchange photos. The last time I saw Rose she was seven years old. She and Jess looked alike then, despite their two years' difference, but I thought time would have changed her."

Benjamin looked at his book, though he was listening. He thought of replying, but couldn't come up with anything to say.

"Ben," Maddie said gently, "if you are attracted to Rose, it's no dishonor to Jesse. It's been almost five years since she died—more than an acceptable period of mourning, even for a widower, and you and Jess were never even engaged. I thought you would be, in time," Maddie reflected. "It took me by surprise when you went away to college without announcing an engagement."

"Yes," Ben said, staring past his book. "I remember how disappointed you were." His lips curved into a tiny smile as he remembered Jesse's comment about her mother: "Sometimes I think she loves you even more than I do—if that's possible!"

Maddie continued talking along her own line of memories. "I admit I encouraged you two, in spite of the fact that Jesse was only sixteen when you met. And those next few years made me see how right I was. If you hadn't gone away to school—"

"If I hadn't gone, Jesse wouldn't have died."

Maddie didn't react immediately. She looked at Benjamin and then stretched her arm across his back. "So that's still preying on you? After all this time? I thought you were done blaming yourself, Ben."

Benjamin studied the left page of his book intently, even though it was a picture he'd seen a hundred times before.

"I know you were torn up inside when Jesse died, Ben, but I thought you were healing. I took it for granted that you were, that first summer you finally came back. And last summer you seemed so much more like your old self."

Maddie moved her hand across Benjamin's tight shoulders. "I can't tell you how glad I am you came back, Ben. You've been a great comfort to me, whether you know it or not. When you're around, it feels like part of Jesse is here—the part she cherished." Maddie's voice was low and choked. She paused, inhaled, and released her breath slowly before she went on.

"But Ben, it's time to move on. I really thought you had. Maybe it's all the studying that's fooled me. I thought you were recovering, as we have been, but you're stuck, aren't you, Ben?" Maddie rubbed his shoulder. "You're stuck in guilt. Not even anger is as destructive. It's one reason our Savior had to die. We were guilty; in sacrificial loving-kindness he died to remove our guilt. But your guilt over Jesse's death is wrong, Ben. I've told you that. There's nothing you could have done. It was an accident."

"An accident I could have prevented." Ben lowered his head and rubbed his temples with his fingertips, an action that had become a habit since Jesse's death.

Maddie straightened. "Oh, really, Benjamin? Are you God, that Jesse's fate was in your hands? Jesse knew how to run a boat, and she knew the lake from childhood. Why she ran into that rock is a mystery. Maybe one we'll never know. It was dark, stormy. Perhaps she got turned around, a wave blinded her for a second…I don't know…" Maddie's voice sounded anguished, "but it was in the Lord's hands, not yours. There is nothing you could have done. Believe me! If you had been with her, two would be dead instead of one. That's all."

The thought struck Ben that perhaps that wouldn't have been so bad, but he didn't tell Maddie so. Instead he squared his shoulders and took Maddie's hand. He held it, thinking that someday Jesse's hand would have been like it—if only she had lived.

"I would have loved having you for a mother-in-law, Maddie," he said, his voice breaking. "I would have loved…" He stood, reached for his book, and was almost out the door when Maddie's voice stopped him.

31

"Ben—"

"Yes?" He didn't turn around.

"I would have loved having you as a son, too. You're a wonderful man, strong and handsome, in mind and in body. But you've got to let the Lord take you through this—all the way through. You're holding on to the past too tightly. You can't let the memory of Jesse cut you off from everyone else."

Ben leaned his palm against the screen door. "Everyone? Like Rose, you mean?" he asked, keeping his broad back toward her. "Maddie, I don't know where I'm heading. I want to go to med school, but I don't know if I can ace the MCAT. And if I do, it's a year of work, then at least another four years of training before I can set up my own practice. I'll have to moonlight the whole time just to meet expenses. And when I'm finished, who's going to want to be the wife of a missionary doctor on the Lake of the Woods? A life of long hours and starvation wages? I'm not even sure that's what I want!"

He faced her. "Maddie, you're right about one thing: I need to get my life in order before I start anything—with anyone."

"I know, Ben. And I pray that's exactly what you will do."

Ben opened his mouth to reply, but no sound escaped. He stared at Maddie for a long moment, then pushed open the screen door with one shoulder and let it slam behind him.

The view from Lilla's one-room cabin was much more contained than Rose's loft vista, but from it Rose could see across a small bay to rows of islands. The panorama also included part of the lawn and lake path, and the first two guest cottages of Singing Pines Island Resort.

Brightly-colored petunias lined the edge of the path. The riotous violet, damask, and white made a stream of color against the spring-green grass, and by the nearest guest cabin was a large circular flower bed. From shiny green foliage hung delicate pink, moccasin-shaped flowers that appeared to have tiny ears and mouths with bulbous pockets for cheeks.

"Lilla, what are those flowers? The pink ones?"

"By the cabin? Lady Slippers. Our state flower and Maddie's crowning glory. I think she transplanted them from the woods years ago. People come from miles around to see them. The whole place is a garden! I can show you the rest of the grounds later, if you want."

Rose looked from the burst of color to Lilla. "I'd like that. I'm feeling a little restless."

"I can relate. So, um, Rose, think you'll survive the summer? Why did you come up here, anyway?"

It was the first personal question Lilla had asked. Rose turned, wondering if she should have accepted Lilla's invitation to come to her cabin. She hadn't felt she could refuse, not after their easy conversation at lunch, and especially not after Aunt Maddie's threat to make Rose do the dishes if she didn't go. Rose liked the petite blonde's vivacity, but she wasn't sure if she was ready to share anything of herself yet. She regretted spilling her life's story to Eric. She wouldn't be made a fool of again. At least, not twice in the same day.

"It's really beautiful here," Rose said, trying to change the subject tactfully.

"Yeah, it's beautiful all right, but not what you're used to, huh? I know. I came here from Chicago and thought I had really bought the farm!" Lilla walked the short distance to her bed, threw a pillow in the air, caught it, and settled it behind her head again as she reclined.

"Maddie almost had to tie me down the first summer I was here! If Ben hadn't come, I would've abandoned her for sure. Glad I didn't. Don't worry, Rose, you'll get the hang of it, and like it, too. You're just used to life from the top of a golden pedestal. I can tell. What you need is a friend like me who can help you to start living in the real world. This place and everyone here have done wonders for me, but I wouldn't have stuck around if it wasn't for Ben. I would have up and gone!"

Lilla smacked her palms together, sliding one hand past the other into the air. "But thanks to Ben, I'm here; and I'll be here for you, too."

Lilla's willingness to reach out made Rose want to do the same. She moved from the window and sat near Lilla on the edge of her bed, saying the first thing that came into her head. "How did Ben change your mind?"

"Are you crazy? Um, I mean, Ben is gorgeous, Rose. I think so, anyway. Or don't you go for blonds?"

Rose considered the question and thought of Frederick's blond hair. "I guess I do—or did." She laid back on the bed, put her arms behind her head, and closed her eyes, willing a vision of Frederick to appear. When it did, she wondered why she always supposed him more handsome when she wasn't actually seeing him. His aquiline nose and sallow scholar's cheeks, while so aristocratic sounding, seemed somehow less than ideal to look at.

"Who are you thinking of? Someone tall and dark?"

"Medium-sized and light, actually. My ex-fiancé, Frederick."

"Frederick? Frederick! What's wrong with plain old 'Fred'?" Lilla snapped to a sitting position, whacked her pillow, and put it

34

back down so Rose could share it.

Rose laughed and let Lilla slip the pillow under her head. "You're the second person today who's suggested that he shorten his name." Rose could just imagine her ex-fiancé's face if she ever did call him Fred. His blond eyebrows would raise, his forehead would wrinkle, and light would shoot out of his pale blue eyes.

"Fred sounds like a drip to me," Lilla said, when Rose related her vision. "Open your eyes, Rose. Right in front of you is a man a hundred times his value!" Lilla stabbed the air. "You might as well scoop him up, with your…let's say, favorable looks. I bet he thought Jesse had come to life again the first time he saw you."

"So that's it! Ever since I came here, everyone's been staring at me. I wondered why. I'm glad I didn't start getting a big head about it." Rose laughed. "So I look like Jesse?"

"Especially close up, from what I've heard. And good for you—take advantage of it and snare him. I would if I could, but I gave up on that awhile ago. He's been a great friend, but he's never looked at me the way he stared at you all through lunch today. Take my advice and go for it!"

Rose couldn't help catching Lilla's mood. "Go for it? All right, Lilla. How could I pass up a man a hundred times the value of Frederick? Where is this man? Where?"

Rose moved to the window. "I don't see him." Suddenly she noticed a man in white leaving his cabin and approaching a hammock. "Oh, you mean him?" she asked coyly.

Lilla joined Rose at the window. "Eric Savon?" She groaned. "That spoiled French Canadian! No way, no matter how many bucks he has!" Lilla snorted. "He had his chance—and he blew it. I haven't looked at him since. No, the man I'm talking about is—hey! He's over there! On the lake path!"

"I don't see anyone…" Rose scanned the path.

"Just coming from behind that big pine. See?"

Lilla pointed to a man with tousled blond hair and an athletic body clad in jeans and a T-shirt. He was carrying a bulky book and walking along the lake path.

"Not what's-his-name!" Rose protested.

"Ben," Lilla said in reverent tones. "If Nick and I weren't having so much fun, I'd still be after him. What's the matter with you, Rose? Don't you recognize perfection when you see it?"

"Maybe." Rose shifted her gaze back to the man lounging in a hammock outside his cabin. "Maybe, Lilla, but he's got some explaining to do."

Ben intended to take the lake path past Lilla's cabin and keep walking directly to his own, but something stopped him. He halted as if to listen. *Is it you, God? Could this be of you?*

Although Ben didn't hear a clear answer from the Master in Heaven, he knew he should obey the mistress of Singing Pines and grant her request. Maddie had said Rose was at Lilla's cabin. Fine. Why make a big deal about it? He would show Rose the island and go back to studying. Easy. Make Maddie happy and only lose an hour or so of the day. Otherwise she would just hound him until he did, and that could mean shooting the *whole* day.

Ben turned from the lake and trudged up the rise to Lilla's cabin. He rapped on the screen door. "Hi, Lilla. Rose there?"

"Good guess, Handsome. We were just talking about you."

Rose walked to Lilla's side. "Hello, Benjamin," she said coolly.

"Hi. Maddie would like me to show you around the resort. If you can go now, it would be a good time for me. I've got an hour or so before I should get back to studying." He stepped aside expectantly.

"No, I don't think—" she began, but then appeared to reconsider as her glance went past his shoulder. "Yes, Benjamin, I'd like that," she said, becoming unaccountably animated. She opened the screen door and reached for his hand.

"Lead on, Benjamin! We can start with that cottage over there," she said, and they made their way toward the Savon cabin.

Freshly-cut grass stuck to Rose and Ben's shoes as they walked across the lawn. Rose could hear the hum of Uncle Mark's mower, though she couldn't see him or his machine. Several yards from Eric's cabin they passed a stand of crab apple trees displaying pink globes of delicately-scented flowers.

Benjamin led the way toward a pair of shady oaks and shook the hammock spread underneath. "Rose, this is Eric Savon."

"Hey, what's—" Suddenly Eric saw Rose. "Well, Rose! Hello again!"

"Hello," Rose said demurely. She moved closer to Benjamin, a sweet smile on her lips.

"I should've known this guy would be around before I could find you again," Eric said, rising and grinning. "I turned to get my bag and you were already with your aunt and uncle. I thought I should let them have some time with you before I butted in."

Rose felt slightly confused. "But why did you let me think you were going somewhere else? Why didn't you tell me you were coming to Singing Pines, too?"

"I thought you knew! Didn't I tell you that when I met you? I thought that was why you opened up in the first place." Eric made a sweeping bow. "My dear Miss Anson, I am sorry I made you misunderstand me. I hope you'll give this poor French Canadian another chance."

Rose felt foolish for being angry with him and now wished she wasn't holding Benjamin's hand.

Benjamin, however, didn't give her the chance to let go. "I plan to monopolize Rose now, Eric," he said, "so if you'll excuse us—" Benjamin clapped Eric on the shoulder.

"No need to rush away, Ben. You don't have to run back to your books so soon. Watch him, Rose. He'll go far someday. And anyone who studies as much as he does deserves it."

"Oh, that's right. You did say you had to study, didn't you?" Rose recalled, looking at Benjamin. "Are you taking correspondence courses?"

"No, the MCAT, the Medical College—"

"Admissions Test. I know." In Rose's mind, an association began to form between her ex-fiancé and the man holding her hand. Unconsciously she tensed.

"You've heard about the MCAT?"

"Yes," Rose said crisply. "In detail. My…an old friend of mine told me all about it, and I wouldn't think of keeping you away from your studying." She withdrew her hand from Benjamin's, symbolically breaking yet another of the chains binding her to Frederick.

"Eric can show me the rest of the island. Aunt Maddie won't mind, and you'll probably be relieved. I know how men are when the MCAT is at stake." She relented a little and patted his arm before slipping away. "Good luck, Benjamin."

"Yeah, good luck!" Eric quickly instated himself as Benjamin's replacement. "So long, buddy."

Wordlessly, Ben wheeled toward the lake path and his own cabin, carrying a textbook where seconds ago a feminine hand had rested.

Each cabin on Singing Pines had its own collection of flowers and trees. One cottage stoop would be outlined in brilliant gold and orange petunias with rust-colored markings, another was set off by luminous blue lobelia. Maddie had marked each plant type with its own placard on a wooden dowel, so Rose's walk with Eric over the resort was like a guided botany tour.

The belated resort guests had arrived later that morning, so Eric avoided them by ending Rose's tour at the back side of the Winters's cabin near a garden almost the size of the building itself. Its edges were marked by foot-high sunflower plants and orange, yellow, and red marigolds.

In the far north corner of the garden, a raised bed of rhubarb spread its canopy of leaves over the tilled ground, creating a barrier between the garden and the first trees of the forest. There, the air was moist and sharp with sap and fresh leaves, the balm of Gilead and poplars throwing their acidic scents as far as they could reach.

"I think that's everything on Singing Pines," Eric said. "Let's take a break." He sat down in the shade of the lilac bushes at the corner of the log house. Rose joined him and plucked a lilac bough, twirling it absently in her fingers as she and Eric listened to the symphony of nature. Full-throated blackbirds warbled, their songs gurgling up and overflowing. Magpies lit in the tops of bammies and muttered their electronic noises. Somewhere in the woods, a partridge drummed.

"So many mingled melodies. Is that why they call this island Singing Pines?"

"I don't know. Sounds more like noise to me." Eric laughed. "I'm glad you enjoy it, though."

After breathing a few more draughts of lilac, so fresh and powerful, Eric felt his throat beginning to sting. He stood and took several paces away from the bushes.

"What's beyond the garden?" Rose asked.

"The woods. More rocks and pines. Weeds, wildflowers. Blueberries, too. And mosquitoes. They haven't developed that part of the island yet. Probably never will. Maddie's a real nature buff. She and my mom take walks back there and won't come back unless they spot at least ten different kinds of birds and twenty plants. They used to try to win me over, but I'm a city boy. I like coming here for the summer, but I have to get away every now and then, take the *Wanderer* to Warroad, my boat to Lakeshore City. I've got a sleek little racer. You've got to see it!"

"Thanks. I will later, Eric."

"Hold on!" Eric caught her hand. "No reason we can't see it now."

"No." Rose glanced toward the cabin. "Aunt Maddie is probably waiting for me. I've been gone a long time. I should be helping her with...something. I guess I don't have any idea about the work involved in running a resort, but my aunt must be busy. I should at least offer to help."

"All right. Promise me you'll go on a cruise tomorrow, then."

"Maybe. We'll see, tomorrow. Now I have to go. I think I saw a movement through the master bedroom window; it's probably Aunt Maddie. Bye, Eric. Thanks for the walk." She pulled away.

Eric sprawled on the ground under the lilacs and watched until Rose rounded the corner, then he took the lilac bough she had left and began picking off the blooms.

"She loves me; she loves me not," he chanted, plucking each purple blossom and sending it flying into the air until he rested among a shower of tiny purple blooms.

He frowned at the final flower left on the stem, then tore it in two. As he tossed the last half over his shoulder, he finished his chant. "She loves me." He smiled. "Yeah, this time, she *will* love me."

Four

⁓✦⁓

After an informal home church service with Uncle Mark as pastor, Rose hurried down the path to the small series of sheltered docks that served as Singing Pines's marina. She began sketching the morning scene, humming as she drew, but she hadn't finished outlining the nearest island when footsteps made the dock shiver.

She looked up, expecting to see another guest with a bad case of fish fever heading out to the lake. But it was Eric.

"What a sight!" he said.

"Isn't it beautiful? What color! I should be painting, not sketching."

"I meant you, but now that you mention it, it is a beautiful morning."

He sat beside Rose as she drew, and she explained the finer points of her sketch. But soon his interest waned.

"Come on, Rose! We have to go for a cruise. Look at the tops of the pines—no wind. It's the perfect day for it." He gave her one of his slanted grins. "I didn't get to see you at all yesterday once you went to find your aunt. I plan on seeing a lot more of you today, I hope."

"I'd love to, Eric, but not yet. Wait until I finish. I've made a pretty good start, don't you think?" She held up her picture to him.

"Great start." He wet a finger and held it up. "Hm. Wind's from the northwest. Got to watch the weather today. Hard to say what it might do. Looks good, but I don't want to take a chance."

Rose added a few more lines. "Why don't you get a boat that can handle rough water?"

"My boat can handle it…I think. Anyway, once you've felt 225 horsepower, there's no going back. It would take all day to get to Lakeshore if I drove one of those heavy slow things the locals drive. In my speedboat, Lakeshore's only a cruise away. Warroad too, as far as that goes, but I don't like to travel the open lake much. I'd rather take the *Wanderer,* like everybody else. But around here, my boat's great. What a ride! She almost flies! Come on, you've got to experience it."

Rose paused to take in the vista before her and made two thick pencil strokes on paper. The lake was a shimmering blue and the sun reflected off the waves, smearing the horizon of land and water. "Look at this place! I wish I had brought my acrylics; the color of the sky is like gentians."

"No clouds," Eric observed. "That's good. No white caps either…yet."

Rose stretched her wrist and laid her pencil in the inside pocket of her pad. "Now I'm ready for a break, but let's take a walk before we go. I haven't been down the lake path yet. That's the one part of the tour you skipped yesterday. Aunt Maddie told me it skirts the entire length of the island." She tucked her pad under her arm.

When Eric didn't reply, Rose followed the lake path with her eyes. "What's that, near the point, just off the trail? It looks like the corner of a building."

"Ben's cabin. And that's where he stays, most of the time—there or alone on some island, studying. I think the guy even studies while he fishes!"

"Well, if he's going to take the MCAT—"

"I know, I know. Like I said, he'll go far. But look, Rose: clear sky, hot sun, calm lake. And my boat. All those things together mean pure, unadulterated fun. No MCAT or anything else is worth wasting this day for! I'll walk with you as far as the point, but then you have a date with me on the lake, all right?"

"I guess, but—"

"All right, then. Come on!"

Rose followed Eric as he bounded from the dock and sprinted down the dirt path. Tangled, gnarled pine roots and ridges of exposed bedrock kept Rose watching her feet instead of the scenery as she tried to keep up with him. "Eric! Eric, slow down!"

He slackened his pace, but Rose still felt too hurried. The walk among the petunias was more like a race, and before she knew it, she was once more at the marina, Eric holding her hand and pointing proudly to a boat.

"There she is."

Rose moved closer to the flat, low speedboat with its huge motor in back. The body was metallic black. A short windshield of smoked glass shielded two black leather chairs set on either side of a narrow aisle. The aisle had a strip of gray-black outdoor carpeting, but most of the floor was wood. The dashboard and steering wheel were a combination of chrome and black leather.

"This? This is what you dragged me over the lake path to see?"

"Yeah!" Eric catapulted from the dock into the boat. "Let's take her out."

"If I do decide to go, I should tell Aunt Maddie—"

"Rose, there's an old saying I live by: *carpe diem.* 'Seize the moment.' And the moment is now. It's not every day I can take the boat out. She's sensitive. Today's perfect, clear and calm, but the wind could come up, so we have to go now. We'll be back before Maddie even knows you're gone. Come on! You're going to love it!" Eric swung her into the seat next to his. "There you are, Miss Anson. Now sit back and leave the driving to me."

Rose began to protest, but Eric's verve was infectious, and the lake was so blue and shimmering. And there were islands out there to explore! "All right, Eric. But just a short ride."

"Whatever you say."

Benjamin stared a few minutes more at the cutaway diagram before he closed the book. He had been studying the human heart, an organ he was intimately acquainted with—physiologically. Emotionally he could make neither head nor tail of it, not since Jesse had died five years ago to the day. Mark hadn't mentioned it in the morning service except during prayer time, but Maddie's face had been full of remembrance.

"Hello? Are you in there, Benjamin?"

He sighed and shook his head. Maddie was on the prowl. She

was always restless on this day. "Yes, Mad. Coming."

He pushed open the screen door for her and stepped aside to let her into the living room of his one-bedroom cottage. "Have a seat."

Maddie removed several heavy volumes from the couch to clear some space to sit. "Well?"

Benjamin occupied the wooden rocker next to her and cocked his head as if he had no idea what she wanted to know.

"Well, how did it go, Benjamin?"

"Okay, Maddie, but the human heart is a complex organ, and I think I'll be working on it a few more days. The cutaway shows it in detail. Here, see for yourself...." He began thumbing through his text.

"Not with studying. How did it go with Rose yesterday? I've been meaning to ask you, but I've been so busy with our new guests. I thought I'd catch you this morning, but you shot out of the house after the service as if your cabin were afire. So tell me."

Benjamin shrugged. "It went okay."

Maddie leaned back. "Oh, so that's why fifteen minutes after I send you to her I saw her wandering around the entire resort with Eric Savon! What happened?"

Benjamin lowered his book to the floor. "That, too, has to do with the human heart, I think. Rose just doesn't go for me, Maddie. She's not Jesse reincarnate after all." Ben rued the words the instant they left his mouth, knowing that today, of all days, he should have left Jesse's name out of the conversation.

"Now that's a real surprise, Benjamin! Love at first sight happens once in a lifetime—maybe. Don't expect it to happen again!"

Maddie's voice sounded bitter, and Benjamin knew his words had hit a tender spot, an old wound that had not completely healed even five years after it had first opened.

As Benjamin wondered how to make amends, his eyes drifted to the window where a flat, aerodynamic boat was pulling out of the marina and picking up speed. He watched it slap across the wake of a passing boat and shoot forward, gaining velocity and a bit of altitude.

"Where is Rose now?" Maddie asked.

"Well, if you want my guess, I'd say she's one of the two people I just saw leaving the marina in Eric's boat."

Maddie leaped toward the window. "What? Not in that flat-bottomed duck boat! That little thing's like a piece of driftwood in a storm, all speed and no heart. What's the girl thinking?"

Benjamin figured that some of Maddie's anger stemmed from the fact that her only child had died on this day in a boating accident, and now her sister's only child was boating away from her too. The parallels were disturbing—for Ben as well, now that he thought about it.

He joined her at the window. "That question is beyond me, Maddie." Benjamin kept his voice light for Maddie's sake and put his arm around the short woman. "I don't know what that girl thinks. I thought I was being a charming tour guide yesterday, but she dropped me cold as soon as we neared the Savon cabin. I don't suppose you'd know anything about that? She and Eric already seemed to have an understanding."

"She met him on the *Wanderer*, that's all I know." Maddie's eyes were glued to the foamy wake left by the speedboat. The boat itself had careened around an island and was no longer visible. Maddie turned from the window and sank into the couch. "Out of the frying pan, into the fire."

"Care to explain that statement?" Ben hoped to let Maddie blow off some steam before she went back to the cabin and continued grieving for Jesse. Maddie always felt better after she aired her tongue.

"The girl's got me boiling, Benjamin. Imagine going out on the lake in that thing without even telling me! Benjamin, Rose is smart, lovely, and has absolutely terrible judgment, if this running away with Eric is a sample." Maddie shook her head.

She looked at Benjamin, her green eyes sharp. "And I think I might know the reason she isn't too warm toward you. I'm afraid she's been brainwashed by her upbringing. Her first impression of you as a manual laborer no doubt put you out of her social picture immediately. And she's still recovering from a break-up with her fiancé—a doctor. I don't know the details, but she and her mother wrote a little about it to me. Nadine was mad as hops, in her cultured way, of course. Rose had some big squabble, I believe, with both the fiancé and then her parents. I could be mistaken—I was reading between the lines—but some big conflict happened, sure as day, and Nadine was furious with Rose, and vice versa. They're still not on the best of terms. After thinking and praying about it for some time, I wrote to Rose and invited her to come up here for the summer."

Maddie spent a few moments in silence, and Benjamin watched her anger cooling.

"I thought a little time away from home might be good for Rose. For all of them, really. It reminded me of the hullabaloo that broke out with the family when I was considering marrying Mark. Everyone thought he was the wrong one for me, my folks and Nadine included, but I just bulldozed over them all. If I'd been a little less hot back then, maybe I'd be closer with my sister and her family right now. I made up with my folks in time, but Nadine still seems distant. Things are getting better, though. I'm glad Rose will be spending a few months with us. I believe it'll help strengthen the family ties."

Her eyes focused on Benjamin. "Forgive me. I was rambling." She smiled. "My mouth gets ahead of me sometimes. Was anything I said helpful to you? I forget exactly what it was you asked."

"Most of it was helpful, Maddie. So Rose's ex-fiancé was a doctor. Maybe that explains her attitude when I mentioned the MCAT. She turned me right off. And she hasn't looked at me since."

"I expected as much. Maybe she figured you and her fiancé had some pretty strong similarities, both so interested in medicine and such. Most likely she wants nothing to do with another man like him right now. Hard to tell what she was thinking exactly, but from now on, I'd advise you to tread lightly on the subject of medicine. Take a tip from Eric: Take her on a boat ride. Better yet, take her on a fishing trip. If you can break through that princess coating, I bet you'll find an exceptional young woman underneath—not that I'm pushing you together, mind you."

Maddie was sounding more like her generous self, and Ben knew it was because she was on one of her favorite topics: matchmaking. Instead of repulsing her efforts as he usually did, he agreed. "Maybe I will, Maddie."

She looked at him with a trace of suspicion in her eyes. "Well, I'm glad you're finally coming around, Benjamin, but don't take your time. Eric almost had Jesse mesmerized before you entered the scene, remember? Your courtship skills may be rusty, but now's the time to take them out of retirement. Now—"

"Or never?"

"Exactly!" Maddie mirrored his smile. "For both your sakes. I have a feeling about you two. I won't call it a word from the Lord yet, but it's more than a hunch, I can tell you that. Rose needs a man who can give her the love and the room she needs. And you need a woman who can tease you out of your seriousness and bring you back into the land of the living with her love. Give Rose a chance, Benjamin. Maybe she's the one. There's no harm in trying, anyway."

"None whatever, Mad, but I think you've got it wrong. I doubt she'll give me a chance."

"But you'll ask her out?"

"I'll ask."

"Fine. And I'll see to it that her answer is yes."

Benjamin laughed. "You are a remarkable woman, Maddie, and an incurable matchmaker."

"Only when there's a match that needs making, my dear boy. You notice I never pushed you toward Lilla. I love the girl, but you're not right for each other. Eric wasn't either. Nick may be the one for her, but I must admit I'm keeping my eyes peeled— just in case he's not."

"I'm sure you are, Maddie. And thanks for not siccing that female shark on me. Lilla's a great girl, but you're right. I don't have the stamina to keep up with her. She's like…like a whirring butterfly with wings of steel: aimless and happy and harmless— but determined."

"And Rose is a flower waiting to unfold. Remember that,

Benjamin. Patience and love are the water and sunshine that will make her bloom."

"Patience and love," Benjamin echoed. "It's been a long time since I felt either, not since Jess—" He bit his lip, but Maddie appeared not to have heard all of his last statement.

"Well, there's no time like the present, Ben." She laughed. "I believe that's a paraphrase of Eric's motto, isn't it? Take another tip from him, Benjamin. Don't wait around. That boy! I remember the first time Eric came here. Took one look at Jesse and off he went. You two had quite a tussle over her, didn't you, Ben? Well, that's best forgotten, perhaps, along with many other things." Maddie stood and walked toward the door.

Benjamin moved to open it for her. He wanted to tell Maddie that he missed and remembered Jesse, too, especially on this anniversary of her death, but he feared his words would only give Maddie more grief and make her worry about him besides. Instead, he hugged her. And when he finally let her go, something in Maddie's eyes seemed to say she understood.

Five

❧

A little more than an hour after leaving Singing Pines, Eric's boat had torn past so many islands that Rose no longer bothered to count them. They all started to look alike: green mounds on blue water with steep drops or jutting rocks at their bases. Her neck began to ache from turning it to see the islands on every side of her, so she began observing only the view dead ahead. It came on with bewildering speed and diversity: now a small bay, next a narrow waterway through thick weeds, a sharp curve near a high cliff, or an obstacle course of green and red buoys.

So absorbed was she in the scenery that she hardly noticed Eric's last burst of speed. Ahead were islands with houses on their shores, some of them stately mansions with multi-colored trim, sprawling decks on both stories, attached boat garages housing at least one or two high-powered crafts. These were the domiciles of the lake elite, Canadians like Eric who had the money to make the Lake of the Woods their playground. Some of the residents were known to Eric, he explained, and he waved at familiar figures standing on verandas and in boat houses.

Eric's boat sped on, and the shores began closing in. Soon other boats were zooming alongside them as they made their way to what looked like a large floating marina. Rocking wakes forced Eric to slow or else capsize. He reluctantly pulled back on the throttle.

The shore was a series of long piers with boats of all descriptions tied, docking, or racing away from their berths. Behind a concrete retaining wall peeked distant towers and office buildings, the mark of civilization.

Eric docked at a floating gas and bait shop, told the boy who caught and tied the boat to fill it and add dockage, and handed him a wad of bills in advance payment.

"Welcome to Ontario, Rose. See the Canadian flag over there? And here I am without anything but American cash on me. Some patriot. These places take American money just as gladly, though; more so, because they can take advantage of the exchange rate."

The sound of boat motors made the air whine, and gas coated the dark water, spreading in an oily iridescent film, its fumes overpowering the scent of the lake.

Eric pocketed his change, hopped out of the boat, and held out his hand to Rose. "Let's go!"

"We're leaving the boat here?"

"I paid dockage. They'll take care of it until we get back. Come on. You need to stretch your legs."

Rose looked back toward the direction they'd come.

"I know Sunday afternoon isn't the best time to visit Lakeshore, Rose, but there's a few things we can do to keep us occupied, so relax. You won't be bored."

"That's not what's bothering me. You said we'd just go on a short ride, and it's already been at least an hour. No one on Singing Pines knows where we are, and to take off to Canada without a word—"

"All right, I'm sorry. I guess I got carried away. The lake was so calm, I just couldn't turn around. But don't worry. We'll take a walk and be back before anyone even knows you're gone. Maybe we can even find those acrylic paints you were telling me you needed. All right?"

"Well, maybe we can get the paints. I guess we can do that much."

"Great." Eric reached for her hand, and soon they were moving down the boardwalk toward the high concrete ramp that led to shops and stores on the other side of Lakeshore City's retaining wall.

Lakeshore was a lake town in the truest sense of the word, relying heavily on tourist commerce. For that reason, everything that might cater to visitors was open all weekend and most waking hours on weekdays. Many of the major establishments were built near the water's edge to lure casual boaters to spend an afternoon, or perhaps a day or two, on its mainland shores. Gas and bait shops, hardware stores with boating equipment, and marine mercantile made up the first wave of establishments, but as Rose and Eric walked on the street above the retaining wall, a softer edge of the town came into view.

Charming souvenir shops offered lake mementos such as tiny clamshell paintings, authentic Chippewa moccasins, carvings etched in dried mushrooms more than two handspans wide, and wooden and clay objects of all sorts. Rose was delighted with these treasures. She examined each carefully, wishing she had some money with her to take away a few of the best samples.

"Anything you want," Eric said magnanimously, and the shop's owner rushed over to help Rose select some of the more expensive items.

"Oh, thank you, Eric. I'll pay you when we get back."

"Don't worry about it. I'd like to give you a gift or two, Rose," Eric said, as she walked toward the watercolor sketches in the rear of the store.

"Miss, these moccasins—genuine deerskin leather, hand beaded by Chippewa natives, see?"

Rose politely inspected the soft shoes thrust at her by the dark-haired proprietor who looked as if she might be one of the Chippewa natives in question. "Did you make these?"

"Oh, no," the woman answered disdainfully, the indentations in her round cheeks becoming more pronounced as she pursed her dark lips. "Reserve Indians." She jerked her head in a southerly direction. "I own this place."

"Oh. Do you buy all these crafts, then?"

"Yes. And everything here was made from materials on Lake of the Woods. Genuine deerskin, tanned and sewn locally," the woman said, trying to interest Rose in the moccasins.

"The paints are made here, too?" Rose asked knowingly, as she pointed to a watercolor lake scene with a frame of arranged driftwood pieces.

"Well, I think so. Yes. Made from...sand and weed dyes."

"I see." Rose smiled. "And the acrylic paintings hanging there? Those on the *china* plates?"

"Done by local native artists," the woman replied, her black eyes beginning to flash at Rose's subtle challenge. "Everything here is done by artists from Lake of the Woods."

Rose noticed the rewording of her former declaration, but let it pass. "You have very good local artists," she said, disarming the shop owner. "And I'm having a hard time choosing from so many fine pieces of art, but I think I'll take this."

She brought to the counter the watercolor sunrise with its frame of driftwood. "So compact, and such balanced composition. The tones are perfect! Who is the artist? The signature is so small, it becomes a part of the weeds of the shoreline."

"G. Nightsky—George Nightsky—a very good painter," the woman said, taking tissue paper and wrapping up the frame. She placed several layers of newspaper around it and put it in a paper bag before asking for the thirty dollars due her.

Eric gave her two American twenties. "Keep the change," he said, and took the bundle and its new owner outside into the sunshine.

Ironically, the only business in Lakeshore City that seemed to be closed was the art shop. Rose could just see a display of acrylics through the darkened window.

"Sorry about that, Rose. Tell you what: to make up for it, I'll treat you to lunch anywhere you choose, all right?"

Rose wished again that she had worn her watch. "I suppose we shouldn't stop to eat, but I am hungry. It must be past noon. But after we eat, we're going straight back to the resort."

"Anything you say."

Eric and Rose made their way back toward the retaining wall. Rose walked past several diners and hotel lobbies before she halted. "Let's go in this one, Eric."

They were standing near the wrought-iron entrance of a

brightly painted blue-and-white outdoor wharf restaurant. "A crow's nest! Look at the spiral stairs leading up. I'd love to see the lake from there, wouldn't you?"

"I'd rather have lunch on the deck, Rose. We can see the lake from there, too, and it's not so high. With my luck, I'd spill my drink, glass and all, on some poor guy below and be guilty of manslaughter." Eric gave Rose's hand a squeeze. "I'm not my best at heights, but I'll climb that pole thing and eat in the sky if it'll make you happy."

"Oh, no—my mother is afraid of heights, too. I wouldn't want to put you through that."

"I'm not afraid of heights," Eric explained, after tipping the seafaring waiter to lead them to the best table nearest the lake. "Not much, anyway!" He grinned. "We can climb up there before we leave if you'd like, but I don't want to eat up there, all right?" He continued to hold her hand as they weaved around blue-and-white scalloped tables with deck chairs that matched.

When they walked under the platform with its tall iron braces, Rose saw that the crow's nest was merely an observation deck. All the tables were on the main deck below, which was still ten feet or so above the water. The deck extended as far as the retaining wall and ended in a wooden railing painted a blue that was several shades brighter than the lake underneath. She and Eric were seated at a table for two near the railing.

A man in a captain's uniform that matched the restaurant's motif presented them with two-foot-high menus made to resemble ancient treasure maps.

"Order whatever you want," Eric said to Rose. "Are you drinking this afternoon, Miss Anson? No? Well, I'll have a double Windsor, straight up."

The waiter snapped a salute and went to fetch it.

Rose settled on the almond walleye platter. Eric ordered filet mignon. "I'm not crazy about fish. Sometimes I wish fishing weren't so good up here. My dad forces Mom and me to dine on everything he catches. I'm always glad when the weather changes and the fish lose their appetites for a while."

"They do that?"

"What?"

"Lose their appetites."

"Yeah, a storm hits, churns the water, or the weather makes a shift from cold to hot or vice versa. It takes a while for the fish to calm down again. And then they migrate, and sometimes Dad can't find them, so we get a break and eat at some of the lodges on the other islands. When the fish flies come the first part of July, no bait on earth can tempt the fish. We go to Flag Island for meals then. That's when I wish Maddie served food to her guests. Most of the other places do, but on Singing Pines it's only a continental breakfast and bag lunches. Suppers we're left to fend for ourselves."

"You poor thing," Rose teased as they sampled the "chips" the waiter brought to the table. "Why did they put gravy on the French fries?"

"Gravy and chips are the Canadian equivalent of ice cream and apple pie. Like it?"

Rose nodded.

"I thought you would." Eric picked up a glass bottle. "Here, put a dab of vinegar on the chips, too."

"Vinegar and gravy and French fries? That's too much!"

"You're supposed to put it on the chips alone. Try it. If you don't like it, you can go back to your catsup."

After a tentative dip, Rose discovered Eric was right. The tangy vinegar added a kick to the fries that Rose could tell was potentially addicting. But she preferred the gravy, and she still ate some of the fries with just catsup.

Their meals came on sizzling platters served with such a flourish that Rose felt she was back in Wayzata at one of her favorite posh restaurants. The flavor, appearance, and texture of the breaded walleye and its accompanying braised vegetables satisfied her hunger and aesthetic cravings at the same time.

When Rose at last put down her fork and pushed back her chair, she felt entirely content. The unique piece of art in the bag at her feet, her satiated appetite, and Eric's promise of a quick ride home put to rest any anxiety about being away from Singing Pines too long.

Eric poked at his meal for another ten minutes and finally suggested Rose climb the crow's nest while he finished his food and his third drink.

The stairway to the top of the pole was made of iron. Rose hung loosely to the winding rail and watched her footing on the narrow webbed steps. The platform was at least fifteen feet in the air, and when she reached the top, she sank into a deck chair.

"Ahoy!" Eric called. "What's the weather doing, Mate?"

His voice was louder than necessary to carry up to her, and Rose wondered if his drinking were the cause. She watched him stand unsteadily, throw his checkered napkin on his plate, where it landed in a pool of steak sauce, and cup his hands to call to her again.

"Halloo, halloo! Let's have the weather report, Matey!"

"Quiet, Eric!" Rose called uneasily. "Come up here if you

want to see the weather." She stood and looked down at him.

"No, thanks, Ma'am," Eric said, sitting heavily. "I'll just have a little drink while I wait. You can tell me the lay of the land when you come down. The lay of the sky, I mean…no, the lay of the lake!" He snickered and passed a handful of green to the waiter, waving the waiter's protestations aside.

Rose pulled her stare from Eric and looked across the lake. The sun was still shining on the undulating water, but a row of clouds made a dark line on the horizon. The lake looked black underneath them.

Lakeshore City's marina was as rough as it had been before, with the wakes of various cruisers landing and leaving the marina a quarter mile or so from the restaurant. Waves splashed the concrete retaining wall, though now Rose heard but couldn't see their impact, as she had during their meal. She turned and made her way down the stairs.

"So, was it worth the climb?"

"Yes, it was. Eric, let's go now. We've been gone so long. What time is it?"

"I never carry a watch. It ruins too many good times." He laughed and waited for Rose to join him. She didn't.

"All right, we can go if you like. Sure you don't want to see any more stores? Maybe we can find an art shop that's open."

"No, let's go. I haven't had much weather experience, but I saw some dark clouds from the observation deck and—"

"Not to worry. Leave the driving to me. We'll go now if it'll make you feel better. It's just a short walk to the marina, and before you know it you'll be back at Singing Pines." He flashed her a wide grin. "Rosy will be home very, very soon."

Six

❧

How long have they been gone, Maddie?" Benjamin stood by the Winters's picture window and watched the white pines tossing like weeds in the wind. It had not yet begun to rain, but the lake was an ominous slate color. As he had walked to the lodge for a mid-afternoon snack, Benjamin almost tasted rain in the gray clouds gathering above.

"I don't know, Ben. Rose never showed up for lunch. I was sure she would have told me if she planned to be gone longer than that. Lilla and I have been working in the cabins since I saw you this morning, and I didn't realize Rose hadn't come back until her place at the table was empty. I checked with Edna Savon, and she said Eric hadn't been seen since morning either. She said he often disappears without saying anything, but with this weather, she was worried, too."

Maddie folded her arms and clasped her elbows as she drew alongside Benjamin. "The temperature is dropping, and the barometer with it. A call just went out over the marine band about a severe weather warning. It's for the whole lake, both sides, from Warroad to Lakeshore City. And Rose may be out in it!"

Benjamin stopped just short of nodding. "Didn't you say she's an artist? Maybe she's out somewhere sketching and lost track of time. Maybe she's in the woods behind the resort," he said, but doubted his own words.

"Maybe. Maybe so. And it's only three now. Not so very late...."

"Right. Hours to go before it gets dark. I mean, before sunset," Benjamin amended, for already the sky was growing dark.

"Yes, but the storm, Benjamin. And if she's gone out on the lake with Eric..."

Benjamin held his tongue. *If* she had gone out? *When* was the only question in Benjamin's mind, and he knew sooner or later that Maddie would have to face it, too.

"Maddie," he said gently, turning away from the glass, "I think she has gone out on the lake with him. Neither of them have been seen all day. Eric's boat is missing from the marina. And we saw him leave with someone this morning."

"Well, perhaps she just went out to do some sketching as you said. It's bound to start raining any second, the way those thunderheads look. She could wander in any moment."

"And maybe not," he said, hoping he wouldn't have to brace Maddie for worse news in the future. "If there's any chance at all that they're out there, someone should be looking for them before the storm hits—just in case. So I'm going." He said the words in a tone of indifference that belied his real feelings.

Maddie nodded and continued to stare through the picture window. The storm front had brought an eerie greenish light to the sky, and though the storm had not yet descended, the lake was frothy with white caps.

"Well, Maddie, any second I waste is a second longer they

may have to wait out the storm. I hope and pray that—Oh, don't mind me; you know what an alarmist I am," Benjamin said, seeing Maddie's eyes widen with fear. "They're probably fine. Don't worry; just pray, and I'll find them if they're out there. Eric's been coming up here for years. He knows the lake. Maybe they'll wander in all on their own, like you said." He hugged her reassuringly before he grabbed a slicker and headed out into the whistling wind.

Maddie watched him walk down the path until he disappeared behind the island's hump. He reappeared again at the marina, a stick man who jumped into a small outboard boat, threw off the invisible lines, bent over the motor, and steered out into the white caps.

Dear God, Maddie prayed, *protect him. And please put your hedge of safety around Rose and Eric, too, wherever they may be. I know…I know they're in your hands.* Maddie leaned against the window trim and watched Benjamin's boat blend into the gloom.

"Eric! It's coming in faster than I can scoop!" Rose sent another bucket of lake water back into the mother waves. Even the water she managed to bail out, more often than not, blew back into the boat as she heaved it overboard.

"The pump's on high! There's nothing else I can do!" Eric yelled, flinching as another wave hit Rose in the face. "Quit bailing and come up here, Rose! I don't know how you can stand it! The boat hasn't swamped so far; it's not worth it! Come forward!"

He turned back to the windshield. Rain swept the boat in

pounding sheets as it had for hours, and the craft reeled drunkenly from crest to trough of the three-foot waves.

Eric held the steering wheel with wet, white hands, trying to steer a course by compass toward Singing Pines. "Can you see anything?" He yelled over his shoulder, but the wind snatched his words and hurled them overboard as if that was what it intended to do with his body, crew, and craft the first chance it had. The waves climbed higher.

"What?" Rose staggered forward a few steps on the slick hardwood flooring, nearly falling.

"Careful, Rose! Are you all right?" Eric longed to help her but knew he couldn't leave his post, or the risk of capsizing would be even greater. He watched her steady herself, and then he faced ahead, though waves were his only view—waves and blankets of swirling clouds.

He tried to peer through the rain, but the stinging drops and bleary patches of gray and black on every side made him drop his head. The boat could have been floating in the air; the horizon and water were the same mixed-up shade.

As the boat tossed up and down, higher and harder, Eric felt himself losing all sense of direction. He glanced at the compass and again corrected his course. If it wasn't for the instrument, he would have had no idea which direction they should head. "Can you see anything, Rose? Land? An island? Anything!"

"No, Eric." Rose's voice sounded garbled and weak. "I don't see anything."

"Come up here! Please! You've done all you can. I can't move; I've got to hang onto the wheel." Eric put every drop of vocal force left into his words, and the wind dropped briefly enough for them to carry to her.

She felt her way toward him, hanging onto the boat gunnel. Eric hoped she wouldn't lose her footing before she reached the carpet. The floor was flooded with water, and as the boat pitched violently, another wave spilled over the side.

The boat righted for an instant, then lurched back near the water's surface. Eric looked over his shoulder to see a wave tearing at Rose, as if trying to sweep her away. He willed her to hold on even as he willed the boat to come into safe harbor.

Rose held on until the wave passed, leaving the imprints of her fingernails in the wooden trim. Eric watched her catch her breath, wait for the boat to become more level, then force her body forward.

The journey of a few feet took such a long time. Eric looked around wildly for something with which to lash the steering wheel so he could help her, but at last she managed to reach the seat next to his.

"There's nothing, Eric, nothing. No land, no sky, just water...."

The roaring wind did its utmost to drown out her answer, but Eric leaned close to support her drooping head with his arm, and he heard every hopeless word.

"Hang on, Rose. We've come this far." He spoke through clenched teeth, cold sober from his fight with the elements. "There's got to be an island soon. We can't be in the big lake; the waves would be higher. I've tried to keep us on course. I don't think we've overshot Singing Pines. It's got to be near. There's got to be some island near."

Rose was shaking wildly, and Eric pulled her closer. "Rose, sit down here, under the dashboard. You've been fighting the wind and water for hours. You're cold as ice!"

"No, I'm all right. I should keep bailing."

She looked as if she intended to rise and battle her way to the back of the boat again. "Rose! Forget it! I've been behind the windshield most of the time; you've been out there with no protection. You're soaked; you have to get warmed up! Come on, you can sit right here. Come on, please! Keep my legs warm with your back, all right?"

"All right." Rose allowed Eric to help her to the floor. "I am tired. If I could just close my eyes for a second...."

Eric turned toward the compass and tried to right his course. "Might as well drop this wheel, much good as I'm doing," he muttered. "There's no steering in this wind. Why we haven't capsized yet is beyond me. This boat is built for speed, not rough water. The sides are too low. If we don't find an island soon, well..."

Despite the pouring rain, the screaming wind, and the motor's labored sputtering between blasts, sleep born of exhaustion and exposure began to deaden Rose. A wave slammed into the side of the boat and made it pitch hard, catching her off balance. She slipped toward the aisle, hitting her head on the metal base that supported the passenger seat.

Eric put out his arm and stopped her from falling toward the back of the boat. She looked up at him unsteadily.

"Here, Rose, sit closer; that's it. I've got you now; you won't slip again, not unless the whole boat overturns. Try to rest. You've done a great job."

Rose curled into a sitting position near him, grasping her knees for warmth. Eric knew his legs on either side of her would give stability but little heat.

She didn't seem to care. Her head hung lower, and Eric felt

her weight heavier against him, felt her breathing deepen.

"Hang on, Rose." Eric was positive she wouldn't respond, but he spoke anyway. "I think it's darker ahead. That could be good. Could be an island." He put his hand on her back, knowing that the blurry black shape in front of the bow could also be a rock or the frontal clouds that marked the storm's real fury.

"Hang on." His voice dropped to a whisper. "You can't die. You can't. I won't let it happen again. Just hang on," he urged, but felt sure that the woman at his feet could no longer hear him.

Rose stood, surrounded by haze. Ahead was a light, and she moved toward it, the fog falling away in front of her until she saw doctors and nurses in a cluster under the light. Groaning seemed to come from the center of their huddle.

"Anesthesia," someone ordered, and soon the groaning ceased.

Rose stepped nearer, looking past a stocky nurse. Eric! It was Eric who lay on the operating table! He was in restraints, and his left shoulder was a bloody mess.

"So you finally came to, Rose?" The nurse asked acidly. "Maybe now you can be a help instead of a hindrance."

Rose looked up and recognized Nurse Schaply, who seemed to be growing larger by the second.

"Suture," the doctor said, holding out his hand.

"But, Doctor," Nurse Schaply replied, "wouldn't it be easier to take the appendage off altogether?" She put a gloved hand to Eric's arm. "Help me pull, Rose."

"No. No! Stop!" Rose moved to grab Nurse Shaply, but

someone held her back. It was another doctor in scrubs. "Frederick!"

"It's for the best, Rose."

"Let me go! We have to stop her! You should understand. Doctors are supposed to help, to try to save—"

"There's nothing you can do." Frederick began pulling her away. "I'll take you home, Rose. I'll take you home.…"

The scene faded, and suddenly Rose was in Eric's tossing boat. He had only one arm. His shoulder had a red bandage on it, and he was trying to steer with one hand, but the boat was floundering. Rose bailed faster. The water poured in, driven by screaming wind.

"Eric, we're not going to make it! Eric!"

The wind shrieked, beating her with its fists. The boat pitched and Eric staggered, tumbling over the side.

"Eric!" Rose cried, but the gales forced the word back into her throat and ripped at her, pushing and pushing until she felt herself falling, falling…

The scent of burning wood and a deep, aching cold were Rose's first impressions upon waking. She stretched a hesitant hand to the wall near her and felt cool, moist rock. She seemed to be in a cleft just large enough and weatherproof enough to provide shelter. Eric squatted at the opening, fanning smoke from a small fire outside.

"Eric?" *He'll never hear me over the wind,* she thought, then noticed howling no longer filled her ears. She heard the fire's crackle and the rain outside: small, lovely noises, no longer the raging madness of a storm.

How heavenly the still earth is, she thought, and wondered if she would ever want to step into a boat again. Her voice gathered strength as she realized she was truly out of danger. "Eric?"

"Rose! Thank God!" Eric dropped the piece of wood he held and scrambled toward her, cracking his head on the low rock ceiling. It didn't slow him down a bit. He took her hand as if afraid she would evaporate before his eyes. "You're all right!"

She was relieved to see both his arms intact. "Eric, what happened? Where are we?"

"I tried to steer a course for Singing Pines, but...I'm not sure where we are. On some island, but it's drizzling outside and the visibility is low. The clouds have lightened, but they're still thick. I'll have a better idea where we are when they lift, that is, if they lift before night falls."

Rose nodded and stretched her legs toward the fire. "How did we get here? I don't remember anything except bailing water and trying to shout to you, unless that was a dream, too. How did you find this island?"

"I thought you might have heard that much. Just when the waves were beginning to build again, I saw a dark shape on the horizon. I hoped it was an island that we could land on. It was. I managed to steer the boat...well, really, we were tossed into the lee side of this island, and then I was able to steer behind a rock face that led into a narrow inlet. There was barely enough room for the boat to pass through, high rock on both sides. The walls gave enough shelter from the wind and waves that I got you out and some supplies before the wind changed again and the waves piled into the channel. I found this rock hole and thought it might work for shelter, so I pulled a few branches over the cracks and got you and our supplies settled in."

"Where's the boat?"

He shook his head. "It was being driven into the shore the last time I saw it, trapped on three sides by granite. Probably not much left of it by now."

"I'm sorry."

"*You're* sorry? Rose, I almost killed you! You didn't even want to go today! I wish—"

"Oh, Eric, it's all right. We're safe now." She closed her eyes and felt the heat of the fire warming her, melting her bad dreams away. She held out her arms and let the warmth prickle the undersides of her limbs. "All we have to do now is wait for the storm to let up and for someone to find us."

A smile of confidence spread across Rose's face. She looked outside. "Look, the rain is so much lighter. The storm will probably blow over in no time."

Eric's smile held nothing of hope in it. "That's right, Rose."

Rose rubbed her arms and began rolling up her jeans. The heat made them steam. "Oh, this feels so good. Eric, sit closer to the fire. You're wet, too."

He obeyed and mechanically held his arms to the flames, but turned his face toward the rock opening.

"Eric, what's wrong?"

He kept his face averted. "Nothing. You're right. We'll probably be fine. The fire does feel good."

" 'Probably?' Aunt Maddie will send out searchers. They'll comb the islands until they find…" Rose stopped and sought Eric's eyes. "You've no idea where we are?"

He turned toward her, his face a strange combination of pallor overspread with ruddiness where the fire was heating him. His black eyes were lusterless. "No idea at all, to be honest. I tried to steer by the compass, but it was hard to make any headway against the wind. Toward the end I was getting punchy. We could be a few miles out of Lakeshore or close to Singing Pines." He shrugged, evidently hoping she would interpret the information in its most favorable light.

"Or we could be miles away from anything." Rose grasped his real meaning immediately. "That's what you're thinking, aren't you? Lake of the Woods has more than fourteen thousand islands. That's a lot to search."

"Yes. A lot. I'm sorry, Rose. I didn't mean for this to happen." Eric stared into the fire. It was beginning to die down even as the raindrops grew thinner and more scattered outside.

"Eric, exactly what supplies did you get from the boat?"

"The first aid kit and a box of emergency things. I opened it up. A few flares, some matches, some dehydrated dinners and water purification pills. A couple of blankets. We really should use them and dry out our clothes."

Rose looked steadily at him. "How long can we make it?"

"A long time. There's plenty of potable water around without using any of the pills, and enough food to last a few days. And people have been known to live for weeks without food—"

"How long, Eric?"

He dropped his gaze. "Three weeks."

Rose neither spoke nor moved.

"I'm sorry, Rose; I'm so sorry. I'm the dumbest, most idiotic, brainless, asinine—" Eric got progressively violent and descriptive as he went on.

Rose couldn't think at all, but stared blindly at the coals. This was worse than a dream.

When Eric ran out of self-vilifications, he sat quietly. At last he reached for her, laying his arm across her shoulders. "As soon as the storm lets up, there could be search boats coming by, maybe even planes." Eric attempted a smile, but the smile was comfortless.

Rose bit her lip, forcing back the questions that flooded her mind and threatened to spill out of her mouth. She yearned for Eric's assurance that everything was going to be fine, but in her heart she knew that unless he lied, he had no assurance to give. They were marooned.

Seven

❧

Morning on Singing Pines started with a hint of light in the east that deepened into coral and was quickly replaced by the canary yellow of the rising sun. The mist burned away, its remnants visible only on the beads of dew clinging to purple wildflowers close to shore. Surrounding the halo of bright saffron, a light azure, signaling a calm, clear day spread across the sky. The sliver of glowing moon and the bright morning star near it faded as the sun ascended and sparkled across the reposing lake.

From his solitary cabin, Benjamin studied a lake map as he finished a hasty breakfast he could not taste. He'd searched the islands nearest Singing Pines, but the blackening clouds and shifting winds had driven him home prematurely. His heavy, high-sided boat had been in little danger of capsizing, but Ben knew if he holed up on an island until he could venture farther, he would worry Maddie and Mark needlessly, and perhaps tie up any rescue efforts. Reluctantly, he skirted the islands until he saw the lights of Singing Pines.

Sure enough, Maddie and Mark were standing at the dock

holding a lantern when Benjamin pulled in. He hadn't needed to tell them his search was unsuccessful; his empty boat and the beaten slump of his shoulders were testimony enough.

"Come on to the house, Ben. You can try again tomorrow," Maddie consoled, patting his back as he stood by her on the dock.

He remained motionless a moment more and faced the black horizon before following the couple up the rise to their log cabin.

At the dining room table, in front of a plate Maddie heaped high with food, Benjamin related his search, and he and Mark plotted their efforts for the following morning.

"I radioed the neighbors again," Mark said, after their plans were laid. "If it's clear tomorrow, I know we can count on at least five men to join us. That'll be good, eh?"

"Yes. Good." Benjamin rubbed his left temple with one hand and took another bite of mashed potatoes with the other. He poked at the broiled chicken, feeling no desire whatever to put it in his mouth. He knew it was no reflection on Maddie's culinary arts that the entire meal was unappealing.

"Benjamin, would you like a slice of rhubarb custard pie? It's the first of the spring crop. I just picked it today. Really, I should have left it another few weeks, but…"

Benjamin let Maddie talk on, reminding himself that this was her safety valve; anyway, her chatter was preferable to his own dark thoughts.

When she wound down, Benjamin replied, "I'll pass on the pie, Maddie. I'm pretty full. Great meal. Think I'll catch some sleep and get an early start tomorrow." He rose and pushed in his chair.

"Oh, some cider, then, at least, Benjamin. You're soaked to

the skin. You should have kept your hood on and worn waders, too, along with your slicker. Here. Just a few gulps."

Benjamin took the mug and drank the fragrant cinnamon cider. The warmth did him more good than the meal, and he felt his hands thaw along with his throat and belly.

"Thanks, Maddie." He drained the mug and set it on the table. "Mark, go ahead with your plans tomorrow morning. You know mine. We can meet back here at nightfall and figure out something else if we haven't found them by then. Goodnight."

"'Night, Benjamin." Mark rose with him. "Stay put, Maddie; I'll show him out."

Mark gripped Benjamin's shoulder and walked with him to the porch door. "I'll be back in a minute, Maddie," Mark called, before closing the door behind them.

"Now let's really talk, Benjamin. How many islands did you cover today?"

"Twelve," Benjamin answered miserably.

Mark nodded. "Add to that my six and Jack Savon's five, and it's still way too short. We're not going to get far on foot, eh? It's mail day tomorrow. I'm hoping Ned can make a few passes with the mail plane before he goes back to Warroad. The boys and I will be looking all day, and I know you and Jack will, too, but it's not sounding good. I contacted the Ontario Provincial Police. They might have a few men available to make a search. I got a relay message to Lakeshore City, too. Eric and Rose were spotted there. A boy at a floating gas station remembered Eric's boat and the dark-haired woman with him. He said they left around 1:00 or 2:00 P.M., and Eric...had obviously been drinking. I didn't tell Maddie.

"The storm hit Lakeshore City pretty hard, Ben. A lot of

boats were missing, torn from their riggings. There was damage to the marina, and the waves even poured over the retaining wall in some places, causing localized flooding. If they left Lakeshore at 2:00 and headed straight home, well, they headed into the eye of the storm. It passed in a huge diagonal swath between here and Lakeshore. The worst of it hit right in the middle."

Mark's words had sounded over and over in Benjamin's head all night, and after a few hours' interrupted sleep, a haggard Benjamin prayed and waited for dawn to break. After breakfast, he went to the Winters' cabin to pick up the bag lunch he knew Maddie would have waiting for him in the porch. Then he went straight to the marina, started his boat, and began his second day of searching.

Another calm, beautiful day on Lake of the Woods, Benjamin thought bitterly. *The killer lake. Quiet one moment, deadly the next. I bet on the dawn after Jesse's death, the sky looked just like this....*

Maddie had conveyed to Ben the details surrounding Jesse's funeral, concentrating, as was her wont, on the tint and nature of earth and sky rather than the color and qualities of the casket or those attending the small ceremony. The earth had been washed anew and was fresh from birth, like a gleaming dragonfly drying its wings in the sun minutes after emerging, Maddie had said. The lake was a soft baby blue, without a ripple. Benjamin was glad he hadn't been there to see it.

Now he cut through the water as if trying to hurt the entity that had killed her closest to him. In Benjamin's mind, Rose and Eric were already dead, too, and although he was rational enough not to blame Eric and wise enough not to blame God, he could almost hate the chameleon lake, the fickle sky, the sun that failed to light the way yesterday and five years earlier. June 8 would now have the added distinction of being the anniversary of Eric Savon and Rose Anson's deaths as well.

The sun burned in the sky, a searing globe radiating brilliant rays on the green foliage, lush and healthy from the rain. Brand-new leaves of poplars and bammies uncurled in the heat, and the dew of dawn quickly dried. Benjamin passed the islands he had already searched, scarcely noticing the purple, yellow, and white wildflowers opening to the morning heat. The glare of the sun on a procession of islands was all that Ben was aware of. He saw only row upon row of islands, each capable of hiding two survivors—if they had managed to survive.

Ben watched the shallow waves glimmer in the sunlight. The lake was again tame, gentle as a new mother, but Ben was sure its treacherous skirts hid the bodies of two more victims.

The water was the color of Benjamin Haralson's eyes, but the sorrowful mistress of Singing Pines was blind to its beauty as she stared at it. Her prayers still climbed to Heaven, but her hope was failing. No answer had come. No news from anyone.

Maddie kissed Mark as he finished his breakfast and quickly gathered his supplies to start searching. She stood at the window and watched him pass from sight down the same path he, Benjamin, and Jack Savon had taken the day before for the same purpose. She watched Mark materialize at the marina, a figure in miniature who climbed into a boat and scooted across the level lake.

It seemed too horrible to be real, too similar to what had happened to Jesse, and memories Maddie had thought crumbled with time resurrected as specters. The worst part was waiting, as it had been while they searched for Jesse five years and one day ago. The search had ended with the recovery of a body fit only for a funeral, and the fact had changed Maddie forever, had changed the lives of Mark and Benjamin, too.

Every June 8 and 9, the anniversaries of Jesse's death and the day of her funeral, the Winters household was subdued. Maddie wondered if soon they would have a new reason for sorrow. She couldn't imagine how she would ever relate the news to her sister, Nadine. It had been bad enough breaking the news to Edna Savon; the woman had nearly become hysterical.

Now Edna was holed up in her cabin, staring at the lake, refusing to see anyone. Maddie knew how she felt. She herself had done the same thing while Jesse was missing. As long as there was any hope of Jesse's return, Maddie hadn't wanted to be distracted by anyone. She felt that if she watched long and hard enough, Jesse would come back—but she hadn't.

The lake claimed a few lives every so often, just when everyone began to treat it carelessly. Among the sheltered American and Canadian islands, drownings were much rarer, collisions and boat wrecks more prevalent. Few were fatal.

The big lake, however, claimed victims regularly. As many as one every six years, some old-timers insisted. Maddie recalled no death for the past five. She prayed the truce would last.

As Maddie looked across the velvety lake, a boat laden with four exuberant riders pulled a slalom skier over the stretch of water past the marina. Maddie watched as the skier cut turns and made a beautiful rooster tail of spray behind her.

Had Maddie been closer, she would have seen the rainbow that arced the spray, and known that the rainbow, not the skier herself, was what made her friends clap and point. But from Maddie's field of vision, the rainbow was as invisible as Rose and Eric.

The boat passed from sight, and Maddie turned her gaze to the islands. Any one of them might conceal the two people most on her heart and in her prayers. Maddie rested her hand on the trim surrounding the picture window, unconsciously taking the very stance she'd assumed for so many hours as the men of the lake searched for her daughter.

Now she watched and prayed, sending messages to Heaven one upon the other like waves, each a living, moving thing that wended its way skyward until it lapped upon the shores of eternity.

Rose sat listening to the water gurgling at the base of the island. Such a soft sound, full of music; so different from the towering whitecaps that had foamed with deadly fury the day before. To think this mirror of blue before her, echoed in the sapphire sky, was capable of such moodiness! Now all was still with the subdued colors of dawn. The moon and morning star were already gone, and the citron-colored sun climbed higher each minute, grew a lighter, brighter yellow as it rose, casting heat and shadows.

It's paradise again, Rose thought, *not purgatory any longer, thank God.*

Rose let the thin foil blanket around her shoulders slip a little, and she stretched her legs toward the sun. What a difference dry clothes, rest, and a little food made! She was almost ready to risk taking another lake adventure. Almost.

"Rose?" Eric's voice sounded far away.

She turned in its direction. "I'm over here, Eric! Did you see anything?"

"Wait a second."

Rose heard muffled sounds, and several minutes later, Eric emerged from the forest and came walking toward her across the high granite shore.

"You know, Eric, the first time I saw you, you were much more debonair," Rose teased, "but stubble on your face and twigs in your hair do something for you."

"Yeah, make me look like a savage, right?" He lowered himself, sitting on a patch of moss instead of the granite.

Rose eyed him pensively. "No, you don't look like a savage; more like a backwoodsman, I think."

"All right, hold the jokes. I want to give my backwoodsman report."

"You know where we are?"

"All in good time, Miss Anson. First of all, the boat must've sunk. There are pieces of it floating down the channel—"

"Yes, I saw them this morning when I went outside. I really am sorry, Eric."

"It was probably a defective model, anyway. I know where I can get another one. But listen, Rose! I know where we are, or at least I have a pretty good idea!"

He sat looking at her triumphantly. In contrast to his torn, stained, and water-damaged outfit, his lofty expression seemed almost comical. Rose smiled and touched his sleeve. "All right, Daniel Boone; where do you think we are?"

He moved nearer. "About two or three miles from Singing Pines and a mile or so off one of the main drags! They're going to find us, Rose. It might take awhile, but they'll find us. I did it! I kept the course!"

Eric hugged her and didn't let go as he continued. "If it takes too long, I'll just swim to the main channel and wait. It's June; there'll be lots of tourists—"

"Eric," Rose said, struggling away from his smoke-smelling chest, "just how strong a swimmer are you?"

"I can swim as well as I can drive."

"That's what I was afraid of. Maybe you should stay here a few days and play Robinson Crusoe with me. I'd make a wonderful Friday."

He cupped her face with his blistered hands. They felt rough on her cheeks. "A prettier Friday there will never be. You know, Rose, this is the first time we've really been alone together. I'm not so sorry we had to go through that storm after all."

"You're not? Eric, it was terrible! Don't you remember the wind and rain? The boat rocking, the blackness and cold?" Her body tensed at the thought, and her eyes grew dark. "I didn't think we'd get out alive."

"But we did, Rose! Man was pitted against nature, and man won! Excuse me, we won. I knew we couldn't die. And here we are: Adam and Eve in paradise. If I could only find some fig leaves," he said, looking around him as if in earnest. "Well, you can't have everything. I'll settle for you."

Rose laughed, but the expression in Eric's eyes told her he was only half joking. She looked across the lake. "It is good to be alive, isn't it? I feel like celebrating, too, but let's wait until the rescue boats get here, all right?"

Eric smiled and dropped his hands from her face. "All right. I get the point. Okay if I hold your hand at least?"

"Absolutely. And I'm glad you're in a better mood this morning, Eric. I never blamed you for what happened. I know this lake can get dangerous. My cousin Jesse was killed on it a few years ago, and from what I've been told, she knew it inside out. And she knew her boat, too, a good, solid one. Accidents happen."

Eric took a sharp breath and stared at the granite. When she looked at him, he gave her a tight smile. "Yeah. You're right. Accidents happen." He turned quickly, and this time he did not look back.

The first rescue boat came later that morning when the sun was high. Rose and Eric had just decided to take a swim. They were discussing what to do for suits, Eric still favoring fig leaves, when the slow-moving kicker boat putted into view.

Eric took off his shirt and waved it as a signal. Soon the boat made a wary landing near the rocks on which the two castaways sat.

"Thank God!" Rose said. "We nearly drowned in the storm yesterday, and our boat sank. Could you give us a ride to Singing Pines Island?"

The man in the boat spit a brown stream into the lake, wiped his dripping chin, and regarded her calmly. "That's what I'm here for. Your name's Rose, ain't it?"

Rose nodded.

"Thought so. Your uncle radioed me." He spat again. "Ten of us've been combin' the lake all mornin', lookin' for you two, an' there was searchers yesterday, too. Let's get you home so everyone can get back to his work." The man's slitted eyes rested briefly on her. "Grab your things, if you have any. Time's wastin'."

Rose scrambled up immediately, but Eric had other ideas.

"Hold on, man," he said, putting his hands on his hips. "We've been through a lot, you know? Let's just take it easy here. We'll get our things and be back as soon as we can." He spun on his heel and walked slowly down the trail after Rose.

She was gathering the blankets and supplies when Eric stepped through the shelter's opening. "Do you want to take that last meal?" she asked. "No, I didn't think so. It's already opened on one side—"

"Wait, Rose. Sit down. We're not in such a big hurry." He put his arms around her waist and pulled her to him.

"Eric!" Rose broke away. "Stop it! That man's waiting for us, and I'm sure Aunt and Uncle—"

Eric smothered her protests. "You were meant for me," he whispered, when he ended his kiss. "Nothing can change that." He caressed her cheek with his lips. "Still want to go?"

Rose gathered her reserves and stood, if somewhat shakily. "Yes, I do want to go, Eric," she said quietly. "And I'd appreciate a hand. Pack up the rest of the supplies, and I'll take these back to the boat. I'll see you there."

Rose did not look back as she left the small rock shelter. She heard Eric mumbling behind her.

"Sorry, I can't hear you, Eric," she called, "but you can tell me all about it in the boat." She carried her burden down the path to the waiting outboard, hesitating only an instant before she climbed in.

Eight

⤜⟡⟐

I won't tax you with a lecture, Rose," Aunt Maddie said, sitting at the kitchen table, "but you had us petrified, as I'm sure you're aware."

For the first time in nearly twenty-four hours, Maddie was able to abandon her post at the window and rest in a chair. Now, even with the hugging and crying over, her body still trembled, and she was thankful for the sturdy chair frame that supported her.

"I *am* sorry, Auntie. It all happened too fast! I know that's not much of an excuse, but first Eric said he wanted to show me his boat, and before I knew it, I was inside and he said we'd take a quick spin. If I had known I'd be gone for more than a half hour, I would have let you know; please believe me! He just headed straight out into the islands, and I lost track of time."

"Yes, and when you landed in another country, you didn't think anything was wrong? You didn't even bother to let us know where you were? They do have radios in Canada, Rose. You might have tried relaying a message."

Rose pushed in her chair and stood at her aunt's side. "Aunt Maddie," she said, draping an arm around her shoulder, "I really am sorry. And I don't want to blame this on Eric. I was irresponsible, too. I know. But he did tell me we'd only be gone a little while, and before I knew it, we were at Lakeshore City. We just stopped at a few shops and had lunch. I guess the hours ticked by."

Maddie met her niece's eyes and softened slightly. "I believe I understand, Rose. Time has a way of doing that when you're young and in love."

"I'm not in love, Aunt Maddie!"

"You aren't? Then why the change in your attitude, Rose? When you first came, you were pleasant enough, but withdrawn, cool. Now you haven't stopped talking since Allyn Fishman brought you and Eric back. And somehow I don't think it was Al's bouncy personality that brought about this difference in you."

"No." Rose reseated herself. "No, I just feel better about things, somehow. On that boat, I thought we were going to die. I was sure. You can't imagine how it was, Auntie! The waves were coming over the sides, I was bailing and couldn't even feel my fingers or hands or legs, I was so cold. The boat kept tipping farther and farther, and water kept spilling inside. The wind was so loud and the waves crashed so much that I could hardly hear a word Eric yelled to me. At first I blamed him, but when the waves got even higher and the sky turned black, I was scared, not angry. And then, as we fought for life, there seemed to be a purpose for living, a reason. I almost felt like we had to fulfill...some kind of destiny!"

Maddie examined her niece's face more closely. A deep flush

lay over her cheeks, and her eyes, though bright, had the glossy look of fever. Maddie put her palm on Rose's forehead.

"I'm all right, Auntie. I'm only tired. I think I'll rest in the loft."

"Hold it a moment. You're pretty hot, and you're not talking exactly coherently, Rose—a little too forced and dramatic. Here, I'll fix you a cool washcloth and meet you up in the loft as soon as you get into bed. I'll bring a glass of lemonade, too. I got some fresh lemons on the mail plane today. You head on up."

As Rose stood, Maddie had second thoughts. "Wait—why not sit here until everything's ready and I'll follow you up? You're not looking too steady, and a fall from the ladder could lay you out for good. Sit awhile and relax. I can squeeze a lemon fast as anything."

As Maddie bustled around the kitchen, Rose sat, talking non-stop. Maddie realized her niece was making less and less sense, but she thought it better not to contradict Rose for the time being.

"I can't believe the way I feel is caused by a fever, Auntie! Everything seems so much better. Eric and I have beaten death! We can beat anything! My life before I came here seems so long ago. Frederick…Mother…Father…. They're miles away, buried under eons of time. The boat ride…was a test…a…rite of passage." Rose made a strange gesture in the air. "And we survived! We conquered! Do you know what I mean, Auntie?"

Maddie gave a brief shake of her head and turned back to the counter.

"Oh, well." Rose lowered her own head on the kitchen table. "Eric said it first; maybe only he understands."

"All right, Rose, that does it." Maddie set down the washcloth

86

and glass she carried. "I'll bring these after I see you safely to your bed. You start first. I'll follow."

They began the climb, but Rose did more talking than moving. "I appreciate your helping me, Aunt Maddie. It's so hard to pull myself up the ladder today. My body feels so heavy."

After only one rung, Maddie canceled the climb. "I don't think this is a good idea, Rose. Here, back down; I'll help. You've only gone up two feet anyway. You can rest in our bedroom. I think I'll ask Benjamin to look in on you later."

When Rose was settled into her aunt and uncle's big bed, a cool cloth on her forehead and a cold glass of lemonade in her hand, Maddie rose from the rocking chair near her.

"Wait, Aunt, please don't go yet. If you don't have to work, I'd like to talk a little more."

"I think it would be better if you slept—"

"Just talk to me until I feel sleepy, please?"

"If you wish." Maddie smoothed the washcloth on Rose's forehead, felt its heat, and turned it over gently. "I'm so thankful to have you back, my dear. I thank God. And I'm ashamed to say that I thought you and Eric were gone for good. I thought I'd never see you again, like Jesse, and that I'd have to tell your mother...."

Rose's eyes were closed, but she murmured, "No, no. Everything's fine, Auntie."

Maddie smiled and patted her hand. "Funny that you have to tell me that, young woman. Yes, I know. The Lord was watching over you. It's just that I was so certain he was watching over Jesse, too. All that night when she was missing, I knew they would find her and she would be fine. I had great faith that God would protect her—and me, I guess. I stood by that picture window and watched, as I did while you and Eric were missing, expecting each minute to see her returning in her boat and waving to me from the marina to let me know she was back. I knew she'd run up the path and hug me, and I'd give her a hot meal and tell her how worried we'd been. But I never had the chance."

"I'm sorry, Aunt. I thought about that this morning." Rose opened her lids halfway. "Jesse died around this time of year, didn't she? That must have made everything so much more horrible. I'm sorry we put you through all this."

Maddie took the washcloth from Rose and freshened it in a bowl of water. She wrung the washcloth and laid it on Rose's forehead. "In a way, it's almost like getting Jesse back, like God saying, 'I can bring the dead to life.' When he didn't bring Jesse home alive, a little of my faith crumbled. I had trusted him and he failed me. I know that wasn't the case, but it seemed like it to me. This time, I had such small faith, and yet he remained faithful."

Rose's lips moved slowly. "No, no, Aunt…, Eric said we…couldn't die."

"I think that's fever talking, Rose, but if it isn't, you're somewhat confused. Your efforts and Eric's efforts didn't save you. God did. There were other boats caught in the storm, other people not so blessed as you. One man died, an experienced guide from an island only a few miles from here. He and a girl were out in a kicker boat. She was driving when it overturned—they must've smacked into a deadhead or some such thing. He was helping her swim to shore when the storm hit. He didn't make it in himself, or maybe he slipped from shore during the night. She's not sure. She just woke up this morning and he was gone. The boat was floating offshore in the weeds. She swam out to it, climbed in, and came home with her story, poor thing.

"Now why should Glen have died when he was such a strong swimmer? The girl is a little thing, a poor swimmer, unskilled in boating, yet she was the one who lived. Why, Rose?"

"I don't know." Rose's words were slurred. "The…luck of the draw?"

"There's no such thing as luck, my dear. As Job said, 'The Lord gave and the Lord has taken away. Blessed be the name of the Lord.' All that happens in life is in his hands. Jesse and Glen are gone, but I thank God that he restored the girl, and you, and Eric to me. The Lord is merciful, beyond all."

Rose's eyes closed with finality. "Maybe…you're right, Auntie," she mumbled.

"I believe I am, Rose. Now you rest. I'll bring you something to eat later on. Goodnight, my dear. May God continue to bless you as he has already today." Maddie kissed her niece on the forehead and left the room.

"When can I see her, Maddie?" Benjamin had been pacing the floor since he'd arrived, and no amount of cajoling or even a direct order could make him sit down.

"You're making me nervous as a kitten, Benjamin! If she doesn't wake in another hour, you may go in. In fact, I'll make you go in even if you don't want to. She was feverish when she came home, but I think it's slackening."

"Did you give her any aspirin?"

"Yes. Two of them."

"Good. That should bring the fever down, unless it's something serious. She probably caught a cold from exposure."

"That's my guess. I don't think it's too much of anything, but I'd like your opinion, Doctor." She smiled. "That reminds me. How's the studying going?"

"Hm?" His face showed no expression. "Oh, that. I haven't touched it since I heard they were missing. And I don't think I can until I'm sure she's safe."

Maddie noticed that Benjamin didn't seem quite so worried about Eric as he was about Rose, but thought it unwise to point it out. "I understand, Ben. Praise God she's safe! It's a little like getting Jesse back, isn't it? Rose and I were talking about that—"

"You told her about Jesse and me?"

"I told her about Jesse and me," Maddie said staunchly. "What was between Jesse and you is just that. I didn't figure it was my place to say anything. I know I say too much occasionally, but I didn't this time."

"Thanks, Maddie. I think I will sit down."

"Good. And have a little lunch, too. I'm late today, I know, but it's about done. You can sample it and tell me if I'm on the right track."

Benjamin tried the portions of roast beef, parsley potatoes, and leftover rhubarb custard pie Maddie set before him on a piece of china.

"China?" Benjamin queried, brushing a fingertip over the plate's blue floral design. "I don't recall you serving lunch on this before."

Maddie was chopping carrots on the counter. She smiled at him before she continued her knife strokes. "We're celebrating Rose's return. In fact," she said, popping an orange slice into her mouth and crunching it, "I don't know if I'll put up the china again. Why not use it? Life is a celebration. Each day the Lord gives us should be lived in thankfulness to his mercy, not just the days our blind eyes can glimpse it working."

"You're right, Mad. The Lord sure answered my prayers this time, even though I hardly had the heart to pray."

"It was the same with me," Maddie confessed. "I think we must feel a little like Martha and Mary when they got Lazarus back from the grave. Our God is the God of second chances." Her voice was shaky, but Benjamin didn't appear to notice.

As he cleaned up the last morsel left on the china plate, he said, "I'm looking forward to what he's got planned for me this time around."

Maddie braced her hand on Ben's shoulder and bent to retrieve his dirty dish. "I think he's got a lot planned for you, Benjamin," she said hoarsely, holding the dish and standing behind him so he couldn't see the tears collecting in her eyes. "For you...and for Rose." She gave his cheek a pat and hurried toward the sink.

Rose's fever was down by early evening, but when Benjamin came to check on her again, Maddie announced that Rose was not to leave the room that day or the next. She was taking no more chances with her niece.

"You may go on ahead and see her, Ben, but don't stay long. I know I'm overdoing it a little, but after what I've been through, I deserve it. Humor me, dear boy. Temporarily forget that you know more about sickness than I do, won't you? Now go on in." Maddie closed the door behind Benjamin, and he stood just inside.

"Flowers? Thank you." Rose wore a pink sweat suit and sat

against the headboard. She reached out her hands for the wild-flower bouquet Benjamin held. "Beautiful. I wish I had a vase for them."

"I can ask Maddie—"

"No, it's fine. I'll just set them in my water glass for now. Well, do you think I'm healthy enough to get out of bed yet, Doctor?"

"Just between you and me, I think you're at least capable of going back up to your own bed, but I don't think your aunt agrees, and I doubt she'll let you up for a while."

Rose sighed. "I guess that's how I pay for my crime." She looked at him. "I suppose you think we had no business out on the lake, too."

"It was a sudden storm. No one knew it was coming." Benjamin shrugged. "Could've happened to anyone. You're not the only ones who got caught out on the lake."

"Yes, that guide and his girl. I know. Auntie told me." Rose's voice grew soft. "I'm sorry for all the trouble we put you through. I hear you braved the storm to go out looking for us, along with Uncle Mark and Eric's father. I think I understand why they did. But why did you, Benjamin? I've been wondering. Why did you risk your life for ours?"

"I wasn't in much danger—not like you two. I couldn't make it far before night fell, and the storm wasn't as bad here. I stayed near the sheltered parts of islands, and my boat is sturdy, made for rough weather."

"Not like Eric's speedboat?"

"I didn't mean—"

Rose's chin came up. "You didn't?" She looked directly into

Benjamin's eyes. He didn't flinch. He almost seemed to welcome her stare.

"Well, maybe you didn't," Rose conceded. "I'm sorry. I'm a little touchy, I guess. I feel silly, lying here in Auntie and Uncle's bed like an invalid. Do you think you could talk Auntie into shortening my sentence? For good behavior or something?"

Benjamin smiled back at her. "I've already been warned not to. But I'll make your imprisonment as pleasant as I can. I brought some books for you."

Rose took the volumes. *"The Scarlet Letter* and *Pride and Prejudice?* Aren't these a little heavy for a convalescent?"

"Maybe. They're a couple of my favorites, though. I thought you might like them, too."

Rose fingered the bindings. She was familiar with the titles. They were, in fact, among her favorites as well, though she hadn't read them in a long time.

"If you feel like resting your eyes, I could read them to you."

"Did Aunt Maddie send you here to be my nursemaid, or are you taking this on yourself?"

"I came of my own free will. I can leave freely, too."

Rose laughed. "I guess you do have your limits. I'm sorry. I'll try to get into a better mood."

Her eyes wandered to the pages of paper lying on the night-stand. She quickly folded the letters and put them inside the drawer. "If I get them out of my face, maybe I can get them out of my mind."

"Letters from home?"

"Yes. Mother must have written the moment I left Wayzata, or maybe she began when I started packing. She and Father weren't too happy that I decided to come here. I'm glad I did, though. If it hadn't been for Aunt Maddie, I'd probably still be—" She stopped. "I'm sorry. You can't be interested in this."

"I can and I am. Don't forget I 'risked my life' for you."

Rose couldn't help returning his smile. "Going to play that up for all it's worth, are you?"

"Only if I have to." His grin widened. "Only when you start shutting me out again. I'm not dangerous, Rose, really. In fact, Lilla says I'm actually not all that bad. She says—"

Rose laughed aloud. "I already know what Lilla says about you. She hasn't quit telling me of your virtues since I came." Rose tilted her head to study him. "Maybe I should do a sketch of you, as long as I'm bedridden. I could call it "Rugged Adonis" or something. That's one of Auntie's names for you, by the way."

"Everyone seems to be pouring it on pretty thick." Benjamin sounded embarrassed. He was silent, then smiled and lowered his voice to a whisper. "That's good—means I've got them completely fooled."

"Them—but not me."

"What'll it take until you're tricked, too?"

Rose thought about it. "You could start by going up to the loft and bringing me my drawing pencils. Don't let Auntie see you, whatever you do. She thinks my activities should be limited to conversation and napping."

"I don't know—"

"Please, Benjamin. They're in the closet, I think. There's not much else in there besides dusty packing boxes. You shouldn't have much trouble finding them. You should be glad to get off this easily!"

He stood, but looked unwilling to leave.

"Go ahead, tear yourself away from me. I'll be here when you get back. And maybe you can start reading one of those novels to me when you return, all right?"

"Okay. And there's a song I want to teach you, too. If you like songs, that is. Maddie said you do. I'm not the best singer, but I think you'll like it anyway."

"You're really taking advantage of my 'sickness,' aren't you?"

"Like I said, only if I have to. I'm here to help."

"Then get my pencils, Benjamin. And my sketch pad. And hurry! Auntie could come in any minute. I'm surprised she hasn't already."

"I'm not," Benjamin said, slipping out the door. "Don't try to escape while I'm gone."

Rose waved him away and, as she turned back, caught the image of her face in the large vanity mirror across the room.

You can wipe that smile right off your face, she chastised herself. *A doctor is a doctor—even if he doesn't have his M.D. yet! Don't go falling into trouble again just when you're starting to get yourself out.*

But the smile refused to fade.

Nine

✎

Benjamin stayed most of the evening to keep Rose cheered up, and he and Lilla spent a lot of time with her the next day, but Maddie still wouldn't let Rose get out of bed for anything except necessities. It was late afternoon before Maddie said Rose might be allowed to move back into the loft—provided she stay there until the following morning. Benjamin joked that Maddie had only made the concession because Mark didn't like sleeping in the guest bedroom.

Around 3:00 P.M., Aunt Maddie bustled in, fluffed up Rose's pillow, and was about to leave when she moved toward a piece of thick paper sticking out from under the bed.

"And what is this may I ask?" Maddie clucked her tongue and held up the drawing.

Rose smiled. "It's a sketch of the point where Eric and I got marooned. Precisely at that spot I watched the sun rise across the water the morning we were rescued."

Maddie sat down on the bed. "It's very good, Rose. Much better than my scribbling. You like working with charcoal best?"

"Not really." Rose swung her feet out of bed. "But I was

going through a charcoal stage when I left Wayzata, and I only packed my charcoal pencils, sketch pad, and a few canvases."

"Has Benjamin seen this?"

"I'd like to show it to Eric first, but I haven't seen him since Mr. Fishman brought us back. I thought he'd visit me today for sure. Did he get sick, too?"

"He's fine, but he and his parents left for Winnipeg yesterday. He didn't come to tell you about it, I gather?"

"No." Rose frowned slightly and turned her attention to the drawing in her aunt's hands. "Auntie, what do you think of the lines here?"

"I couldn't say, Rose; I'm not an artist, just a dabbler. And looking at a sunrise in black and white is a new experience for me. Do you use watercolor or acrylics, too?"

"Yes, but I don't have any with me."

"And I suppose you sneaked up to the loft to get these drawing materials when I wasn't looking?"

"No. Benjamin did." Rose smiled.

Maddie sat down next to her niece. "Rose, did you ever stop to think what you were doing when you sent Benjamin up to the loft? He hasn't been up there since Jesse died."

Rose looked puzzled. "Was Benjamin in love with—"

"I would've thought Lilla had told you everything by now." Maddie wiped her hands together briskly. "Well, it's not up to me to say anything—not a word!"

Rose stared at her aunt. "Lilla did mention something. I guess I didn't think about it much."

"Maybe you should, my dear." Maddie stood. "But now I have something for you."

She went to her closet and stepped on the seat of a chair so she could reach the top shelf. She took down a dusty cigar box and wiped its surface with her sleeve before handing it to Rose. "And you may as well get out of bed. You're not getting any rest anyway if you're drawing all the time and making Benjamin do your dirty work. And I guess you are quite well at that. Here. Think this'll do? It was my old set. And I think I can dig up some watercolors for you, too."

Rose opened the hinged wooden box and found twenty or thirty tubes of acrylics with their names and a dab of identifying color on each label. "These are perfect, Aunt Maddie! I'll start right away. Here, give me that black and white thing."

"No, no. I'm beginning to like this sketch. Very unusual. Believe I'll frame it and hang it in one of the cabins, if it's all right with you."

"Absolutely fine. Auntie, I've wanted to talk with you about the cabins. More guests arrived this morning. You're busy, aren't you?"

"June always is. We won't have much slack time until after July 4."

"Yes, Lilla told me. I'd like to help you in the cabins, if you don't mind. I'd like to do more in exchange for my room and board than contribute second-rate drawings now and then. I...I want to work...to do some...manual labor."

Once Rose had made her disclosure, her words flowed. "I'll probably be worthless at first, but I learn fast. How much can there be to cleaning anyway?"

Maddie laughed and threw her a towel from the closet. "Tell you what, Rose. You take a shower and I'll get your clothes from the loft. Tomorrow, if you're still feeling well, Lilla and I will show you exactly how much there can be to cleaning. How's that?"

"Suits me just fine." Rose slung the towel over her shoulder and headed to the bathroom. "Won't Eric be surprised when he gets back? He's as spoiled rotten as I am. Maybe I can talk him into helping Uncle Mark around the place, too. It's time we got off our golden pedestals and learned how to be useful."

As Rose swept into the bathroom, Maddie chuckled. She couldn't for the life of her envision her pampered, silk-appareled niece tackling dirt with a scrub brush or cleaning someone else's bathroom grime.

Maddie closed the bedroom door and finished doing the dishes. From the window above the sink, she saw guests strolling the grounds, but the Savon cabin was dark and uninhabited. Behind her, Rose was singing in the shower, a bouncy nautical tune Maddie recognized as often coming from Benjamin's mouth. There had been many changes in Rose Anson since she'd first set foot on the island, and Maddie felt that in the next few days, there would be even more. When Eric got back, Maddie wondered if he'd like what he would find.

"I still don't know how you got me into this, Benjamin," Rose complained. "It's not even light out yet!"

"Watch out!" Benjamin touched her waist to guide her. Rose wondered how he could use his big hand so gently.

"You almost walked into that pine bough, Rose. Here, walk with me."

Rose held onto him for balance and direction. The sky was not quite pitch-black. It rarely was in the islands, Rose was learning. Usually a sprinkling of stars or a harvest moon acted as lanterns until the sun's awakening, but this morning was full of shadows. Only a single star shone by the moon, and neither gave much light.

By the time Benjamin led Rose down to the marina and into his boat, a faint pink crept along the eastern horizon. A soft glow made the landscape dimly visible, and ordinary objects took on a fantastic, almost surreal depth and color. The dock seemed a brilliant gray, the trees chartreuse.

Except for the muffled squabbling of cliff swallows diving through the dusky air, the world was hushed. A wind like a slow exhalation came from the west and breathed without ruffling the water.

Benjamin choked the motor and pulled. The engine revved and settled into an even firing. A wood duck, crabby from being awakened, flew by the boat so low his wing tips almost brushed the water.

Benjamin headed east, and the uneasiness Rose had felt at being in a boat again was purged by the ethereal beauty of pre-dawn. Now no star was visible, although the moon still hung, faint and slight. A translucent layer of clouds veiled the stars and allowed a pale blue to diffuse the sky.

Weaving through the islands, Benjamin steered the boat toward a beach and slowed near the lee side of it. A huge hunk of reeds drifted ahead of them. At first Rose thought the mass might be the bow of an overturned boat, and her anxiousness returned. As they drew closer, she realized it was only a chunk torn from one of the weed beds.

Benjamin explained that the storm's high winds caused a lot of damage not only to the manmade buildings and docks but also to God's creations. Sturdy old pines, almost three feet in diameter, had been caught in the gales and tipped over. One such tree on shore lay before them, its roots still clinging to the shallow earth that had once anchored it to the granite.

The rattle of Benjamin's pole against the aluminum boat punctuated the bird chorus. Rose sat still, listening to crows caw-ing and white-throated sparrows giving their cry: "Pure, Sweet Canada, Canada, Canada!" they said, according to her aunt.

A gull flew in front of Rose, clutching a fish on the fly. Pelicans landed near the boat, hoping for handouts. Rose didn't bait her hook, although she did hold her pole as if in preparation to fish, and she studied Ben's movements when she wasn't watch-ing for the sun.

The boat rocked slightly as the breeze grew in strength. Waves echoed off the hull at different pitches. Rose shook her head, remembering the clutching waves of a week ago. The memory of them had not been altered by the seven days of hard labor Rose had served on Singing Pines. From an angel of mercy, Aunt Maddie had become a drill sergeant, drumming out orders.

"Rose, you wanted to learn the cleaning business and you will!" Aunt Maddie had decreed. "But if you ever need a break, let me know," she added with a smile.

Rose's pride became her enemy, and even though Aunt Maddie had made her take rests while she and Lilla marched on, Rose rejoined the forces as soon as she was able. She had come to know the meaning of sore, work-tested muscles.

"Benjamin, I'm glad you took me out here," Rose said, sud-denly grateful for a break. "I needed some time away from the resort." The haze began to lift, unveiling the closer islands even as all other things in the distance remained a smoky blue. "I needed some color in my life, now that—"

"Eric's gone?" Benjamin looked away. "I'm sorry, Rose. I shouldn't have said that."

"Maybe not, but you're right. Eric and I had quite an adventure together, and I do miss him. I wonder why he's staying away so long?"

Benjamin didn't reply.

An uneven wind moved across the rolling water, causing it to pucker. A gray-blue haze enveloped the lake's surface, and white mists covered the distant islands. The whole scene suggested a fairy land to Rose.

"Pretty good breeze for so early in the morning." Benjamin moved his pole up and down in a movement that reminded Rose of his shoveling the day she'd met him.

"Could get some walleye chop today, Rose."

"Walleye what?"

"Chop. Just enough bounce in the waves to make the lure appeal to walleyes without having to jig it yourself. That's my definition, anyway. Ever jigged?"

"Do I look like I have?" Rose quipped.

Benjamin laughed. "I thought you made a face when I baited my hook. Never been fishing before?"

"Never. And if Auntie hadn't threatened me with all the laundry and the cabins by myself if I didn't go with you, I wouldn't be on my first fishing trip now—though morning on the lake is beautiful," Rose added, realizing how rude she must sound. "I appreciate the chance to see it." She smiled carefully, trying to thank him without encouraging anything.

Benjamin dipped his hand into the bait bucket and caught

her line. "Here. I'll bait your pole for you. You don't like the look of the leeches, do you? I didn't either my first time fishing with Jes—" He shut his mouth, but not in time. He glanced up to see Rose's reaction. She looked at him with interest, but he didn't finish his sentence.

He bent over Rose's pole, putting the leech on the hook and releasing the line, telling her just how much monofilament to let into the water and how to work the pole.

Rose listened and tried to quit noticing the color of his eyes. Benjamin was a nice guy, she had to admit, and nice looking, but she was not interested in another doctor, not even a doctor-to-be, although she'd reminded herself of that fact several times over the past few days.

They sat without talking much, although Benjamin started to say something several times. Finally the lake creatures took pity on him, and a flash of silver jetted from the water and landed in a belly flop.

"Did you see that fish jump, Rose?"

"No, but I heard the splash, and I see the ripples."

"Keep a sharp eye out. You'll see another. Maybe you'll get a good idea for another one of your sketches. By the way, what's your favorite medium?"

Rose tilted her head to consider the question. "It varies. Right now I'm most interested in working with those acrylics Auntie gave me."

"Perfect! Look at the changing colors then. This island, the lake, and the sky will be transformed as the morning progresses. See the moon? It's risen, fading away. And now the sky is lighter."

"Yes, but where's the sun?"

"Behind those islands. It'll appear soon. The pink is deepening and spreading, like offshoots of the rising sun buried in the mists."

Rose smiled inwardly at his description and looked toward the east to see if it was accurate. It was, and she began to catch his enthusiasm as the beauty he spoke of cut through the haze and piqued the artist in her.

"Look at those clouds: brush strokes of pink," she said, pointing. "The moon is so high and pale, I can hardly see it anymore. And still no sun, but the sky is getting lighter and more like day every second."

She inclined her head and listened. "Benjamin, is there...a waterfall around here?"

"No. But it sounds like one, doesn't it?" He seemed pleased. "It's the waves hitting the shore."

Rose turned toward the island behind them. "Oh, look at the colors onshore, Ben! I've never seen ones so deep, with such variety. I wish I had brought my paints. The island looks like it's in 3-D! The pines have become such a rich green, and every tree, every leaf seems to have its own shade: verdure, malachite, viridian—"

"The colors are magnificent, Rose, but if you keep looking there, you'll miss the sun. It should appear any minute now."

Ben gestured ahead of them. "Keep your eyes in the east, but don't look directly at the sun or you'll burn your retinas. Watch. Watch—"

They both held their breath and leaned forward, their eyes fastened on the same spot, a glowing aureole on the crest of a pine-topped island in the distance.

"Watch...watch...there it is!"

Benjamin and Rose released their breaths simultaneously and glanced at each other to make sure neither missed the spectacle. Involuntary smiles lit their faces. Rose quickly looked back at the sun, but felt Ben still watching her.

"Ben, look!" Rose cried, aware he stared at her and wanting him to see the wondrous sight before them. "Gorgeous! It's like a thin disk—suspended there like a clock pendulum. And so big—it looks bigger than the island below it! And the color—"

"It's the most beautiful color in the world," Benjamin said, easing himself closer to her as she gazed raptly at the rising sun. "It's the color of rose."

Ten

&ex;

You haven't said much since sunrise." The boat drifted over a reef, and Benjamin let his line down to the walleyes and saugers feeding there. "Anything wrong?"

"I was thinking again. A bad habit for me lately." Rose tried to laugh. "I got another letter from home. Uncle Mark brought it to me yesterday afternoon, and I keep thinking about it. I can't understand how Mother's keeping up the pace. I'm glad there aren't any phones around. She'd be at me every minute."

"There's a phone on Flag Island if you ever really need one. Maddie refuses to have them on her island though." Benjamin looked at Rose. "Your mother still wants you to come home?"

"More than ever. I was afraid she might start in on Auntie, so I wrote to her last night and tried to explain how I feel. I said I was beginning to enjoy life again. That should satisfy her, I hope. She's a worrier, like Aunt Maddie. Way too overprotective. But she does want me to be happy."

Rose looked upward. The sun had lost its redness and now hung like a bulb. Underneath, the lake resembled a paint-by-number picture. Each tie-dyed wave contained rings of color, almost like the rings of a tree, but shimmering: myrtle greens, dancing scarlet, and violet on dapple gray, each ring outlined in black. "I could stay here forever. And maybe I will! There are a million scenes to be painted, a million things to be sketched."

"Time to see another one of the million." Benjamin reeled up his pole and stowed it, starting the motor and checking the map for the next nearest reef. He expected a return from each fishing hole, and if he didn't get one within the first ten minutes, he was off to another reef. It was the way Jesse had taught him.

At last they settled down to a hot spot—for Benjamin. After watching him catch five plump walleyes and two wriggling bass, Rose wasn't content with her losing score of three bait-eating strikes, one empty clam, and two broken lines. "I don't feel like sitting around all day watching you have all the luck, Benjamin. Teach me how to catch fish."

He was just unhooking a small sauger from his line, one hand keeping its dorsal spines down, the other hand slipping the barbs from the fish's ashen lower lip. Once the operation was complete, he eased the fish into the water, holding it a few seconds before releasing it. The sauger flipped its tail twice and dove into the depths.

"I've told you everything I know already, Rose. You fish on the bottom, keep your rod jigging so the lure bounces and attracts fish, and then when the strike comes, set the hook."

Benjamin jerked his own rod violently to demonstrate. "Then keep the tip up, but not too high—never too high—and reel in as he gives you slack. I'll net for you."

"Are you sure you're telling me everything? I've been trying to do all that, but it hasn't worked."

"Well…" Benjamin didn't look at her. "Maybe it would help if you held onto my pole while I caught another fish. Maybe you'd get the feel of it then."

"That might work."

Benjamin pushed aside a boat cushion and made room for her. "Here, sit in front of me. I'll, uh, hold the pole, and you can put one hand here and the other on the rod base, okay?" He indicated the handle and a point just above it.

He watched her station herself with clinical interest. Though she sat so near him she had to feel the quickened rising and falling of his chest and his breath past her cheek, Rose appeared impervious to any sensation other than a fish's tug on her line. Benjamin, however, was acutely aware of the warmth of her body next to his chest, warmer than even the sun on his back.

Benjamin shifted uncomfortably and held his arms out to avoid touching her slim waist and tapered forearms. If she could be so inhumanly cold, so could he—if he could just get his mind off her. He tried to find a relaxing position.

Rose swung her head around to look at him. "Something wrong?"

Her tone had an edge to it, and Benjamin shook his head, trying to occupy himself with catching another fish. But other senses, not the least aquatic, kept stirring within him.

Her whole body is less than half of mine, he thought. His eyes followed the curve of Rose's shoulders down, and he fought an impulse to rub her gleaming hair with his cheek.

"Benjamin—"

"Yes?"

"Do you feel it?" Rose's tones were low but excited.

"What?" Her bluntness took him by surprise.

"The fishing pole! I felt it move! Didn't you?"

"Uh, no." Ben was thankful that although he had misinterpreted her words, he hadn't made a fool of himself.

"Oh. Maybe I didn't feel it move, then." Rose clunked the tip of the rod against the boat in agitation. "I just can't get the hang of this!"

"The rod might have moved. I can't say. I wasn't paying much attention to it." Ben decided to come clean. "Rose, I can't concentrate on fishing with you by me like this."

"Should I move?"

Her look was sincere as she turned her face toward him, but the face was far too lovely. Perhaps the effect was due to the angle of the sun or the way the light reflected off the waves, or maybe Ben was seeing her through the filter of his heart; in any case, Rose's face appeared radiant. The green in her eyes glimmered, her cheeks glowed. Her dark lashes and chiseled features intensified her beauty, making it, in Ben's eyes, almost unbearable. He leaned forward to take her face in his hands.

"Rose, if you do move...if you ever move from me again, I'll—"

"Benjamin! The pole!"

There was a clunk and a splash in rapid succession. Rose shook Benjamin's shoulder. "Look! The pole, the pole!" She pointed to it sinking beneath the water's surface.

Another splash sounded, this one heavy, and Rose was amazed to see Benjamin diving after it. He came up with the rod in one hand and swam to the boat. His smile broadened as he reached the aluminum edge and handed the rod up to her. "Take it. And remember what I told you."

"What? Oh!" Rose felt the strong tugs of a hooked fish. She jerked the pole and pulled in line, keeping the tip up.

"That's it!" Benjamin crowed from the stern. He heaved himself into the boat. "Play him! Pull him in, but let him think he's winning. The drag's set light; that'll encourage him, but keep reeling in whenever he lets up."

"What's the buzzing noise? Oh, you are wet!" Rose said, as Ben put his hand on her shoulder.

"Sorry." He wiped his hand on his dripping cut offs. "That sound is the drag letting out line. You're doing fine. Keep it tight. Keep the tip higher."

"I'm trying." Rose stared into the water where her line disappeared at a sharp angle. "It's hard to reel in!"

"Must be a big one then! I'll get the net." Benjamin rummaged around until he held the dip net near her pole, looking ready to pounce as soon as the fish showed itself. "Okay, he's getting tired. Whoops, another jump," he said, as Rose's pole tip bowed and straightened. "Must be a bass."

"Oh, Benjamin, you take it! My wrist's aching!"

"That means he's got some size. You really want me to take over? You're almost there. Pull back easy and bring him in, now."

Rose kept winding, and the pole arched as she leaned back. "But what if I lose him?"

"What if you do? You won't though. You have fine form." He laughed and rested his hand on her wrist.

"Don't distract me."

"You distracted my fishing first."

Rose smiled, and for an instant let the rod tip down. The

fish, feeling slack, drew back and charged. The line snapped and swung back, weightless.

"You lost him. Never give them slack. Well, that was a good fight. Either a huge walleye or a good-sized bass, I bet." Benjamin lowered the net and took the rod away from her. "I'll put on more tackle for you."

Rose rubbed her wrist and sat. "I would have had him if you hadn't made that last comment."

"I'm sorry." Benjamin put down the pole. "And I'm sorry I tried to kiss you, too." His tone was light, but an underlying tension warned Rose not to answer flippantly.

"And I'm sorry I dropped the pole in the lake, Benjamin. You just—you took me by surprise."

"You've been taking me by surprise ever since you fell into that hole with me." He leveled his gaze at her. "I fell much harder, though I didn't want to admit it. But you knew, didn't you?" He rested his palm on her cheek. His fingertips brushed the hair along her temple.

"No, Benjamin, I didn't. I'm sorry—not sorry that you feel…like you do. I'm sorry I didn't realize…how you felt." She squirmed uneasily. "Benjamin, it's uncomfortable talking like this!"

"I just want to know what's going on between us. I'm not fooling around, Rose. I'd like to know you're not either."

"What? Oh, you mean the day I had you take me to Eric? Yes, I was using you then. And I do like Eric, Benjamin."

She took his hand away from her face. "I appreciated all the time you spent visiting me while I was sick, and I'm enjoying our time together now, but I don't want you to get the wrong idea, Benjamin. We're…well, we're *different.*"

"What do you mean, 'different'?"

"We're from different worlds," Rose explained.

"What do you know about what 'world' I come from? If you're talking about status, maybe I should remind you that technically you're a maid now yourself."

Rose looked at him askance.

"Oh, yes, you are," Ben said resolutely. "When you cleaned that first cabin, you stepped over the line into the working class. For all you know, I may be slumming with you."

"I chose to clean cabins. I volunteered!"

"Maddie chose it, too. So did Lilla."

"Yes, but they're doing it for a living." The subtle logic of her argument weakened under Benjamin's steady gaze.

"Oh, that's not what I meant!" Rose abandoned her case and tried another argument. "At least Eric and I understand each other. With you, I don't know…"

"What? Ask me anything. I'll answer. But first I want you to know why I'm asking you all these questions. I've been in love before, Rose. Only once. I never expected or even wanted to feel anything close to it again. But with you I feel kind of what I felt then. Stirrings, beginnings toward love, a real love. And now I'd like to know what you think."

"Benjamin, I don't want to think. You're a doctor all the way through, aren't you? Analyze everything, demand reports on everything! Well, I want you to know that I don't—"

"Wait." Benjamin put his hands lightly on her shoulders. "I'm sorry. I didn't mean to upset you. I know what you've been through—part of it anyway. As much as you've told me. I know there must be more. Maybe this isn't the right time. I withdraw the question. And I promise not to analyze anything else until you're ready. Let's try fishing again, okay?"

Rose resumed her position before him, but sat ramrod straight. As Benjamin began sharing more pointers, she slowly relaxed against his chest, until her smooth black hair flowed past his cheek.

"I'm glad you came fishing with me, Rose. I didn't think you would."

"Auntie made sure of that. You sure have an ally in her."

"So do you. She thinks—" Benjamin cut off his sentence. "I'm glad you came, Rose, for whatever reason. It's not often that I give myself a whole day off, and this one is June Beauty itself, begging to be put on your canvas. Look at the lake, leaden on the surface and deep sky-blue in the distance. That's part of the Chippewa name for Minnesota, you know: 'land of sky-blue waters.'"

Rose relaxed further against his shoulder. "Chippewa?"

"Ojibway. Anishinabe. Indian. We call them Chippewas since that's what they call themselves. They were the first people up here, the first to see the sun rise and change from rose to orange to yellow. So bright, now, hanging just above that island. Watch it dance in the waves. Watch the sun trail."

Rose glanced from the burning star to its reflection in the water, an equally burning stream of light leading directly toward their boat. She closed her eyes and felt the sun's heat on her cheeks and a moderating northern breeze.

"Look, Rose, a loon. To the right, very near."

The loon was so close that the red of his eye was startling against his dark head and neck; so, too, were his white collar and speckled design against his ebony body. The loon swam closer, its sharp, black beak stirring the water.

"He's waiting for a handout. Stay still, and maybe you'll hear him call."

The loon paddled about with an invisible, soundless motor, made three passes before them, and moved away. Rose was about to speak when the bird thrust his breast forward, lashed his wings backward, and raised himself on the water. He craned his neck and uttered a call so wild, so clear, and so joyous that Rose's mouth opened in amazement.

The bird repeated his display and his call, cocked his head and listened, then sped across the lake's surface and flew away.

"It sounded just like a laugh!" Rose said.

"Yes, but when he cries in the night, it's often a much sadder sound."

"I'd like to hear it."

"Maybe you will. Who knows if I can get this motor going come twilight? We may float out here 'til the moon is high."

"Won't Auntie worry?"

"I know the lake, and she knows that. If we came home early, she'd worry. But not if we came home late."

"You're very sure of yourself."

"No, I'm not. And especially not of you. I'd like to be."

"You are insistent, aren't you? All right, then. Let's talk, Benjamin Haralson. But if you don't mind, I'll ask the questions. First of all, why are you taking the MCAT this fall? Isn't spring the usual time?"

"The usual and the best. But I wasn't sure this spring that I wanted to take it, and I'm still not sure I want to take it this fall. But I'm going to."

"What made you change your mind?"

"I don't know. It took some time away from school to make me decide. Finishing four years of pre-med seems pretty empty if you don't go all the way and take the MCAT. Maybe I'm looking to it to tell me if I'm really cut out to be a doctor. Rose, I'm not as sure of myself as you think."

"No, I guess you're not. I guess you're a lot different from how I thought you were at first."

"You mean, not like your ex-fiancé?"

Her body tensed at the thought of Frederick, but then her mind shifted to Benjamin. She recalled his reading to her, his interest in her art, his love of natural beauty. "No, I guess you're not like Frederick after all."

"Want to talk about it?"

"Not much. I'm tired of hurting, Benjamin. I thought I was in love with Frederick. I thought he loved me. Even now I half expect him to come walking back into my life. And if he ever did ask me back, I…I really don't know how I'd react. Sometimes I think I'd laugh in his face and tell him that when I threw his ring in the lake, I was throwing him away, too!"

She stopped. "I didn't mean to tell you that."

"Why not? Still shutting me out?"

"Benjamin, I don't even know how I feel about Frederick, or Eric, or you! I just want to forget everything that's happened. I want to start new, like the sunrise. I want to get on with life. I don't want to hurt anymore! Do you know what I mean?"

"I think I do."

She looked over her shoulder at him to see if he was serious. He seemed to be, and Rose allowed her eyes to linger. She looked at the strong lines of his well-formed cheek and jaw. His forehead was partially covered by fine blond bangs that lifted slightly in the wind. But it was his eyes that arrested her, intelligent eyes the color of the lake at dawn—a blue-gray that looked as if it, too, could change with the weather.

Rose surveyed him with an artist's sensitivity, reading in the arched brows and faint lines above his forehead a matching sensitivity and buried grief. But along his mouth, with its full, upturned edges, she discerned humor and hope.

"All right," she said resignedly. "I'm not promising anything, Benjamin, but you're right. There is something between us. I've been thinking about you, too. But I want you to know I'm not sure. I don't want to hurt anyone, and I don't want to be hurt again, not by you, or Eric, or anybody. But I am having a good time today. I like being with you." She looked at him. "I want you to know that."

The hope spread from Ben's mouth to his eyes, and as he fixed them on her, she raised a warning finger.

"Remember, I promise nothing," she said. But when he moved forward to kiss her, her lips were already on his, and her arms hung lightly around his neck.

Eleven

❦

I n a sheltered cove of an island lined with cedar trees, a small kicker boat rested. A narrow, golden beach about ten feet wide and partially hidden from view stretched from one side of the cove to another. On the beach, on two colorful beach towels, lay two women in swimsuits.

The blonde, short-haired woman wore a blue bikini and sported a deep, golden tan. The other woman, a taller, more slender, dark-haired nymph, was clad in a green tank suit that matched her eyes, though now they were halfway closed.

The island, located only a few miles from Singing Pines, was Lilla's favorite. Rose had been hearing about the place for weeks and was glad when Lilla invited her to come for an afternoon of tanning and small talk.

Rose listened as Lilla spoke, periodically opening one eye to look at her, as if seeing helped her to hear better.

"They met the end of June, on a morning when everything was still, he said." Lilla wiped moistness from her forehead and flicked a few grains of sand from her cheek before settling back onto her beach towel and into her story.

"Ben never told me how he came to the resort or why. It was like Jesse was the reason, even before he knew her. Like God had told him in a dream like Joseph's that he should come, and he came, expecting nothing, receiving everything. That's how he put it, anyway."

Rose turned on her side and let her gaze stray over the lake. The waves hitting the shore sounded like a sloshing washing machine. "When did he tell you all this, Lilla?"

"The first summer he came back. He was really moody then, and I was doing my best to cheer him up. I dragged him out on a fishing trip one day and chattered away all afternoon. Finally he started talking too—almost an hour straight. I just sat and listened, even though I was dying to ask questions. I knew as soon as he quit talking he probably wouldn't start again. And you know, I've never heard him open up like that since! Something about the boat or that day loosened his lips."

Rose nodded and watched the waves.

"He faced the opposite way the entire time. Never looked at me once, just jiggled his pole and looked at the lake, kind of like you're doing now."

Rose self-consciously glanced at Lilla and saw her friend's teasing grin. "Don't be too smug, Lilla. And I wouldn't face the sun so much if I were you. Freckles are popping out all over your nose."

"Oh, no, really?" Lilla sat up suddenly and dug in her beach bag for a mirror. "They are not, Rose. Whew! Freckles are cute on Nick, but not me. You had me going there. Freckles used to be my nightmare."

"I guessed so from your coloring. Now we're even. Keep telling your story."

"That reminds me, you never did give me the lowdown on why you and Ben ended up coming home so late last night. When was it, midnight? Or even later? Every time you guys go out, you come back later and later, ever since that first fishing trip. He pop any...um, important questions last night?"

"I'll tell you if you ever finish your story."

"Incentive! Just what I needed." Lilla closed her eyes and paused, as if setting the scene in her mind. "Ben said it was love at first sight. Jesse was sitting on a checkered blanket under the fir tree by the house when he saw her, playing with a batch of puppies Queenie had."

Lilla opened one brown eye and looked at Rose. "You didn't know Queenie, did you? She died last year. Anyway, it was her last batch, and they were adorable! Black short-hairs, like Queenie, but with white patches from their roving Dalmatian father, a guest's dog. Real love 'em and leave 'em type. You know the male counterpart, right? How many days has Eric been gone, anyway?"

"I lost count. Go on."

"Okay. Ben saw her and before he knew it, they were both on the blanket, playing with nine fat, squirming puppies. They spent the whole afternoon together, talking and laughing as the puppies climbed all over them. They didn't even realize it was getting late until the mosquitoes came out and the pups were all snuggled close by, sleeping. Ben says that pretty much set the tone. They spent his whole vacation together: swimming, fishing, exploring islands, doing everything that is pure, lovely, and good, he said. I guess it's a Bible verse or something. Anyway, it was Jesse who taught Ben about the lake: how to run a boat, how to ski, stuff like that."

Lilla put her hands behind her head. "He must have been quite a wimp before Jesse got hold of him. Poor little rich boy and all that."

"What? Ben?" Rose nearly choked.

"Sure. A regular heir. Didn't you know? His parents are loaded. He's disinherited now, though, not that he would've touched a penny anyway. Something about refusing to go into the family business. I don't know the details. He planned to work his way through college, with Jesse's blessing. He never saw her alive again after the day he left for his freshman year. She died that next summer, a few days before he was supposed to come back. He didn't come back to Singing Pines at all, then, not even for her funeral. Maddie didn't know if he'd ever come back."

Rose felt they were intruding too much on Ben's private life, so she shifted the conversation away from that sacred ground. "So it was Jesse who wanted him to go to college?"

"Yep. I don't think he would've done it otherwise. He was a goner—totally whipped. Jesse wore the pants in their relationship, he said, not that I could ever believe it. She put him on the Singing Pines work crew, took away his dress whites, and gave him blue jeans—made a man of him. Ben picked up guiding jobs here and for other resorts after Jesse taught him the best fishing spots."

"No wonder Eric's money doesn't impress him," Rose said softly. "I'm sure I didn't either, with all my talk about being from different worlds. Lilla, I'm probably a lot like Ben before Jesse got to work on him. I couldn't have cleaned an oven or cooked a meal to save my life!"

"I know, Rose, I know. Remember who helped train you. It wasn't all Maddie." Lilla gave her friend a longsuffering look.

After Lilla had received proper thanks, she continued. "They planned to get married after he came home from college. I don't know if he was pre-med then, but he must have been. I think they both were ready for a long separation, but it turned out to be permanent."

Neither woman said anything for a while. Lilla shifted on her towel and joined Rose in looking out across the lake. "The first time I saw Ben, he looked like an ogre or something, tight and angry. It was hard to believe Maddie when she told me how he was before Jesse died."

"A big difference?"

"Humongous! Maddie said that before Jesse died, she never saw him frown. Not ever! He was always cracking jokes, always helping out. He became part of the resort, part of the Winters family. He and Mark chummed around; he used to help Maddie clean cabins, even, if Jesse had too much work. And the only time he left Jesse's side was to take a shower or sleep or guide."

Lilla fell silent and Rose raised herself up on one elbow. "Why doesn't Ben guide now?"

"He does, but not often. He only took a boat out a few times that first summer he came back, and only toward the end. I think Maddie had a talk with him or something. Last summer he stayed longer, helped on the resort, and guided more, but he was still a loner. I don't know why he comes back. Maybe it reminds him of Jesse, fishing the spots she taught him, looking at the islands they saw together. All those memories must give him some kind of happiness, or he wouldn't come back, I guess. Hasn't he talked about her?"

"Not much. The first time we went out he said he'd been in love—"

"I guess!" Lilla interrupted. "If Nick and I ever get a love like that going, I'll never let him go. Neither should you, by the way—let go of Ben, I mean. So, do I get to hear what happened on your latest date? You went fishing again, didn't you? Any action? Besides the fishing, I mean."

"I know what you meant." Rose let a handful of sand shower her friend's foot.

Lilla shook it off. "If that's the worst you can do, fire away, but I want to hear everything!"

"I've told you most of what happened during the morning and afternoon…"

"Yeah, but it's the night I want to hear about!"

Rose's eyes fastened on the blue waves. "Well, we had a shore lunch, talked some more and…"

"Kissed like crazy," Lilla suggested.

"No. We're going slowly, as we decided. It makes everything—I don't know, more relaxed, more special."

"Honey, I don't doubt that! Anything with Ben is special. What else did you do?"

"We fished and talked. I feel so comfortable with him, Lilla, more every day. But there's something about him I don't like, too. I'm not sure—"

"Afraid of getting in too deep?"

"Maybe that's it. I don't know. Last night he wanted to stay until the moon came out and the loons gave their night cry. We planned to do that on our first date, but the rain sent us home early. But last night was perfect. We sat in a fern gully on an island, close by the shore, and listened to the loons calling to each other back and forth across the lake. Everything was so still in the sunset, and as the colors deepened, and the sky darkened, I swear they started crying—just like humans. Or maybe it was me. Everything was so beautiful." Rose gestured helplessly. "Lilla, can you understand?"

"I think so," Lilla said quietly. "Everything was so beautiful, you were afraid the bubble might break."

"Something like that."

As Rose stared hard at the lake, she felt Lilla's arm around her shoulder. Rose smiled and squeezed Lilla's hand, then released it to wipe her eyes. "Thanks, Lilla. You amaze me, you know? I was afraid you'd make fun."

"Of love? Not me!"

"Not love, Lilla. It's too soon for love."

"I don't know. You've been dating a week already, haven't you? How long do you think it has to take? Ben's a quick boy, Rose. He fell for Jesse at a glance, and he fell for you the same way. I knew it the first time I saw you and him at lunch. I told you so, remember?"

"Lilla, do you think he…do you think he only likes me because I look like Jesse?" Rose studied the sand. It was the question she longed to ask of Ben, but she could never get it past her lips.

"At first," Lilla answered judiciously, "he might have. But there's something about you, Rose, something beyond your looks. I felt it. Ben must feel it. You're…steady, reliable—but fun, too. I feel like I know where I am with you. You make people feel—I don't know, like they're on solid ground, and glad to be there." Lilla shrugged.

"Thanks, Lilla." Rose exhaled deeply and flicked the sand with her fingertips. "I hope you're right. I hope Ben likes me for something inside, not for how I look outside."

"You sound like you doubt it."

"Maybe I do. I'm an artist. I know how beauty affects people. It can be intoxicating, can sweep you away, can even feel like love sometimes. I know I'm not a raving beauty, and I don't mean to sound like it, but I do look like Jesse, and Ben loved her. In his eyes, she was probably the most beautiful, the most perfect woman ever created. I guess I need more time before I can believe Ben loves me for me—if that's how he does feel."

"He hasn't said it then?"

"Not in so many words."

"Well, I won't tell you what to do, Rose, but even without the words he's shown you some pretty good actions. Relax and don't worry about it."

Lilla slid back on her towel and spread herself out languorously. "Feel that sun! Enjoy the day, Rose. It's girls' day out; no men, no worries."

"No worries," Rose echoed, but her voice lacked the carefree reassurance of Lilla's.

"What time was it, Benjamin? One A.M.? Two?" Maddie teased, sitting in Ben's rocker and drinking the iced tea he handed her. He watched the glass sweat and pool up in the cork coaster after she set the glass down.

"I don't think it was that late. Nearer to midnight." He stretched out on the couch and looked at her unflappably.

"You're not going to tell me anything, are you?"

"Nope." Ben let his face broaden into a slow Cheshire grin.

"I'll just get it from Rose when she and Lilla get back. What time did they leave?"

"Around 10:00—okay, you caught me," he said, seeing Maddie's smirk. "I was watching for her. I thought she might come to the cabin this morning before she took off with Lilla."

Maddie took a sip of her iced tea. "That's what she probably thought about you, too. Both of you are more stubborn than matching mules! Well, don't fret. They shouldn't be gone too much longer. What a scorcher! They'll get more sun than they bargained for, and with Rose having gone out with you all day yesterday, too, well, I bet she's in for a nasty sunburn. Know any remedies, Doctor?"

"A few." Ben set down his glass on the coffee table. "Maddie, I'd like a little advice."

"About Rose? I'm sticking to my guns, Ben. Go slow. Go very slowly with her. She's been hurt a lot."

"By her fiancé, I know. She told me." Ben touched the side of his glass and made a trail through the moisture. "Don't worry, Maddie. We're going as slowly as I can stand."

"Good." Maddie drained her glass and deposited it into the kitchen's tin sink. "Now I'll leave you alone. Get some studying done before she gets back. You've been spending a lot less time with your books lately, and if Rose isn't too sore, I bet she'd like to see you when she comes home. Be sure you have some cures for sunburn handy."

"Okay, Mad." Benjamin walked with her to the door.

"Remember, Ben, anytime you want a confidante—"

"I'll know who to come to: you and Lilla."

Maddie laughed. "You've got that right. But Lilla's slicker

than I am. She's probably wormed the whole thing out of Rose by now."

"Maybe," Ben mused, "but Rose can keep her own counsel when she wants to. Even after seeing her every day for a week, I'm still getting mixed signals."

"And I'm sure the feeling is mutual." Maddie sighed. "How hard it's going to be to sit by and watch you two waste time! But I'll do it for your sake, Benjamin." Maddie waved as she went through the doorway and let the door slam behind her.

Ben watched the short woman attack the lake path and move quickly out of sight beyond the point. *Maddie's probably right,* Ben thought. *Rose and I probably will waste time.* But the prospect seemed only pleasing to him. He retreated from the window, walked to his desk, and went to work.

CHAPTER

$\mathcal{T}welve$

❧

As the boat bounced over the waves, Rose and Lilla could see a figure in white on one of the docks of Singing Pines's marina. As they came closer, Rose recognized Eric, standing by a new speed boat almost the duplicate of his old one.

Lilla slowed the motor and steered the boat alongside the dock, moving past Eric's craft and throwing him a line. "Make yourself useful," she commanded, "and tie us up."

"Anything you say, Lilla." Eric stopped the boat's forward motion with one foot and then tied the rope in a halfhitch to the post. "Hi, Rose. I've been hoping you'd get back soon. You were out a little too long in the sun today, I see."

"Well, you're in no danger, Eric. How can you stand wearing so many clothes?" Lilla, still bikini-clad, transferred her bag and towel to the dock. Eric took her hand and helped her out, then offered to assist Rose.

"No, thanks. I'm fine." Rose hopped onto the dock. She wore her towel sari style over her tank suit, and she felt Eric's eyes on her. "Is something wrong?"

"Rose, you look terrific, even with a burn."

"Thanks. Nice boat." Rose shifted her eyes from it to her friend. "Ready to go, Lilla?"

"Sure am. Bye, Eric." The two young women swept past him.

"Rose, what's the matter?" Eric caught hold of her shoulder. "That was a pretty cold reception! Didn't you miss me?"

"Did you go somewhere?" Rose asked, not missing a beat in Lilla's stride as they climbed up the rise to her cabin.

"I'm sorry I left without telling you." Eric walked alongside her and reached for her hand. "I didn't know I was going," he added in lower tones.

Rose tilted her head and continued walking, though she fell a little behind Lilla.

Eric dropped his voice further. "Rose, my parents flipped after our boat ride in the storm. They were convinced it happened because I was a drunk, and they took me to get…dried out." His face was drawn.

Rose stopped in her tracks. "Lilla, go on ahead. I'll be there in a while." She stared at Eric. "What did you say?"

"My parents brought me to Winnipeg for…treatment."

"Eric, I was under the impression it took months to get dried out. You are talking about treatment for alcoholism, aren't you? Or are you inventing this story so I won't be angry that you left without telling me?"

Eric's laugh was hollow. "No, it's true enough. My dad threatened to disown me if I didn't go. The doctors saw I had no problem, but asked me to voluntarily commit myself to appease my parents. I humored them for a while, took their tests and listened to their sermons, and then they released me. I came back here as soon as I could."

"I'm sorry." Rose touched his upper arm in apology. "I didn't know. No one told me. I thought you left me flat."

"After all we've been through? No way! Rose, I'm not that bad a guy. What's Lilla been telling you? Or is it Maddie?"

Rose felt a blush deepening the redness on her face.

"Or is it Ben?"

Rose couldn't keep her eyes from darting.

"Well, crafty ol' Benjamin! Tossed the books right out the window, did he? How much time has he been spending with you?"

"Eric, I'm sorry you got dragged off by your parents, but that doesn't give you the right to quiz me on my life in your absence."

"I'm sorry, Rose. I can't blame you. I know it must've seemed like I left without caring. But I do care." He brought her hand to his lips and kissed each fingertip. "I...thought about you a lot while I was gone.... I wanted to explain what happened, but with no phones and the mail coming only three times a week, by float plane at that...I figured it would be better to explain myself when I got back."

He finished his finger kisses and turned her hand over so her palm was up. "I didn't know it would take so long for me to get back, but those doctors were blind! When I did get out, I knew you'd be upset, so I brought a token of peace."

From the pocket of his silk slacks, Eric pulled out a small jewelry case. He set it on Rose's palm and opened the cover. Against a background of crushed white velour nestled a gold ring. The setting was ornate, made up of tiny gold-flaked leaves with delicate intertwined stems that held in place a green stone shaped like a rosebud.

"I couldn't leave Winnipeg without getting this for you." Eric transferred the ring from the box to Rose's right-hand ring finger. "See, I even remember the size of your finger. I don't want to hear any blather about how you can't accept it, either. I had it made specially for you. The band design matches the one on my ring, and the stone is exactly the color of your eyes."

The deep green of the stone did match her eyes, and the band fit well enough, but Rose slipped the ring off and pressed it into Eric's hand. "I...appreciate the thought, Eric—"

"Thought, nothing! Appreciate the ring," he said with a slanted grin, and tried to put the ring back on her finger.

"Eric, I can't. Don't ask me to explain, please!" Rose wrenched her hand free and hurried up the rise to Lilla's cabin. She didn't turn around until she was inside.

Eric stood, looking after her. Abruptly, he stuffed his fists into his pockets, turned, and strode toward the marina.

The dish towel went around and around the china plate, polishing the front side, then the thin edges, decorated with their blue flowers, then moved on to the underside. Maddie watched its action and said nothing until the towel went back to the plate's front and started over.

"Rose, I think that's dry enough." Maddie gently took the plate from her niece and put it away in the cupboard. "They don't need polishing tonight."

"What? Oh, I'm sorry." Rose picked up another piece of china and began her motions anew.

"Is something bothering you?" Maddie avoided Rose's eyes as she put a dripping glass into the dish rack. "You didn't have much to say at supper. Ben didn't, either. You two have a fight?"

"No."

As Maddie weighed an appropriate response, Rose placed her plate in the cupboard, carefully closing the door.

"Auntie, why does everything have to be so difficult?"

"What do you mean?"

"Well, sometimes I wish I was a kid again. Since I grew up there's been nothing but problems, and they all seem to involve men."

Maddie laughed at the spin Rose gave the word. She shook her head. "I admit men can be troublesome, Rose, but a comfort, too. Mark and I have been together so long now, I can hardly remember life without him. And I hate to think of it that way ever again."

"Auntie, when you met Uncle Mark, did you know, right away, that he was the right one?"

"Dear me, no." Maddie pulled the plug on the empty sink, listening to the sound of the drain clearing its throat.

"What I mean is, when were you sure it was love, Auntie?"

Maddie ran the dishrag over the chrome faucet, following it with a towel before she answered. "I don't remember a certain time," she said, rubbing a spot near the base. "In fact, on my wedding day, I still had a few doubts. It's hard to be completely sure, you know."

"But you were sure enough to marry him."

"Yes, but you asked if I was sure he was the right one, a different thing altogether." Maddie set her towel on the counter. "I was used to what you might call 'playing the field.' Mark was my favorite boyfriend; I was sure of that, and I wanted to marry him. But even after we were married, I used to wonder if he was the right one. Marriage is difficult, after all. During the hard times, it's easy to think you might have made a mistake. But then the good times return. I think it's only now that I'm sure he was and is the right one. But I loved him long before that."

Rose wiped the last dish and the last piece of silverware, and hung her towel to dry on the rack near the fridge. Then she turned and walked with her aunt to the kitchen table.

"I was so sure of Frederick, and he wasn't right. Then Eric came along, and while I wasn't sure of him, at the island I began wondering. We went through quite a crisis together."

Maddie sat down. So did Rose.

"And then there's Ben. He's so different from Frederick or Eric. I don't know what to think about him. Today he gave me some ointment that he mixed up just for my burn. I put it on and it feels so much better now. Look." Rose lifted her sleeve. "The red isn't so fiery."

"He'll be a fine doctor."

"He isn't so sure."

"It's a hard thing to be sure, as I said." Maddie stood. "Often, the only thing, the only being I'm sure of is God."

She walked to the fridge and opened it. "Want some lemonade? I think this conversation should be continued on the porch. The sun's going down soon. Mark won't be home for at least another hour—he's guiding again, and by then we could do real justice to these lemons."

"Sounds fine, Auntie. I'll help."

Rose soon carried a pitcher of lemonade to the porch. Maddie held the glasses and set them down as she sat on the swinging bench Mark had made. "Fill up the glasses, leave the pitcher on the end table here, and come sit down. The show is beginning."

The two women sipped and watched the sun sink. Though by this time Rose had spent many evenings on Singing Pines and had seen many sunsets, Aunt Maddie had told her that each one, like each day, had its own personality.

She was right. Tonight, dark clouds shaded part of the horizon, growing thicker as they went higher until they blotted out most of the sky. Part of the sun's rays were deflected by these clouds so that hazy spots of red and orange were displaced, and the sunset was spread over the sky in peculiar blotches. The lake reflected the pageant faithfully.

Maddie gave herself over to memories, recalling past boyfriends and escapades, which she described to Rose's laughter. Each adventure seemed less and less likely until Rose declared she couldn't believe a word that streamed from Maddie's mouth.

"And then—I pushed him," Maddie said.

"You didn't really!" Rose protested.

"Yes, I did." Maddie bobbed her head emphatically. "And he fell right into the lake." She made a graceful diving motion with her hand, and Rose surrendered to another laughing fit.

"Oh, Aunt! You were awful!"

"That I was," Maddie affirmed complacently. "I often wonder why the good Lord never chastised me for it. Here I am, with Mark, happily married for a quarter of a century. He's played me no tricks like I played on him and a score of other young men. Not that I meant any harm. I was young myself."

"I see. And will that excuse work for me?"

"Certainly not!"

They both laughed until the sun was covered in clouds and the lake turned a steel blue. As the night grew cooler and darker, Maddie stretched out her legs and dropped them to the floor with a bump.

"Well, my dear, time for bed. Mark will be along any time, and I have some reading I want to do. I'm finishing up *A Tale of Two Cities,* and the heroine's husband has just been recalled to prison after being released. Nobody knows why, but I'll find out before Mark gets home."

"Do you have any good books for me? I finished the two Ben gave me, and I think I might have a hard time getting to sleep tonight."

Maddie collected the glasses and tucked the empty pitcher under her arm as they walked indoors. "There are some good books in the loft by the bay window, but I think I could rustle up some reading for you that you'd enjoy and that might solve your dilemma at the same time."

She led the way toward a wall-sized bookshelf in the living room. Maddie ran her fingers across the bindings in one row and stopped on a worn, black book. She pulled it out and handed it to Rose.

"The Bible? Thanks, but I've already read it." Rose held it back out to her.

"So have I. Many, many times. After my visit with Charles Dickens, I'm going to read part of it again." She pressed the book into Rose's hands. "I suggest you take this and read just a short passage that I'm sure will help you out."

Maddie touched the golden lettering on the binding. "Look

at the bottom of the front cover."

Rose turned the Bible over and read the name in faded gold. "Jesse Winters's. This was Jesse's!"

"Yes. We bought it for her on her thirteenth birthday. We told her we wanted her to read the gold right off the pages. And she nearly did." Maddie flipped through the book and moved the ribbon bookmark to another page. "Right here, Rose. This is what you should read tonight. And if, in the morning, you think I was mistaken, if you don't find it just what you need at this moment, I won't bring it up again."

Rose looked skeptical, but she hugged her aunt. "All right. I'll try it. Good night, Auntie."

"Good night, Rose," Maddie said, and watched her niece climb the ladder to her loft, one hand holding the Bible.

Rose glanced at the passage before setting the Bible on her nightstand. She turned her light off while she undressed, locating her nightgown in the top vanity drawer. She switched on a lamp, climbed into bed, and settled her pillow comfortably about her shoulders before she began reading.

"If I speak with the tongues of men and of angels, but do not have love, I have become a noisy gong or a clanging cymbal," Rose read. "And if I have the gift of prophecy, and know all mysteries and all knowledge; and if I have all faith, so as to remove mountains, but do not have love, I am nothing."

Rose kept reading, drinking in the words, and as the sunlight withdrew from the land, and the stillness of night took hold, the passage turned into a kind of poem.

Love is patient,
Love is kind,

and is not jealous;

love does not brag and is not arrogant...;

Love bears all things,

believes all things,

endures all things.

Love never fails;

There was more to the passage, but Rose closed the book and set it aside. She walked to the bay window. The sky was Prussian blue, and stars had begun to pierce its dark fabric. Rose looked away from the tranquil lake toward the Savon cabin, but it was just out of range. She turned toward the lake path and followed it until it disappeared around the point.

What is Benjamin doing? Rose wondered. *Is he awake or asleep? And if he's dreaming, am I a part of his dreams?*

Had Ben ever read the love passage? Rose recalled he mentioned the Bible frequently in their discussions, especially whenever he had a point to make, and now she knew why. In all her childhood skimming of the book, its words never had such an impact upon her as they had now.

"Love never fails," Rose whispered, and hoped that somehow, Ben believed it too.

Thirteen

Rose studied the waking water, then translated its image to her paper—a thin brush stroke of ultramarine with a hint of amethyst near the horizon. The sun was hidden behind a mantle that hovered over the lake. Rose sketched birds in the distance, white pelicans floating in packs, and aerial towers of swirling sea gulls. Dark, hunched islands provided the background.

After applying another shred of color near the emerging sun on her paper, Rose twirled her brush in the water-filled glass next to her leg. She rested the sketch pad in her lap and glanced toward Ben's cabin. So far, she had detected no motion. She couldn't have missed him. And sitting here on the shore just beyond the point, in full sight of his cabin, she knew he couldn't miss her. And she wasn't leaving until they met.

All night dreams had whirled around in her head, much like the blue-smeared brush in the clear water, until her mind felt as muddied as the glass, as fogged with mist as the sun. Images of Eric, Frederick, and Ben entered and left the stage of her mind, playing their parts, delivering their lines, and leaving Rose, like a judge, like a spectator of her own life, to decide whom to pick.

As Rose took her brush from the water and dabbed it in a bit of silver, she recalled what the three men in her life had said in her dreams during the night.

Frederick had come on stage first, dressed for surgery. His thin hands were encased in latex gloves. He held them before him. He wore a sterile cap and gown of khaki. A white mask covered his nose and mouth. His glasses obscured his eyes as he spoke, and from her seat before him, Rose listened to his muffled words and watched the mask on his face move.

"Love is comfort, love is security," Frederick recited. "Love is not weak. Love does not contradict and is not overreaching."

Frederick adjusted his glasses with his forearm before continuing, peering out into the nearly empty auditorium at his audience of one. "Love performs all things, obeys all things, believes all things. Love never questions."

Frederick bowed stiffly and walked offstage until he was swallowed by a burgundy curtain. Rose looked for him to appear again. He didn't.

She opened the only object next to her, a thick black book with faded gold lettering, and turned to a bookmark. There she compared Frederick's statement with the passage on the page. After due consideration, Rose wrote Frederick's name in the margin and his score: 1. A bell sounded.

Rose heard footsteps. Another young man made his way to center stage. This time it was Eric, dressed expensively as usual. He wore a vest of precious gold threads, woven like chain mail, over his black silk shirt. A golden cape hung behind him and at his sides, and his hands were lost in its folds. His slacks were immaculately pressed and tailored, fastened at the waist with a lustrous gold clasp.

Eric stood proudly, his legs wide apart. At an invisible cue, he dropped to one knee. "Love is exciting!" he boomed, his gestures unrestrained. "Love is new, and is not unattractive."

He strode to the stage's edge and stared down at Rose, his eyes bright. "Love does not settle for second best and is not easily pleased! Love wants all things, believes all things, endures all things!"

With each word, Eric pulled his body down farther and farther to Rose's level, until at last he lay on his stomach on the stage, his black-gloved hand reaching out to her. "Love...never...satisfies."

Eric's eyes closed; his arm relaxed as if in death. Then, all at once, he sprung up, bowed magnificently, threw Rose a golden bracelet, and made his exit, flourishing the curtains behind him.

Rose searched the passage and compared it with Eric's speech, then in the margin she wrote his name and score: 2. The bell sounded twice.

Rose put the Bible aside and waited. The stage was empty and she heard no one waiting in the wings. From somewhere behind her, a spotlight began searching the stage. At last it stopped on center stage, but still no one appeared. The round spot of light illuminated only the wood of the stage floor and the black background behind it, an unending space that extended into nothingness.

Ten minutes seemed to pass, then fifteen, then twenty. Rose reached for her Bible and was about to walk down the aisle and away, when she heard a shuffle. She looked up at the stage. It was still empty, but the curtain to the left, where Frederick and Eric had made their entrances, moved slightly, as if from a breeze.

The curtain wavered, and someone stepped reluctantly from behind it. He was a large young man in a white T-shirt and blue denim jeans. His blond hair was tousled as if from a ride in the wind. He stood still a moment, shifting uncomfortably, then stepped forward. A look of determination replaced his initial expression of resistance. Rose settled into her seat and waited for him to take his place. She opened her Bible in readiness.

Benjamin approached center stage and stood in the light. He squinted and held up his hand to shade his eyes. "Rose? Rose, are you there?"

"I'm here, Ben."

Benjamin moved toward her voice until he stood at the stage's edge, just before her. He took his hand from his eyes and stood erect, his powerful shoulders back, his body in a neat military stance, tennis shoes at a forty-five degree angle, eyes forward, trained on Rose.

The veins on his hands and arms were raised, probably because of the heat from the spotlight, or perhaps because he was so intent on his task. Rose stared at his arm, thinking of Michelangelo's sculpture of David and the cast she had handled of the arm. Ben's arms and hands were just like it, full of strength and beauty, so capable of force, but never used forcefully except when physical work demanded it.

Her attention shifted to Ben's face as he began to speak. His voice was clear and deep.

"Love," he said, coming forward and looking down at Rose until she could no longer meet his gaze, though it was bathed in gentleness. "Love is…"

She heard the sound of his feet moving and she looked up, afraid his next pace would send him crashing from the stage. But Ben swung his big body until he was sitting, his legs hanging inches away from her.

140

"Love," Ben repeated even more softly, "is patient."

The ends of his lips drew into a smile. His eyes sparkled like the sun trail on the lake as he stared deeply at her. She dropped her gaze in response, and something like a shiver ran down her back.

Ben pushed himself from the stage and stood before her, no longer in the glare of the spotlight, which shot above him and illuminated only the gold of his hair. "Love," said Ben, "is kind."

Rose studied the open Bible in her hands, knowing Ben had quoted the first two phrases in perfect humility, so unlike the verses of Frederick or Eric. Rose wondered how and why she had ever listened to them, and was ashamed.

As if reading her thoughts, Benjamin bent down and placed his large, beautiful hand on hers. "Love is not jealous," he whispered, and curved his hand gently under her chin, raising it until her eyes met his.

"Love does not brag," he said, leaning even nearer, "and is not arrogant." Hardly a millimeter separated his lips from hers.

"Say it with me, Rose," he coaxed, and their mouths moved in sequence: "Love hopes all things...endures all things... believes all things."

Rose's vision became blurry, and Ben wiped away the tears slipping like diamonds from her eyes.

"Finish it with me, Rose," he whispered. "Please." He kissed her so lightly she felt as if mist had brushed her lips.

"Love," said Rose and Ben in perfect unison, her voice choked and thin, his steady but so soft it did not drown hers out, "Love never fails."

"I love you, Rose."

As she moved into the fortress of his arms, she heard herself answering him without words, with all the emotion and love that flowed like the tide between them. "Ben, I love you. I love you, too."

This was the dream that had driven sleep from Rose's eyes so early this morning, the vision that had pulled her from her bed at dawn and drawn her to the point outside Ben's cabin to wait and see if the day would match the night or if her dream had been merely fantasy.

She painted and listened, painted and listened, and as the paper gained color and the sky grew light, Rose's head turned more and more frequently to the small cabin beyond the point.

Waves began slapping the shore as the wind awakened, and Rose, intent on catching the peculiar angles of a cloud, did not hear Ben's quiet footfall until he was just yards away.

"Morning, Rose. Been here long?"

"Only since sunrise." She hoped her smile didn't betray her nervousness.

Ben lowered himself next to her, sleep still visible on his features. He had splashed water on his face, for the hair nearest his temples was damp. Faint shadows clung beneath his eyes, and his cheeks were flushed.

Rose dropped her brush into the water and set her paper aside. "Did you have a rough night?"

His shoulders heaved and released in a sigh. He stretched his arms in front of him. "Crazy night. Full of dreams. I kept waking up."

"I know the feeling." Rose wondered how to approach her subject and decided on directness. "Did...any of your dreams include me?"

He didn't answer. Rose thought she might have to ask again when at last he responded.

"As a matter of fact, they did."

He seemed unwilling to elaborate, so Rose probed further.

"I'm in the mood for a story, especially one about me. Why don't you tell me about them?" She tried to smile, but felt as solemn as he looked.

Ben plucked a tall piece of grass and chewed on the end thoughtfully, finally tossing it away. "I dreamed we were married, Rose. And we were living right here, in my cabin."

He reached for her hand. "We were the only ones on the island. There was no resort, nobody else. We were completely alone, but neither of us seemed to mind." He paused.

"And what did we do all day, we two? Or shouldn't I ask?"

"You shouldn't. We were newlyweds."

Ben raised his arm and Rose slipped under it, sheltered close to his chest. He rested his other arm on hers, and Rose recalled her own dream. The feelings she had when he held her then, the feelings of protection and fulfillment and excitement, were precisely what she felt now.

"I'm glad you're with me, Rose. I'm glad you came out here this morning. You were the first sight I saw as I looked out the window. You, facing the sun, your beautiful black hair cascading behind you like a cape." He kissed the top of her head and then her cheek. "What made you come?"

"I had some dreams of my own."

"Like mine?"

"I don't know yet. You didn't finish telling me yours."

Ben laughed. "Okay, I will. My second dream was great, too,

143

but so strange. We had children, two of them. Two girls, with hair just like their mother's." He placed his hand near her part and let it slide down to her shoulders.

"Now that is a dream, Ben. If we had children, we'd have at least one boy, a blond, like you, who grows up to be a gentle giant like his father."

Ben moved his cheek beside hers. "There was no boy in my dream, and the girls grew up so fast before my eyes, like beautiful dark flowers, graceful and lovely. And then…"

"And then? Then what happened, Ben?"

"The girls grew up and went away. They came back to visit, bringing their own children. We grew old together…and one morning I woke up. You were gone." Ben's arms drew Rose closer.

"You mean I died?"

"I guess so. But in the dream you were suddenly not there. All your clothes and keepsakes were; you weren't. I looked for you, but I couldn't find you. Smoke closed in around me, and I couldn't see. Rose, it's the loneliest feeling I've ever had. I tried to get back to sleep after that and couldn't. Every few hours I'd wake up, searching for you."

Ben kissed her neck, and Rose felt a tickle travel to her toes. "Maybe that's why I don't plan on letting you go now."

Rose turned to look at him, her face so close to his that she could hardly focus. "You mean I'm supposed to spend the rest of my life in your arms?"

Ben nodded and rubbed his lips against her cheek.

"Good," she said, and turned a fraction of an inch more until it was no longer her cheek that he kissed, but her lips.

Ben saw the cloudburst coming hours before it arrived. "See those clouds moving in from the west? That gray-blue color means they're heavy with rain. June is the month of rain, and Minnesota is the land of ten thousand weather changes—sometimes all in one day. Let's go inside."

They gathered her things and watched the clouds a while longer before they made their way to his cabin. Ben closed the door just as the first drops struck. He guided Rose to the couch and pushed several thick volumes to the floor. "Here, let me get situated, then come beside me, and we can watch the rain." Ben stretched out his long legs and reclined, gesturing Rose to do the same. "I've been waiting for an excuse to do this."

"It's a good thing this is a wide couch. You take most of it up the way it is."

"Maddie found it for me. It's a pretty old piece of furniture. Mark's dad's. They didn't have room for it in their cabin. It's perfect for me...and now for you, too."

They talked and watched the rain blur the sky, moving in waves across the lake and ricocheting off the aspen leaves. Rose listened to Ben talk about his childhood and family, and she saw the clouds become swarthy, turning the day dusky. The wind grew strong, and Ben spoke between gusts that rattled the windows. Heat from inside the cabin and the cool storm outside made a fog settle on the windows.

Ben's words slowed and his arms grew heavy upon her. The sky turned somber and thunderbolts seemed to strike yards away, rumbling across the heavens and releasing a burst of light that flickered and died. When Rose looked to see Ben's reaction, his eyes were closed.

"Ben? Ben, do you think Aunt Maddie will worry about me? I didn't tell her where I was going."

"You have a way of doing that, don't you?" Ben asked groggily. "If the storm doesn't let up soon, I'll go over and tell her you're safe with me."

His body was warm beside her, and Rose rested her head on his chest again. "Why don't you radio her, Ben? I hate to think of you getting all wet and cold out there."

"I don't have a radio." Ben stifled a yawn. "I'll go over in a little while."

His breathing became deeper, and Rose felt his exhalations stirring her hair. As he slept, she heard the raindrops hitting the roof. They clattered, then thudded, then fell in even patterns, like giant hands drumming their fingertips overhead. Rose let her eyelids droop and listened until she slipped into her own dream, where each raindrop was a piece of Benjamin's love that washed over her and flowed like a river to the ground.

"I'm relieved you finally showed up, Rose," Maddie said, making a tight hospital corner on the last bed of the cabin she and her niece were cleaning, "but you really should learn the art of leaving notes."

"I know, Auntie." Rose handed her a freshly fluffed pillow that she'd just inserted into a brilliant white case. "Mm. How do you get the bedding to smell so good, and feel so good, too? The guests must love it."

"They do. One of the reasons they return, they say. They especially like how I hang the bedding on the line to get outdoor fresh and then mangle it until it's crisp and smooth. You haven't seen that part of the operation yet, have you?"

"No, but I'm sure I will." Rose smiled and ran a dust cloth over the logs. "I think this bedroom's done."

"Good. Do a check on the kitchen and bathroom, will you? Lilla did them before she left, but she was in a hurry to meet her boyfriend, and I want to make doubly sure everything is perfect. She's a good gal, but when she's due for her time off—especially with Nick—she gets forgetful."

Rose went to the bathroom and checked all the white porcelain surfaces, shining the chrome where Lilla had left a fingerprint, making sure the inside of the medicine cabinet and windowsills were clear of dust and dead insects.

"The bathroom is fine," Rose reported, and moved on to the kitchen, polishing the handles on the fridge and oven and rubbing the toaster until its sides were a mirror. She checked the interiors of all the appliances and cupboards, and passed the broom over the floor. "The kitchen looks good, too."

"I'm checking the living room. You go ahead and mop, then shake the rugs, and that'll be it for today," Maddie called.

After satisfying Maddie's orders, Rose stood out on the step and waited for her aunt to join her. The two women walked briskly toward the Winters's cabin, but the wet grass soaked their shoes before they'd taken many steps.

"That was a good rain. Things will really green up if the sun gets a chance to shine. The flowers will burst into bloom again. I think it'll be a good berry year, too—plenty of moisture all spring with mild temps. And maybe I'll have a bumper harvest from the garden this fall, if the deer don't get it, Rose. Rose?"

Rose kept in stride, but didn't answer. Her mind was full of other things.

Fourteen

෧ᆇᆖ

W hat a day! Almost makes up for all the bad weather we've been having lately." Benjamin sat on the island's rocky shore and stuck his toe in the water. "Brr! The rain sure cooled down the lake."

"But not the sun." Rose basked in it.

"Let's go for a swim. You don't want to get burned again, do you?"

"I've got plenty of sunscreen on today. I won't burn."

"You might. Just a short swim. How about it?"

"No." She held her face up to the sun, her eyes closed. "I want my face to get brown before we go back to the resort. Who knows when we'll have another day like today?"

"Okay, okay. Guess I'll just have to go floating by myself." Ben took two inner tubes out of the boat and laid one at Rose's feet. The other he set in the water near shore. He eased himself onto it and glanced down the shoreline. "Rose!"

"Hm? What?"

"Beaver," Ben whispered. "Look down the shoreline a

hundred feet, by that white fallen poplar."

The furry rodent was hunched near shore, his tail over a rock. He was large as a medium-sized dog. He worked on the tree, his teeth grinding on the wood.

"Are beavers dangerous?"

"Not at all, but you wouldn't believe it, would you, to hear him gnawing away at that tree?"

"No, I wouldn't. What are you doing?"

Ben slipped under the water and popped up inside his tube. "I'm going to sneak up on him."

"Why?"

He moved silently away, making a motion for her to keep quiet.

"Well, if you're going, I'm going, Benjamin; but if it turns on us, I'll be dangerous—to you!" she hissed.

Ben's inner tube made a rippling wake. He heard Rose following behind him but kept his eyes on the beaver. The animal was still chewing away at the tree, his stained yellow teeth gouging out chunks of wood which he spit onshore.

As they came nearer the beaver, Rose began shifting her body. Ben treaded water and let her catch up to him. "What are you doing?"

"If that thing comes after us, I'm keeping out of the water." She laid on the tube with her stomach over the hole and held out her arms and legs in the air. "Tow me, will you?"

"Yeah, but no more talking or you'll scare him away."

"Scare him?" Rose muttered. "Why not? He's already scared me."

The beaver had his back toward them, and Ben moved in.

Beads of water dripped from the beaver's repellent fur. The animal waddled around the tree, grasped a thin branch with his small, handlike paws, and snapped his jaws together. The branch, thick as Rose's thumb, was severed. Ben sneaked a look at Rose. She had her eyes glued to the animal and drew in her hands close to her sides.

The beaver caught the motion and turned. Ben didn't dare breathe. The beaver looked at Rose and Ben with his black eyes, wheeled forward, slapped his tail on the water, and dove toward them, disappearing underwater.

"Ben! Ben!" Rose screamed. "It's going to chew your legs off! Did you see the size of its teeth? It'll cut you in half!"

Ben didn't exert the energy to answer. Although he was sure—or relatively sure—that his legs were in no danger, he couldn't help wishing he was out of the water like Rose was.

Hoping his calves didn't resemble any entree delectable to beavers, Benjamin thrashed toward the boat, pushing Rose and her inner tube ahead of him. He tried not to think of the beaver's yellow teeth.

Rose held on as Ben acted like a motor behind her. "Keep kicking, Ben!" She scanned the lake's surface. "It's still underwater. Those teeth! They must have been at least three inches long, thick and curved like claws!"

Her head swiveled as she kept a lookout for the animal. Benjamin pushed her and himself steadily toward safety.

"Ben-ja-min! I see bubbles circling us! Maybe it thinks your legs are trees!"

Bubbles were indeed rising and popping around them. Benjamin swam grimly and waited for blunt beaver teeth to sink into his thigh.

Several feet from shore, Rose sprang from her tube onto the black rocks, landing squarely on her bare feet. She seemed impervious to the pain.

"Ben, come on!" she yelled, holding out her arm to him. "Jump! Jump!"

Ben's tube was surrounded by bubbles, and Ben hastily pulled his legs out of the water and crouched on his tube. His tube moved backwards with the leftover motion from Rose's leap, and as her tube drifted by Ben, he thought he saw a brown whiskered muzzle nudge its underside. He held his stomach well out of the water and tried to keep his balance. His elbows and knees supported his full weight, and where they pressed into the tube, water seeped into the pockets.

"Ben!" Rose pointed down the shoreline where a head broke the water, took in a snort of air, and dove.

Ben turned his head in time to see it and hear the slap of the beaver's tail. He kicked his way to shore.

"It's underwater again, Ben!" Rose warned.

"But it's heading the other way. See?"

A trail of bubbles and swirls was moving away. Ben reached shore with both inner tubes and threw them in the boat as the beaver surfaced near his tree and waddled ashore to resume work.

"Your first wildlife experience?" Ben asked, sprawling on his towel.

Rose nodded and lay on her own towel. "I hope it's my last."

"Not really," Ben said, wiping a stream of water from her neck. "You don't mean it, do you? We weren't in any real danger."

"Oh? I noticed you were keeping yourself as far from those yellow teeth as you could. We're lucky that thing didn't pop our tubes and eat us alive!"

Although Rose's mouth was a serious line, her eyes danced, and she and Ben burst out laughing simultaneously. Ben roared and laid flat on his towel, his memory replaying the scene while Rose laughed with him.

"I guess it was ridiculous," Rose giggled, wiping the tears from her eyes. "You were so funny, paddling into shore, the bubbles surrounding you, and the whites of your eyes wide for fear the killer beaver would attack at any moment!" She shrieked, and a new series of belly laughs racked her body.

"Wait a minute!" Ben turned over on his side. "You weren't laughing then!"

"Yes—y-es—" she gasped, "but I am now!" Another wave of laughter engulfed her.

"Okay," Ben said, bobbing his head as a warning. "Go ahead, laugh."

"I…will!" Rose managed to say between guffaws. "Oh, Ben, it's so f-funny—my stomach hurts from laugh-ing!"

Ben looked at her without a twinge of pity. "Attack of the killer beaver, huh?" he asked in a low voice.

Rose nodded weakly and held her abdomen, which still vibrated in merriment.

"Attack of the tickling man is far more deadly," Ben said, ominously, and set out to prove it.

"All right! All right! Stop tickling, Ben!" Rose rolled over. "I won't laugh at you anymore. But it was funny; you have to admit it!"

"Yes, it was. And you really weren't terrified after all?"

"A little scared maybe." Rose's smile began fading. "The only time I've been terrified is when I did some volunteer work at

Frederick's hospital. I was truly terrified then, and afterwards."

"Pretty bad, huh?"

"Pretty bad." Rose's eyes glazed. She lay silent a long while, then her mouth opened slowly. "One night there was a big accident on the freeway. We were swamped. I spent the whole time helping in the emergency room. It was terrifying. Blood. Screams. Ambulances and gurneys, hacked and mutilated arms, legs…"

"You don't have to tell me—"

"No, I want to." She raised herself to a sitting position and stared across the water. "It's what made me begin to doubt Frederick. I was put under this woman, Nurse Schaply. A woman like a bulldog." Rose shuddered. "I know you have to be tough, professional, but this woman was…inhuman. She could look anything in the face, anyone. No matter how they screamed. And she had no reaction. None."

Ben put his arms around her. "Rose, you really don't have to tell me."

"I've got to tell someone. I guess I want it to be you, Ben. I've kept it in long enough. I still dream about it sometimes."

Benjamin began feeling an intense anger toward the man who allowed this sensitive woman to be put in such a place of death and suffering. *Didn't Frederick know how Rose would react? Didn't he care?*

"Frederick stayed near me the whole time. He helped too, although he was tired—his own practice was long done for the day. He said I should quit if it bothered me so much. It was as if he wanted me to fail! He told me to stick with my art and forget about medicine. He said it was a good thing I'd discovered so early that I wasn't cut out to be a surgeon, since I couldn't stand the gore."

"That's why you were doing it? To see if you wanted to be a surgeon?"

"Yes. And I made it through the two weeks of volunteer service I'd signed up for. Nothing was ever as bad as that night in emergency, but I still heard screams sometimes when I walked down the halls. Every scream brought back that night."

Rose's clenched hand was white. She noticed it and relaxed her hand, laying it on Ben's arm. "After it was all over, I told him that I still wanted to be a surgeon, and that as soon as I finished my bachelor's in art, I was going right back to school for a pre-med degree. He was livid. He tried to talk me out of it, used every reason in the books. Finally he said I was being stubborn and unrealistic. He said that if I overrode him about something as important as this now, before we were married, our marriage didn't have a chance of working."

Ben held her tighter. "My poor Rose. No wonder you were afraid of me, putting me in the same class with him."

Her head raised. "And so I told him he was right. Our marriage didn't have a chance of working. And I walked out."

"You did?"

"Yes. And Mother was furious. She took his side!"

"But I thought he was the one who—"

"Broke it off? No, I did. But I always wondered if I was wrong. Maybe he had nothing to do with pairing me with Nurse Schaply, though I always suspected it. And maybe he was right. Maybe I never should've thought of being a surgeon. It must have hurt him—"

"Why in the world would it hurt *him*?"

"Because it's what he wanted to be, and couldn't. His second

154

year of med school his right hand became unsteady. I always thought it was nerves; anyway, it developed a twitch that wouldn't go away, not with treatment, therapy, or surgery. It destroyed his dreams of being a surgeon."

Benjamin digested this information. "So maybe he thought you wanted to be a surgeon to spite him, to show him that you could do what he couldn't?"

"That's what's always bothered me, though I didn't think of it until a week after I broke up with him. He came over the next day, apologizing and ready for reconciliation. I told him to forget it, and tried to give his ring back. He gave me the most heartrending look and begged me to keep it as a token of our friendship. After he left, I realized he really did love me. I started thinking then. But when I came to the conclusion that I really loved him too, and that maybe I really didn't want to be a surgeon after all, especially if it bothered him so much, it was too late. He wouldn't see me. He hasn't really seen me or talked with me since. Not for almost a year now."

"But I thought you two lived next door."

"We do—or did. That is, our parents' estates are adjoining. But there's an awful lot of space between the mansions. I didn't realize that until Frederick quit crossing it to see me. I caught glimpses of him every day, going and coming from the hospital. That made it worse. That was when the pain really began. I missed him. I knew I loved him. But he didn't love me anymore."

She turned, her eyes wet. "He wouldn't forgive me, Ben. I knew I had said things that needed forgiveness. So had he. But I was willing to forgive. He wasn't. It terrified me, worse than Nurse Schaply or the emergency room."

Her lips trembled. "It was the first time I ever encountered finality, the inability to make something right, to get another chance. It was irreversible. Terminal. Unforgiveness is a...is a horrible thing."

Ben kissed her cheek. "I think I finally understand. But there's more to it than Frederick's unforgiveness, isn't there? You've never forgiven yourself for how you reacted in the emergency room and for how you treated Frederick afterwards. And you're afraid to risk love again, aren't you? Afraid you might fail or find unforgiveness again. That's what really hurts."

She didn't answer, but began sobbing.

Ben pulled her to his chest and rested his cheek on her head. "You can't give up on love, Rose. With God's help, you have to try again, no matter how terrifying it seems. It took me around five years to learn that lesson," he whispered, touching her hair with soothing motions. "I wouldn't recommend taking that long, but if you do, I'll wait, Rose." He kissed her. "I'll wait."

The tiny boat floated in a sea of black. The water, dark as sable, was broken by the boat's slow motion as Ben paddled. Each edge of stirred water caught the moon's reflection and radiated across the bay.

Deep silence cloaked the earth as they eased onshore. The half-moon gave enough light to illuminate the entrance of the trail Ben sought. He led Rose over fallen tree trunks, around boulders, and past perilous crags until the path hit level ground.

Rose planted her feet in Ben's footsteps. They crept slowly, one of Ben's hands behind him holding onto hers, the other hand catching twigs and branches that barred their way.

"Are we there yet? I mean, have we reached wherever you're taking me?" Rose asked.

"No. We've hardly started. We'll hit the rise in a moment. You're ready for another adventure, aren't you? The beaver didn't take it all out of you?"

"The beaver? No!" She laughed. "But the trail isn't so slick as it was at the water's edge, is it?" she asked, remembering how her foot had slipped on the moist rock.

"No. Plenty of brush, and no danger of falling into the lake. It is pretty steep, though, and I won't be able to hold onto you. Watch me, and grab the rocks I grab. You'll do fine."

The trail wound to the left and ascended suddenly. Ben dropped Rose's hand and climbed, keeping near the ground, his legs and arms bent, his back hunched.

"See?" he called over his shoulder. "Keep your center of gravity low—it helps your balance."

Rose mimicked his movements. The brush did help keep her secure, although she had to lift her feet carefully to avoid tripping as she climbed.

"Not much more to go," Ben called. "The rise is getting more gradual now. The climb's a lot easier in daylight, just because you can see what you're doing better."

Rose held her tongue and didn't ask why they hadn't attempted the climb in daylight, then. She concentrated on keeping her legs moving.

"There!" Ben stood tall and held his hand out to her. "Come on!"

"I'm coming," Rose grunted, knocking her knee against a rock before the earth turned level and the moon shone again, unobstructed by the forest. She extended her arm and Ben drew her upright. They stood on an expanse covered with low brush. Pines and other trees made a black border behind them and to their far right.

"What's over there?" Rose asked, pointing to the left.

"You'll see," Ben said cryptically. He draped his arm around her waist, and they walked together along the path through the brush.

"Juniper bushes," Ben said, indicating the prickly, pine-looking growth that sprung from the ground in rough patches. "There are blueberry bushes here, too. It's hard to see in the moonlight, but they've already got green berries forming."

"Like this?" Rose knelt and held up a glaucous-looking berry the size of a pea.

"No, that's a juniper berry, even though most of the leaves surrounding it are blueberry leaves. It's attached to a juniper branch, see?" Ben untangled the limb and held it up. "I've made the mistake before, and in daylight, too. I've even eaten a juniper berry—or at least bitten into one." He screwed up his face. "Awful! Tasted just like a pine needle."

They continued their hike until they reached a small rocky plateau with little undergrowth. Ben untied the blanket he'd been carrying around his middle. Rose wandered away as he fiddled with the knot.

"Is that the lake down there—"

"Rose!" Ben leaped forward and wrapped his arms around her, pulling her away from the edge. As her feet moved, several pieces of rock slid over the edge and made tiny sounds as they fell.

Ben held onto her as they walked in the direction they'd come. "Yes, that's the lake down there. We climbed the cliff."

"You mean that huge rock face we saw by the boat?"

"Eagle Rock, yes. We're on top of it now. But it breaks off easily near the edge. No one's fallen off yet," he said, "and I want to keep the record clean tonight. We can sit nearer the edge over here, where some of the bedrock is bare. It's a lot safer."

Ben guided her to a large, smooth rock and spread out the blanket. They sat down and Rose leaned against him, her fingers intertwined with his.

"A double star scape," Rose breathed. She tilted her face. "I can see the stars in the sky—" she leaned forward slightly and looked past the cliff into the lake far below at its base, "and I can see the stars in the water."

Her body strained against his arms as she leaned farther still. Suddenly, she stiffened.

"Ben, is that our boat?"

"Yes."

The vessel looked like a toy model. "We're a long way up, aren't we?" Rose leaned back against him.

Ben nodded close beside her. "I've been this high ever since I met you."

His lips tickled Rose's ear. She smiled but said nothing.

"What are you thinking about?" Ben asked.

She inhaled deeply before she answered. Pine, earth, and juniper made up the perfume of the night. "I was thinking that I can see God from up here." She lowered her eyes from the heavenly lights and gave a short, self-conscious laugh. "Silly, isn't it?"

"Not at all. I'm glad to hear you say that, Rose. I don't think I've heard you mention God before; I was beginning to worry."

"I'm not used to baring my soul. Especially not so much in

one day. God is very personal to me, Ben. I was raised not to talk about him." She felt Ben's nod.

"I understand. My parents taught me that, too. But there came a time when I couldn't help myself from talking about him. He became such a big part of my life—the source of my life. I learned to love him, and when you love someone…" Ben paused and Rose felt him rest his head against hers.

"Rose, there's something I've been wanting to tell you—"

"No, Ben. No more serious talk, please. It's been a great day. But I…I don't think I'm ready for what you might say. I love the time we shared today. I love this place…" Her voice dropped. "I love…"

The sentence remained incomplete. At last Rose sighed. "Well, thank you for bringing me here, Ben. That's what I want to say, I guess." She squeezed his hand and leaned her head on his chest, listening with all her soul to the silence of the night.

Fifteen

※

Rose had intended to sketch the lake at the moment of its awakening, when the breeze dipped its fingers over the surface and stirred the first morning waves, but her pad was white as the clouds in the east. She couldn't decide where to begin, where to make the first splash of color.

Why should I be able to paint when I'm not able to think? she chided herself, and set down her brush and pad.

The water was lapis lazuli near the horizon, but dark at her feet. Ben had told her that when the hot July and August weather came, algae would tint the lake green, and she had already seen that near the muddy shores, the water looked umber.

The myriad, changing lake, she thought, and took up her brush just as a tremor ran through the wood of the dock on which she sat.

"Morning," Ben said, striding toward her. "Painting again? Good."

"I'm not really painting yet, but I was about to." She presented her cheek for his kiss, then spread a blotch of watery blue on her pad.

Ben made no comment, but Rose heard him hop into his boat. She didn't take her eyes from her work.

"In the mood for a ride?" Ben unwound the bow line and threw it into the boat. "I'm doing some volunteer work at the reserve today. Want to come? Dr. Algers only makes the trip from Warroad every two weeks, and when he does, I try to help him. He calls me 'Nurse Haralson.'"

Rose bent over her pad.

"Rose? Rose, do you want to come with? Maybe it would be a good chance for you to heal, to get into medicine agai—"

"No." The stern image of Nurse Schaply loomed before Rose, and in the background, Frederick's voice. "You're just not destined for medicine," she heard him saying.

Rose summoned a smile. "No, I don't think so, Ben. Lilla and I planned to go tanning today. I told you that last night at Eagle Rock, remember?"

She pulled her hand from the pocket of her blue cotton summer dress and raised it, palm up, to the sky. "Not a drop of rain. Perfect tanning weather."

Rose avoided meeting Ben's eyes by spreading more blue on her pad. Her excuse was legitimate but so superficial: tanning instead of volunteer duty. She hoped Ben wouldn't think less of her, but she wasn't ready to volunteer again. Not yet.

"I do remember a couple things about last night," Ben said, "but your telling me that you were going to spend the day with Lilla wasn't one of them."

When the silence following his words lengthened into minutes, he spoke again. "I'm sorry. I thought you might want to go. Maybe next time. If you ever change your mind, just let me know."

He climbed out of the boat and gave her a hug, then untied the stern and climbed back in. "Tell Maddie not to hold supper for me, will you? I may not get home until late. Don't wait up."

"Will it take that long?"

"Maybe not. But Rob usually doesn't see the last patient until evening. And I'm late. I'll have to make up for it."

Rose watched him pull the starter rope and cast off the stern line.

"Goodbye! And don't plan anything for tomorrow—rain or shine!"

Rose nodded and watched him take the eighteen-foot kicker boat in a northerly direction, its bow high in the air, its motor churning the water into yellow, white, and amber.

She gathered her art supplies and left the marina, ducking her way through the trees to the house, trying to keep from view of the Savon cabin. Eric had made himself scarce again, and Rose had a feeling he was angry with her. She wasn't ready for another meeting with him, and she breathed more easily when she had slipped into the Winters's porch apparently unnoticed.

Lilla lounged in the porch swing. "Hi ya, Rose! Avoiding Eric, huh? Good luck!" Lilla threw down the magazine she was reading and picked up a duffel bag. "Done with your painting for this morning? I'm ready to go."

"Come up to the loft. I won't be a minute." Rose led the way.

"Well, I'll come, but I know what your minutes mean, so I'm bringing the magazine."

Rose hastily assembled tanning equipment while Lilla sat at the window seat. She read and watched Rose pack, then looked out the window. "Hey, Rose, Eric's waiting at the dock! For you, I bet."

"Oh, no!" Rose left her towel on the bed and came to see. "Lilla, could you run the boat around the point and meet me by Ben's cabin?"

"Sure. But you know you have to talk to Eric sometime. Why not today? The sooner the better. Believe me, I let him know how I felt about him immediately—as soon as I figured it out myself."

Rose laughed and went back to packing. "I'm sure you did, but I don't really know what to say to him. I'm still working that out."

"Whatever. I'll tell Eric to take a hike for you if you want." Underneath her bangs, Lilla's eyes glittered.

"Thanks, but I don't think so. I'll figure out something. One of these days. Eric's not such a bad guy, Lilla. He's a lot of fun."

"More fun than Ben? Why don't you just tell Eric straight out that you don't want him around anymore?"

"I'll do it when I'm ready, Lilla."

"Like I said, 'Whatever.' Anyway, I'll get the boat. Meet you in five?"

"Give me ten minutes. I have to sneak through the brush, and I don't want to get too torn up by brambles."

"Okay." Lilla slung her bag over her shoulder and rolled the magazine under her arm. "Remember to pack sunscreen."

"I've got it," Rose called to Lilla's diminishing footfalls. She held the bottle of lotion in her hand. "This, at least, I've got," she said to herself, and carried her bag downstairs.

Ben tied his boat on the rickety dock in front of the reserve school. He could see the small, white rectangular building on the island above him, peeking out from behind scraggly pine trees. It wasn't far away from the boat landing as the crow flies, but Ben knew the hike there would take awhile.

He wore his usual outfit, a clean white T-shirt and faded denim jeans. In one of his hands he carried a bag filled with medical equipment he'd collected over the years.

The rock path up the slope dipped sharply at intervals. It was soft or hard according to whether or not lichens and mosses or tiny eruptions of grass covered the granite and had not yet been worn away by the feet of other travelers. Ben swiped at a few immature wild raspberry plants as he walked and made a mental note to take Rose picking soon.

By the time Ben reached the school, his rapid climb in the hot sun had caused a trickle of sweat to drip down the channel between his shoulders. He was glad shade was ahead, and smiled as he opened the door and stepped into the chaos of the school.

Wailing children, some seated, some wandering, some running wildly, made the interior seem in constant motion. Their mothers pursued them or rocked them or merely yelled at them from their own seats. Several patients or bored-looking fathers watched uninterestedly, and some old folks in a corner looked on with slitted eyes and wagging heads. They shook their canes periodically, no doubt grumbling to one another as to how children ought to be seen and not heard. In view of this cacophony, Ben felt in perfect agreement with their philosophy.

"Benjamin!" Dr. Algers called from across the room. His voice sounded tired.

Returning the nods of several women and the handshakes of some of the men, Ben made his way to Dr. Algers's side. "Hi, Rob. Sorry I didn't make it earlier. I forgot today was the day."

Dr. Rob Algers wiped his sleeve across his forehead and handed Ben the infant he was inspecting. "Take a look at the right leg. What's your diagnosis, Nurse Haralson?"

"Poison ivy?"

"Perhaps. I'm hoping that's what it is, and I'm going to give Jaclyn's mother here some ointment. Apply it three times a day, Mrs. Ketchinon. If it gets worse, stop in at Singing Pines and have Ben here take a look at it. That's all right with you, isn't it, Ben? I won't be out again until the usual time, and this could be nasty by then if I'm wrong."

"Fine, fine." Ben handed Jaclyn to her mother. "I've got to get used to house calls sometime." Ben smiled at Rob, knowing that the older man was establishing him with the reserve people. They still looked at him a bit suspiciously, like the newcomer in medicine he was, but through Dr. Algers's confidence in him and his own volunteer efforts, he was gaining some credibility, even with the older folks.

The day passed quickly, and as Ben assisted, he took notes, writing little diagnoses to himself or commenting on something Rob had said or did that surprised him.

"There's so much to know," Ben sighed after the last screaming child had left the makeshift clinic. "How am I supposed to learn everything I don't know now in the next four years?"

"You learn more in the next four years. You learn all you don't know in your lifetime. Then you die," Rob said, grinning at his comrade-in-arms.

Dr. Algers motioned to a woman with a burgeoning stomach to draw closer. She took her husband by the hand, and they made their way to the examining table, an ordinary fold-down table with a clean white sheet on it. The husband looked none too thrilled to leave the card game he had been involved in, and the woman chattered and pulled at him until he stood by her side.

"Well, Ben, what do you think?" Rob asked.

"Pregnant?" Ben tried to keep from smiling, and the woman roared with laughter.

Dr. Algers chuckled and patted the woman's tight belly. "He's a sharp one, isn't he, Imelda?"

"Sharp," the woman nodded, and laughed again. "Isn't he sharp, George, to know that I'm pregnant!"

Her husband grunted and cast a look over his shoulder at the card game he was missing. "Can we skip the jokes and get on with it, Doctor?"

"Sorry, George. We can go in the back for the examination. Ben, will you take care of things out here while I'm gone? Mr. Knockamus there needs his blood pressure taken, and Isadora needs her heart checked. I'll be back in about a half hour. If you feel like starting other cases as well, feel free."

Dr. Algers led Imelda and her husband to the cramped quarters that offered privacy but little working room. Ben carried out his appointed duties and had just finished his diagnosis of a woman's arm rash when the doctor appeared again.

"As I said, you and the baby are doing fine, Imelda, but you'll be reaching the due date before we know it. If there are any problems, I want you to get into town immediately—day or night. No putting it off, George. And I want her in Warroad at least a week before she's due."

Dr. Algers shook George's hand and waved to Imelda as she walked toward the school door. George rejoined his card-playing cronies and had a brief conversation with them before they rose and followed him and Imelda outside. The doctor stared after them.

"Isadora's blood pressure is good, but her heart is skipping a little, Rob."

"Hm? Oh, fine."

"I said Isadora's heart is *skipping*, Rob."

"Oh, sorry. I was afraid of that. The dosage will have to be upped. I'll send her out a new prescription on the mail plane."

"Mr. Thunder can go?"

"Yes, yes. His meds are fine. I guess that's everyone." Rob Algers gathered his things and looked about the empty room. "Ben, I'm worried about Imelda. Everything's looking fine so far, but she's had complications with her other four pregnancies. There are times, actually, when two weeks seems far too long to be away from here."

"Don't worry. I'll look in on her."

"I was hoping you'd say that." The lines on Rob's forehead smoothed a bit. "I'm beginning to depend on you out here, Ben, and you've got a feel for it: for the people, the work, everything. I hope you're going ahead with med school."

"I plan to take the MCAT in September," Ben said, sidestepping Rob's question.

Dr. Algers frowned. "You won't be able to attend classes this fall, then."

"No, but I need money anyway. I figure if I do well, I'll head down to the cities, work at the job I had last year at the hospital, and get my application to the U first thing next spring."

"You're still thinking of doing missionary work here?"

"I think this place needs a mission, don't you?"

Rob ran his hand along his whiskered jaw line. "Every time I'm out here, I do. And when I see cases like Imelda, who could use an on-call person, I'm convinced you're right. I hate to see you go into a life of debt, though."

"If this is of the Lord, Rob, it won't be a life of debt. The Lord will provide for our needs."

Dr. Algers nodded absently. "Well, that about wraps it up, doesn't it?"

"Think so. I saw another case of poison ivy. Pretty bad this year."

"Yes, and how that baby got into it I'll never know. Thanks again, Ben. I wish I could offer more than my thanks, but if I did get some funding for you, this wouldn't be legitimate volunteer time."

"I know, Rob. I'm grateful for the opportunity. See you in two weeks."

The men exchanged pleasantries and observations about the weather and the fishing as they walked down the trail to the dock. The sun was getting ready to set, and the water was calm. Frogs croaked in the shore weeds, and the two men stood on the dock, soaking in creation's evensong. Gulls cried and spun in mid-air, brilliant against the muted colors of evening.

"Well, Ben. Thanks again. I'm glad you have the time and freedom to do this."

"Freedom?"

"Yes, no strings attached—no wife, no family to tie you down, that sort of thing." Rob climbed into his boat and leaned on the motor cap as he tugged on the stern line.

"When did you get married, Rob?"

"Oh, years after med school. I had to get the bills paid first. School is expensive, you know. I didn't think it would be responsible to tangle a wife and kids in debt until I could float myself. It took about five years of practice before I felt I could support her and the little ones bound to come along. I'm glad you're a single man, Ben, especially with this missionary dream in your head."

Ben pressed his lips together. He opened them and began to speak when Rob's motor cut the air.

"See you in two weeks!" Rob shouted, and his boat pulled away. The aluminum sides glinted in the waning sunlight.

In minutes, Rob had turned behind an island, leaving only his wake and the words he had said: "School is expensive, you know...didn't think it would be responsible to tangle a wife...glad you're a single man, Ben...missionary dream in your head."

But was it all a dream? Couldn't it work out, and with Rose as part of the picture? It was the question Ben was beginning to wrestle with constantly. Was it fair to continue their relationship if Rose didn't know how hard their life might be together? He could offer love, sure, tons of it—but did she need more?

Ben looked up at the little white building on the rock, so shabby, so curiously a part of his greatest ambitions in life. It was the site for a mission. Clearly, somebody needed to help the people on the reserve, as well as those on the islands. But was it his mission? Wouldn't he feel less sure of himself if it was?

He hopped into his boat and started it, making an arc in the opposite direction Rob had taken. *If God really intends this mission for me,* Ben thought, *he's going to have to show me.*

Sixteen

❧

Rose sat humming and sketching beside Ben in what had become one of her favorite places to practice her art—the shore beyond sight of the resort and just below Ben's cabin, where she had come after her dream. She often sat here, even when Ben was gone, sketching or watching the lake and all the creatures living in and around it.

Ben flipped a page of the textbook and underlined a word with his fingertip as he read. Rose watched him and smiled. A day away from him had seemed to clear her mind, and now she was glad to be near him again. She was ready to be open again. Rose would have liked to talk, but she refrained, knowing he should study at least another hour.

As Rose let herself become part of the surroundings, her charcoal pencil slipped from her fingers. She listened to the tone of the frogs along the shore, their pitch changing on the breeze, like a medley of minor chords.

The bammy leaves near her flapped, and the tops of the pines on the nearest island swayed. The oversized jean jacket Ben had lent her kept out the wind; Rose glanced at Ben's lowered face to send him a smile of thanks, but he was too deep in his studying to see it.

An animated glob of spider web floated by. The center of the web was intact, but anchor strands flailed from its edges. The brown spider, no bigger than the inside of a Cheerio, rode his self-made aircraft in search of a fly. "If the prey will not come to me," the spider seemed to say, as he passed Rose, "then I will go to the prey."

A blade of grass trembled near the shore, the ambush site of a wood tick who hung onto it with his back legs. He stretched his body out and pawed the air until he was horizontal to the ground, reaching, reaching for a victim. Rose flicked at the blade until he fell into the water and floated away, his hair-width legs moving like flagella.

Rose sketched the sailing web into her drawing and added the water rings made by the wood tick into an empty spot near the far right corner of her paper. She drew the rings wide, so that they radiated to the shore, at the feet of a young woman with long, black hair.

Ben leaned over to check her progress.

"No fair looking until I'm finished!"

"Okay. I'll wait." Ben dove back into his book and seconds later asked, "Done?"

"No!" Rose laughed. "And you're not either."

"Rose, you've been here almost a month now," Ben said, closing his book and setting it on the ground between them, "and I've never asked how you like it."

"Well, don't ask me now." Rose placed his book back in his hands. "I'm not finished with my drawing, and you've got more studying to do. Only two months 'til the MCAT, remember."

Ben gave her a less than amiable look and resumed studying.

The sun was high and just emerging from a cloud. Rose lifted her face to the heat and closed her eyes. She heard the slosh of water and the hum of an unseen motorboat. A shadow passed, dark and cool. Thinking another cloud had covered the sun, Rose opened her eyes to find herself looking into Ben's face.

"Let me take a break, Rose. I want to talk to you. I've been trying to get up the nerve—"

"Ben, you've hardly studied an hour!"

"Yeah? Well maybe I've studied enough." He folded his arms.

Calmly, she picked up his book and balanced it in the crook of his elbow. "You haven't studied enough for someone who isn't sure he'll score high enough on the MCAT. It's all or nothing, Ben. They don't like candidates who take it more than once, you know. At least, the best schools don't."

"Is that why you decided not to go into medicine?"

"Partly, but it was my art and my bad experience in emergency that really—wait a minute, this isn't helping you study! Now get back to work!"

Ben opened his book and put one arm around her shoulder.

Rose leaned against him and took up her pad, sketching the blooming white yarrow and prolific black-eyed Susans. Lately the tall grasses of Singing Pines had become infested with them, though no one minded. Rose tried to smell them, but all she detected was the spicy aroma of wild pink roses at the forests edge.

"Why doesn't Aunt Maddie plant petunias down here, too? No, don't answer that. I suppose it's because there aren't any guest cabins around."

"No, she thinks the wildflowers would put them to shame, and I, as the sole surveyor of them this far from the main grounds, agree."

"Thank you, Doctor. Now back to your books."

"Not this time. I've finished that section, and I want to talk to you. Something's bothering me—"

"Ben, you haven't decided not to become a doctor, have you?"

"Are you so sure that's what I'm supposed to be?"

"Yes. You're an intelligent man, Benjamin. I know that. And Aunt Maddie's told me about your 4.0 grade-point average and all your honors. You have to go on. Glory awaits you." Her smile was saucy.

"I don't want glory, Rose. I want what God wants for me...and I want you."

Rose turned her head suddenly. "Benjamin! Are you asking me to—"

"No." He smiled wistfully. "Someday I'd like to talk with you about loving, honoring, and cherishing. But there are some things you have to know about me first. You know about my hopes of being a doctor, but I don't think you have the whole picture. I won't be Frederick's kind of doctor, from what you've told me. No riches or position or anything like that. If I can get into med school, if I can get my degree, I want to come back here."

"This would be a wonderful place to practice." Rose settled into his arms.

"I hope to be a missionary doctor. No regular practice, no regular hours, no regular salary."

"You mean you'll live on charity?"

"No, I mean I'll raise missionary support. 'The worker is worthy of his wages,'" the Bible says. I don't want charity any more than I want my father's money. But if God wants me to be a missionary doctor to the people on the reserve and islands, he'll supply the funds. If not…" Benjamin shrugged.

Rose watched a clump of wavering Indian paintbrush, pale yellow like the new sun, with rusty red-orange tips. In their Sunday family service at the cabin, earlier that morning, Uncle Mark had read a passage in the Bible relating to wildflowers, something about their being better dressed than Solomon in all his glory. Looking at the Indian paintbrush, so splendid and vibrant, Rose could almost believe it.

The passage went on to advocate dependence on God and freedom from worry. God cares about the sparrow, it said, and knows the number of hairs on your head. He will care for you. Rose accepted the philosophy in a general sense, but surely Ben hadn't taken it literally, as a promise to himself, even though Uncle Mark had preached a passable sermon urging that very reaction.

"Ben." Rose rested her hand on his forearm. "The missionary plan is a lovely idea, but it won't work. You can't spend all that money getting your degree and then not make any money. You wouldn't even be able to pay your student loans!"

"I don't plan on having any—or many, at least. I can guide up here summers. That's good money. And I can moonlight after school in a hospital. That's practically arranged. And even if I do get accepted into med school, it wouldn't be until next year. I could make a lot of money by then, if I watch my expenses."

"So after all that work, you really don't expect to make anything?"

"I assume you mean money. If it works out, I might, but probably not. It'll be bare bones, not much higher than the way I'm living now. And Rose, I'm used to it. It doesn't bother me anymore. I would trade, I *have* traded, all the luxuries of the city for life out here on the lake: for the clean air, the water, the islands, all these wildflowers, the birds, the fish—everything!" Ben stretched out his arms, then lowered them slowly.

"But I don't know if I could ask a wife and family to give all that up. I...don't know if I could ask you to give all that up."

Rose dropped her gaze. "I don't know either, Benjamin. Not yet. I don't know if I could ever.... Give up everything? For good?"

She surveyed the restless water, the foamy, wind-driven white-caps. "I do like it here. I'm happier now than I have been in a long, long time. But the reality is that I've only been here a month. I can't trade the balance of my life for thirty days! How long have I known you? How many hours have we talked? Many, I know, but not enough. Not nearly enough! Frederick and I lived on adjoining estates. We knew each other our whole lives, but it wasn't until I was sixteen that we started dating, and he didn't ask me to marry him for four years after that! You're going too fast, Ben; way too fast." Rose paused and tried to collect herself.

"I admire your selflessness, Ben.... I just don't know if I can be that selfless." She smoothed the hairs of his arm as if soothing his bruised ego. "You understand, don't you?"

She expected him to shake his head, to walk away and never come back, as Frederick had one terrible day. But Ben's expression was gentle.

"Yes, I understand. I know it's too early to talk marriage. I just wanted to sound you out, to warn you what I'm all about before you get in too deep. Now you know my plans and are free to make your own."

He raised his forefinger to her temple, tracing down to her chin. "Now that's out of the way, I won't be pushing you any farther. I know we've barely met, but it doesn't feel like that to me, Rose. There's so much that we share, and our differences only make me appreciate you. I like your art, even though I don't understand much about it. I like to have you sitting by me, sketching while I study. And I like the music that flows from you when I least expect it, your humming and soft singing. And—"

"That's enough, Mr. Haralson." She laid her hand on his arm and felt the softness of his skin, the hardness of his muscles underneath. "You're a complex man, Benjamin, a contradiction: a man of silk and rock."

"And you're my bird, full of song and grace, a creature of pure beauty."

Rose stopped stroking his arm. Her face clouded.

"'A thing of beauty is a joy forever'," he continued, kissing the back of her head. "I've heard that saying before, but never thought about it."

"It's not true, Ben!" Rose turned to face him. "Beauty is transient! All the images I can catch on my canvas, Ben, they appear and fade—almost instantly! A sunset, a flower, even the quality of light on the lake or wind among the leaves—there and gone, almost as if it had never been at all."

"Rose, that's not true beauty. That's not what I meant. The things of this earth are passing; I know that. I'm talking about the beauty of the soul, God's beauty, the beauty he created and placed in you, which will never fade. You have a beautiful soul,

Rose, a caring, loving attitude toward others and the ability to enjoy God's beauty in nature, even if it is transient. The beauty I cherish in you is eternal...like my feelings for you."

How could she reply to that? No words, no kiss, not even the tears in her eyes seemed adequate. She weakly squeezed his hand, and together they gazed across the white-topped lake. Somewhere birds chirped from their forest perches, and in the bay the wind whipped the whitecaps higher. But all Rose could hear was the even thudding of the faithful heart next to hers. She rested her head over it and listened, hearing in its strong, steady beat the rhythm of the future.

Seventeen

❧

S o, Rose, what are your plans for the Fourth?" Lilla asked, as she carried a big pile of dirty sheets into the laundry room and heaped them at her friend's feet.

"I don't know. Ben's not saying. From the amount of work you keep bringing me, though, I'd say I'll be doing laundry."

"The Fourth is always crazy like this. But don't worry. Maddie'll make sure we have at least the evening off. I'm going to town with Nick to see the fireworks."

Lilla helped to check the pile of bedding for spots and began scrubbing away at a mosquito splatter with a bar of soap. At the next tub, Rose did the same.

"Well, your plans sound like fun, anyway. I like fireworks, but Ben hasn't said a word." Rose rubbed the edges of the sheet together. "By the time I get home again, no one will believe these are the hands of an artist."

She put the sheet in soapy water and stared at her new callouses and the rough redness of her palms. "If anyone told me this spring that I'd be scrubbing someone else's laundry, I'd never have believed it."

The slam of the screen door announced Maddie's presence, but the pile of dirty sheets she deposited did not make her especially welcome. "Couldn't help overhearing, Rose. Life—or God, I should say—is like that. He stretches you. Part of his divine humor, I believe. He listens carefully to what we humans say we'll never do, and then puts us in a position to eat our words. Take heed, Rose, and say you'll never be happy enough!"

The three women laughed and scrubbed together, and soon much of the pile was delegated to separate washing machines or waited for a turn to be washed. The difficult chore of spotting was finished for the day.

"I'm off to the clothesline," Rose said, taking a load of wet, clean laundry from a washing machine she'd filled earlier. "Are you two joining me, or am I going solo?"

"I'll help you, Rose—"

Maddie clucked her tongue. "Not so fast, Lilla. You have two more cabins to clean before you're off to town. Want to help Rose with the laundry, too, or shall we head out immediately?" Maddie had her back to the two women and was counting out towels, washcloths, dish cloths, and bedding for the next job.

"Sorry, Rose," Lilla said. "The fireworks start just before dark, and I want to eat in town and join the street dance before that. Counting the ride there, time to get ready after these next two cabins…well, I'll barely have enough time. You don't mind, do you?"

"Of course not, Lil. I don't even know if I have anything to get ready for. If I finish before you, I'll give you a hand."

"You're fantastic!" Lilla gushed, and nearly knocked over the laundry basket Rose carried in her haste to hug her. "See you!" Then Lilla was gone, clutching a handful of clean rags and running to the next dirty cabin as if her life depended on it.

"I'd estimate we'll get that cabin cleaned in an hour flat," Maddie observed, standing near Rose and watching Lilla's legs fly across the lawn. "How I wish I could motivate the girl half so well when she doesn't have a date with Nick! Oh, well. She gives me my money's worth—in entertainment alone."

Maddie stepped aside as Rose carried her basket through the door. "And don't you worry, Rose. We won't need your help in the cabins. The new guests will be coming by launch later on tonight, and I know Lilla's going to finish the cabins before you're done here. I see we have enough pressed sheets, so you can leave the mangling for tomorrow. Besides, it's getting hot. I'd hate to think of you mangling today."

Rose wiped her damp forehead. "Thanks, Auntie. It's so humid in the washhouse already. I was dreading the heat of the mangle." Rose bent and gave her aunt a peck on the cheek.

Maddie smiled. "You're becoming mighty proficient with your kisses of late, I notice," she said, taking a pillowcase and pinning it to the line before Rose even got her own sheet arranged for pinning. "I don't suppose Ben is tutoring you?" She whisked another case from the pile and hung it deftly.

"Aunt Maddie! Aren't you ashamed of yourself, dawdling here with me while poor Lilla is cleaning by herself at breakneck speed!" Rose clucked her tongue in her aunt's familiar way.

"No, I'm not ashamed of myself, Niece." Maddie took a swipe at her with the end of a sheet. "But I will be going. I sense kissing is a touchy topic with you, no pun intended, and I respect your privacy."

The short woman gave a surprisingly graceful curtsy before returning to the washhouse to collect her towels and bedding.

When she reappeared, Rose was hanging her second sheet.

"Remember, Rose," Maddie called, watching her footing as she carefully descended the washhouse stairs, her arms piled high with linen. "You only have to get the clothes in the machines and hang them afterwards. There'll be time enough for the mangling tomorrow. I want to be sure you and Ben have a nice Fourth of July together."

"Thanks, Auntie. We will." *I hope,* Rose added to herself as her aunt tottered away.

Several hours and many clothespins later, Rose was sitting beside Ben as they skimmed across the water in his boat.

"You're not exactly a knight," Rose said into his ear, "and this noisy kicker boat isn't the white charger of my dreams, but wind in my hair beats soap under my nails hands down!"

"This is just the beginning, damsel. Now that you're out of distress, I want you to know that you're in for what I hope is one of the most pleasant days of your young life!"

Rose tucked her flying hair behind her ears, only to have it blow out again behind her. "The day is more than half over, Ben."

"Not so. The Fourth is officially over at midnight. I hope you're caught up on your rest, because I have many plans." Ben attempted to kiss her and got a mouthful of hair for his trouble.

Rose laughed and tried to contain her tresses with her hands, but they still whipped madly until Ben slowed the boat and turned down a narrow passage.

"Where are we going?"

"Wait and see," Ben suggested, weaving the boat through an invisible obstacle course.

"Are there many rocks?"

"Yes. Just under the surface of the water. Few boats come here. I'm betting we'll be the only ones today—maybe the only ones this year."

Ben turned to the left past a long point and landed the boat on a short stretch of beach. He held his arms out to Rose and carried her to the shore. "Here we are. Welcome to your own private beach for the day."

On the sand were lawn chairs, beach balls, and a screened-in tent with a table inside loaded with fresh fruits and homemade goodies.

"Benjamin! When did you ever have the time—"

"Here and there, madam, here and there. Maddie helped with the cooking. I procured the fruit—I made a deal with Cap. Don't fill up too much, or you won't have room for supper," Ben warned, leading the way into the tent.

Rose sampled a bunch of artistically arranged grapes. "You're making supper here, too?"

"We're going somewhere else for supper. After snacking here and enjoying a swim and some lounging time, along about evening we'll head to our next destination."

Rose made short work of most of the fruit, even though she had eaten Maddie's lunch only a few hours ago.

Ben took the leftovers out on a tray. "How about finishing on the raft?"

"The raft?" Rose watched as Benjamin dragged a colorful two-person inflated raft from the brush and maneuvered it into the water.

"Climb in. I'll hold it steady for you."

Soon they were adrift, Benjamin batting lazily at the water

with a plastic oar and Rose finishing the last slice of kiwi from the tray.

"Are you sure you don't want anything to eat, Ben?"

"Nope. I'm saving my appetite for tonight."

"I see. No snacking until then, hm? You must have something pretty great planned to beat this meal."

"Yep."

"So, when do I get to know what's happening tonight?"

"Tonight."

Ben's paddle strokes were even and slow. The water gurgled and turned circles behind them, appearing, Rose thought, like miniature whirlpools.

"Come on, Ben, give me a hint. What have you got planned? Tell me, or else!" She started to tickle him.

"Uh-uh. You'd better take it easy now. You almost ate enough for both of us."

"You're right." Rose settled herself comfortably in her own seat. "I could probably take a nap if I tried. I worked hard enough today to deserve one. I've never seen so many stained sheets in my life!"

"Busy day for me, too. I was helping Mark fix a couple outboards when I wasn't hopping around trying to get this day set up. I could use a rest myself."

"Fine." Rose stifled a yawn. "Just tell me a story until I'm sleeping, and then you can doze off yourself."

"Okay. A story. How's this? Once upon a time there was a wonderful woman from the suburbs named Petunia who had gorgeous green eyes and long, black hair and a great desire to be a world-famous surgeon—"

Rose opened her eyes. "I've heard that story before. If you're going to tell it, skip to the part where she graduates from med school and marries the handsome prince."

"No problem. That's my favorite part anyway," Ben said, and began his tale in a slow, sleepy voice. Neither one of them noticed when the paddle slipped from Ben's hands and drifted away upon the surface of the water.

The ochre of sunset spread across the horizon and was reflected in the still lake until it reached the beach where Rose and Ben sat. The blackness of distant land framed the bottom of the panorama before them.

Rose finished the last bit of grilled steak on her plate, ate the final morsel of steamed broccoli and cheese, and stared at the strawberry pie in a tin held by Ben's hands.

"Don't tell me you can bake, too! Ben, I can't eat another thing! I've never had a more wonderful meal in my life, and I've never had a more wonderful day—"

"The day's not over yet, Rose. I still have until midnight. Save your evaluation until then. Sure you don't want a piece of pie for dessert? Maddie made it."

"How about if I share a piece with you? That's the best I can do."

"Okay." Ben provided a clean plate and they settled down to enjoy Maddie's famous wild strawberry pie as the colors of sunset grew brighter and the lake became dark and silent.

A faint popping sounded to the right, and Ben and Rose turned in time to see a burst of exploding fuchsia.

"Fireworks! Ben, I didn't think I'd see them this year!" She kissed him on the side of his mouth, getting a dab of pie for her reward. "Thank you so much!"

"Keep a sharp look out. From here we should see fireworks in three directions. There'll be displays in Warroad, Rocky Point, and Baudette. It'll be a three-ring show. Six-ring, if you count the reflection in the water."

He picked up the remnants of the meal and then spread a blanket on the sand. "Here you are. Sit close to me, Rose. Warm enough?"

"No. Evenings on the lake are so cool. Hold me tighter."

"It's not so cool tonight, and if I hold you any tighter, I'm afraid you'll bruise."

Rose turned from the rockets of blue, red, and green and looked toward the sunset, brilliant and glowing. "So much beauty," she murmured. "Beauty from all sides. Hold me tighter, Ben. I don't think I can stand it."

"Rose! You're not crying!" Ben craned his neck to look into her face, colored with the reds and oranges of sunset. "Love, what's wrong?"

Rose shook her head, but the tears continued to spill down her cheeks. "I don't know. I'm sorry, Ben. I'm not unhappy, really! I don't know why I'm crying. I just can't stop!" She sobbed as flames of color arched through the sky—as sunset sank away to burning embers in the west and the sky became dark; the firework displays grew brighter and more showy, even far away and tiny though they were. Ben laid his hand on her head and held her to his chest, stroking her hair.

"Rose, Rose. My love, don't," Ben whispered. "Don't be sad, because…I love you. I've said it in many ways, but I don't want you to wonder, to have to guess anymore. Is that what's bothering you? Then know, Rose Anson, that I love you—not because you look like Jesse, or because you have money," he kissed her, "or talent," he kissed her again, "or beauty," he kissed the end of her nose, "or grace," he finished, kissing away the last teardrop on her cheek. "I love you because I love who you are, who God has made you. I cherish you."

Rose covered her face with her hands, and Ben wondered if he had misinterpreted her tears. Had she been crying because she couldn't return his love? He sat in suspense, daring only to keep his arms around her as he waited for her to speak.

The night grew black and the flashes and reports of the fireworks spread in a half-circle from southwest to southeast. They shimmered like candles in the water before disappearing while others took their places in the firmament. Rose lifted her head and placed her hand on Ben's cheek.

"Ben," she said, her voice and mouth tremulous, "I think—I think I cherish you, too." She closed her eyes and put her lips up to his as the southern sky exploded in a shower of red, white, and blue.

Eighteen

❧

Although Benjamin still kept to a rigorous studying schedule, it was not so tight as before. Often he would take the morning, noon, or evening off to spend time with Rose who, by now, was brown as a Chippewa.

She loved their adventures of canoeing, swimming, island exploring, and walking through the forest of Singing Pines. She enjoyed the art and music lessons she'd started giving him and the physiology and boating lessons he gave her, but sometimes Rose worried that Ben was sacrificing his future for his present.

One afternoon as they were sitting ashore one of their special islands after the long boat ride it had taken to get there, Rose put her thoughts into words.

"Don't worry," Ben answered. "I still average at least six hours of study every day."

"But will it be enough? You used to spend almost the whole day at it. Ben, I don't want to ruin your chances!"

He kissed her furrowed forehead. "You are my chance, Rose. I don't have any guarantee that I'll ace the MCAT, but even if I don't, I'm not giving up the opportunity of a lake summer with you. This I'll remember until I'm gray, long after I've forgotten my score on some test."

"It's not *some* test, it's the MCAT."

"I don't want to brag, Rose, but as you've said repeatedly, my past record is pretty impressive. And I'm feeling better and better about the MCAT. Besides, I still have the rest of July, all of August, and all the days before the test in September. I'm already going into it a lot more prepared than many do. Some of this is up to God, you know. If he wants me to be a doctor, he'll honor all the time and effort I've put into the test, and make my mind clear when I take it. So please don't worry, okay?"

"All right, Ben. I just don't want you to regret the time you spend with me."

"Regret time with you?" Ben looked incredulous. "My love, I'll never regret a millisecond we've had together—no matter what happens in the future. I had my priorities messed up once. Now I know better. Time with God comes first. That I'll never give up. But time with you comes second. Studying is a distant third. Very distant."

She said nothing, afraid to speak in case her voice revealed how deeply his words had touched her.

Ben laid his palms on her hands. "I don't mean to scare you, Rose, or box you in with the strength of my feelings. Anything can happen at the summer's end; I know that. But we have now, and I'll do my best not to waste what time we do have. That's all I meant, okay?"

Rose nodded, but Ben was watching her carefully.

"Something's still wrong, isn't it? Want to tell me about it?"

She looked up, her eyes and face somber. "I got another letter today."

"I thought your mother changed her mind about wanting you home, since you're so happy here." Ben kissed her cheek. "I give myself some of the credit for your continuing happiness."

"It's not from Mother, at least not directly. It's from…a friend."

"Which one? Irene? She's the only one still begging you to come back, isn't she? Or is it—" He stopped. "Not Frederick!"

Rose nodded.

Ben lowered his head. "What does he want?"

"I don't know. His hand is getting better. They figured out what was wrong with it, some nerve condition, like I thought, and it's been steady for more than a month now. He's going back to med school. He thinks maybe now he can be a surgeon."

"And he wants you back."

"I don't think—"

"Of course he does! Why else would he write?" Benjamin sounded angry.

"I don't know. That's what upsets me."

"He wants you back, Rose. You don't threaten him anymore. He figures he can be a surgeon and have you, too." Benjamin was holding Rose's hands. He stared at them. "Have you decided what you're going to do?"

"What do you mean?"

"Are you going back to him?"

"Benjamin!"

He looked up, and Rose saw the pain in his eyes.

"Ben!" She gave him a quick kiss. "Is that what you thought? That I'd go running back?"

"You're not?"

"Of course not!" She kissed him again and saw a shadowy smile cross his lips. "Ben, when I said I loved Frederick, I didn't know what love meant. I'm learning now. You're teaching me. But I haven't graduated yet. I still have a few lessons I want to learn from you."

"You're not going." Ben's words sounded almost like a prayer of relief.

"I'm not going," Rose repeated. "I'm not going, Ben! Don't look so serious!"

He drew her into a hug. "Don't scare me like that again!"

"I'm sorry. I didn't mean to scare you. I wasn't even planning to bring it up, but I keep thinking about it. It's really bothering me. Ben, do you think Mother put him up to it? I know she says it's fine now that I stay, but maybe she's just saying that. She was really upset when I broke up with Frederick, and maybe she thinks now that he's all right, we can go off and be surgeons together. She likes to hatch little intrigues, just like Auntie. In some ways, they're a lot alike."

"I already told you what I thought. He's well, and he wants you back. You're sure you don't want to go?"

"Not unless you're getting tired of me." She laughed as Ben kissed her cheek again and again. "All right, you've convinced me! I'll stay."

"I wish you wouldn't be convinced so easily," Ben said. "I was beginning to have fun. And I needed it, after a shock like that."

She turned and leaned her back against him, bringing his arms around her. "I am sorry, Ben. I didn't stop to think how it might sound to you. The only thing that upset me is why he wrote. I wondered if Mother was trying to manipulate him, or if

191

he was feeling sorry for me. I'm sure he's not trying to start anything. When he told me it was over, he meant forever. He even said so. I'm sure Frederick's moved way beyond me now, just like I've moved way beyond him. To you."

Ben squeezed her gently. "Just keep telling me that for a few days, will you? I might forget it now and then after all the trauma you put me through today."

"I'll tell you anytime you want, Ben. Anytime you want."

The next day was sunny and warm, and Rose finished her resort work by noon. After lunch she went out to the point to sketch and paint, and Ben sat beside her and studied, taking a break every so often to look at Rose's picture or listen to her sing. After two hours he closed his book.

"Rose, are you about finished? I could go for a good ski."

"I'm finished if you are." She gathered her towel and art supplies and headed toward the Winters's cabin.

"Where are you going?"

"To find Uncle Mark or Lilla. They always pull you."

"Always just ended. You know how to handle a kicker well enough now." Ben took her hand and tugged her toward the marina. "You can pull me. I have great faith in you." He jumped into his boat and snapped on his life jacket. He threw one to her as she climbed in.

"Ben, I don't think I'm ready to pull you yet."

He grinned as he started the motor. "That's okay. I want to ski in Tranquil Channel. You have until we get there to be ready."

Rose set her face stubbornly.

"You can do it, Rose!" Ben grinned at her and pulled the boat out of the marina. "Just try it, okay?"

Ben gave Rose last-minute pointers as they traveled to Tranquil Channel. They were there far too soon.

"Ben, I still don't feel ready!"

He unsheathed his ski and set it on the water. "You're ready. You know you are, Rose. Take a chance!" He jumped into the water and hooked up the towline to the stern.

"Oh, all right. But don't blame me if you get killed."

"You'll do fine. I trust you completely." Ben took the other end of the rope and paddled away.

"Okay, start her up. You've got a firm grip on the handle?"

Rose nodded, feeling the motor's vibration transmitted through her hand via the rubber-coated handle.

"Okay, then. Pull away from shore. As soon as the rope's tight, I'll give you the signal to gun 'er."

Rose gave the motor a little gas, all the while watching Ben in the water. He kept his ski tip up and held onto the towline, drawing handfuls of water with his other hand to steady himself. His boating lessons had taught Rose the rudiments of operating a kicker, but she never imagined he'd trust her to pull him skiing. She felt queasy as she watched the towline's slack disappear.

"Ready!" Ben yelled as soon as the rope went tight, and Rose twisted the throttle as far right as possible. The motor roared and the boat leaped ahead.

Despite her attempts to keep the bow moving straight, the wake behind was a crazy zigzag pattern. Ben hung on, but all Rose could see was a towline that disappeared into shooting white water. She squeezed the handle further, and the added speed pulled Ben out of the water.

He cut over the wake in a graceful arc and waved to her as the ski drew almost even to the stern. Rose smiled and nodded her head, not daring to let go of the handle to wave. She was thankful that her long hair, woven in a French braid, was out of the way so she could keep Ben in view with just a glance over her shoulder.

Rose searched the lake's surface for deadheads and other submerged dangers, turning back just as Ben made a tight cut to the left which pulled the boat so hard that he slowed it.

At the height of his motion away from the boat, Ben cut back violently, lifting his towline to take in slack; the boat speeded up, and a beautiful rooster tail of water at least twelve feet high sprayed from the back of his ski. He crossed his own wake as he jumped back over the other side of the boat's wake for yet another spray.

Rose glimpsed the rainbow that formed from the spurting rooster tail just before it disappeared. She knew that spraying was the height of freestyle slalom skiing, and Ben's spray had been magnificent. The faster and tighter the cut, the taller the spray and wider the rainbow. Rose loved to see the water rising like a geyser behind him and hear his talk about it afterwards.

Ben made several more cuts and sprays, and the rainbow accompanied each one. They passed an oncoming boat that disturbed the glassy water but gave Ben high waves to jump. After a few more sprays, Ben gave Rose the signal for stopping and dropped the towline as she circled the boat back to pick him up.

"Ah, Rose, that was great! You've got the hang of it. Best puller I've had in a while, and what a day for skiing!"

Rose pulled in his ski and rested it in the bow. "I missed a few of your sprays, but that first one was excellent. I don't think I've seen one shoot so high before." She wound the tow rope around her hand and elbow as Ben climbed in from the stern, using the motor casing to help him.

"Yeah, that one was the best. Did you see the rainbow?"

"Yes, and I saw it lots of times afterwards, too. The angle of the sun must be just right."

"Probably, but with sprays that high—"

"Let's not brag too much, shall we? Personally, I think it was the fantastic boat handling that allowed you to do so well. I've never seen you in such good form."

Ben reached out to touch the coils of hair curving along the nape of her neck.

"Oh, Ben, your hands are cold!"

"Then warm them up, Love."

The gulls flying overhead heard no more conversation for a while, and perhaps the sight of two humans in each other's arms was appealing, for one gull swooped near the boat and gave a shrill cry that caused the dark-headed human to look up, startled.

"What a day, Ben," Rose said, releasing her grip around his neck and settling herself in her favorite position, cradled by his arms and supported by his barrel chest. "The sun is so hot that I might even try skiing today." She pulled off the T-shirt she wore over her suit. "Might as well. You made me soaking wet."

Ben sprang up and began adjusting the pair of skis he'd stowed earlier. "That's just what I've been waiting for you to say. Slip your feet into the bindings and see how they fit. And here, put on this life vest."

"Ben, I was joking! I don't know how to water-ski!"

"And I don't know how to paint. But you've been spending enough time trying to teach me. Besides, you ski downhill every winter, don't you? Same thing, but better. You'll love it, Rose. And you'll have no better day for learning. The water's smooth as satin, and the sun is so warm I had to spray just to keep cool. Even if you do fall down, it'll only feel good."

The idea lost some of its appeal after Rose felt the shock of jumping into the water. "It's so cold, Ben!"

"Only because the air is so hot. You'll get used to it. Here come the skis!"

Ben leaned over and launched them across the water. Rose caught first one whizzing ski, then the other.

"Now you've got the line, right?"

Rose had just finished slipping her feet into the skis' rubber bindings, and she held up the line and pulled on it, trying to shed the awkward, floating sensations. "Ben, I feel like a bobber!"

"Don't worry. You always feel unstable in the water, but once you come out and glide across the glass, you'll feel like a ballet dancer, like a swan! Now remember: Keep your knees bent and your weight back. Let the rope pull you up, and don't straighten until you're used to how skiing feels. The water inside the wake will be rough, but to get over it you have to jump the wake, and that's tricky. You can probably do it, but wait until you know you can. Then don't try to slide over slowly, or you might wipe out. Go over it with a little speed, at an angle. You don't have to fly over it like me."

"All right. And you don't have to grin so hard," Rose said, at last balancing herself in the water. "Look, I'm as steady as you are!"

"Yeah, but it's a lot easier with two skis. You'll do fine. I'll start the motor; take the slack slowly and wait for your signal. You know all the signals, don't you?"

"Yes." Rose tried to keep her knees from shaking. "Start 'er up!" She bit her lip, but couldn't help smiling.

"Remember to stay clear of the wake for awhile. Now, as soon as you're ready, tell me, and I'll gun the motor. Then hold on!" Ben eased the boat forward until the slack was gone.

"Ready!" Rose cried, and the boat lunged, popping her out of the water like a cork. She straightened her legs too fast as she came out and her weight shifted too far forward. Her ski tips caught the edge of the water and plunged downward, pulling her with them.

Ben wheeled the boat around and retrieved her skis, cutting the motor when he came near her. "Are you okay?"

"Fine!" Rose sputtered. "I drank half the lake, but I'm fine!"

"This time keep your legs bent until you're steady. And don't get your weight too far ahead."

She glared at him. "I expected a little more sympathy."

"I'm sorry. Hey, it happens. You just got too much forward momentum. I'll take it easier on the speed. That'll help."

"Thanks a lot!" Rose swam for the towline and put on her skis. She arranged the rope between her legs and floated, her knees well bent.

Benjamin started the engine and took up the slack. "Yell when you're ready."

Rose took a deep breath. "Ready!"

The boat surged and the line tightened, pulling Rose up with it, but this time she leaned farther back. She found herself zooming across a slightly bumpy surface. It felt like cobblestone.

She looked up to see Ben cupping his free hand over his mouth and yelling something. "What?" She could hear snatches of his voice, but the motor obscured his words. "Wha—"

First one ski slid down the wake, then the other. Rose felt as if she had just slipped off a stair. Her legs shook, the tow rope in her hands wobbled, and her body swayed, but she hung on, and soon the rocking ceased. She became aware of the smooth surface beneath her, so slick she almost felt like she was floating. She straightened her legs a little more and leaned back, imitating the stance she'd seen Ben assume so often.

Ben yelled something from the boat, and although Rose couldn't understand his words, appreciated the bravo sign he gave her. She waved back, nearly fell again, and then kept her hands on the handle.

She skied in a straight line, gaining confidence and balance, and when she had a firm grip on the tow handle, turned her skis and cut over the wake, skiing on cobblestone once more. The rough water made her crouch, and she veered away from it, going over the other wake at an angle. She kept her knees well bent to give her added stability.

Ben pulled the boat nearer the island walls of Tranquil Channel. At first the granite rock so close made Rose move back to the safety of the wake, but the reflection of pines and wildflowers in the water called, and she answered. She skied over green bammies and speckled Canada lilies, seeing them under her skis and at her side, a double dose of God's beauty. Enchanted, she bent even farther and dipped one hand in the silken water as if to stroke the reflection.

She stayed low above the water, making a spray with her hand and opening her mouth slightly to sing an ancient prayer stirring her heart. Her eyes fastened on the mirror images before her. She became a part of the beauty around her, scarcely mindful of the towline or skis now, as a porpoise is unaware of her dorsal fin or a mermaid of her tail, conscious only of the delight, the joy and freedom of movement.

Rose slipped over the water and drank in beauty until an ache in her arms and legs drew her back to herself. She straightened and gave Ben the stop signal, releasing the towline and sinking slowly into the water.

Ben had the boat near her in seconds and was pulling her in. He unfolded her towel and wrapped it around her shoulders.

"Well?"

Rose shook her head and reached for Ben's hand. "It was…" She searched for the words. "It was so.…" Still she searched, and her eyes teared with the effort. She felt stunned, overwhelmed by the discovery of joy, beauty, and freedom so overpowering.

"Oh, Ben! It was…was like being given wings! But even more than that…so much more! It was…it was—"

Ben squeezed her hand. "I know," he said, ending her difficulty by kissing the lips that still reached for words not yet known to humans. "I know."

Nineteen

❧

en, Dr. Algers can't make it today and hopes you can."
Maddie delivered her message even before she was inside
Ben's cabin. "He said to be especially careful of a Mrs.
Nightsky. He thinks she's close to giving birth. Was he referring
to Imelda? I haven't been over to see her for awhile, but I know
she's due soon."

"Yes, it's Imelda." Ben said, pulling on a jacket. "He gave her
a good going over last time and made me read a treatise on emergency childbirth in case something happened. Rose has been
quizzing me on it all week."

Ben downed the last of his coffee while standing near the
window. "No wonder Rob didn't want to come out today. It's
pretty windy for morning. Probably white caps on the open lake.
Could be rough by tonight."

"Is that when you'll be home? I hate to have you miss lunch
and supper both. Good thing you got a big breakfast."

Ben slung a slicker over his arm. "Yeah, breakfast should fuel
me for a while."

"I packed you a few things in case it doesn't." Maddie handed him a bag, then glanced out the window. "I don't like the wind, and this dawn was red as blood. You know what they say."

"'Red sky at morning, sailors take warning.' I know. I saw it too."

"Were you doing some early studying?"

"Yes, but not about medicine. Maddie, do you know where Rose is in her relationship with God? I tried to ask you that once before."

"I believe that's a question you should ask Rose, if you're wondering. I do know that she's been reading her Bible quite a bit lately and asking good questions. She talks to Mark a lot after his sermons. I'd say she knows the Lord, but she's a young Christian."

"That's what I'm thinking, too. But you're right. I should ask her. I don't know why I keep putting it off. I told myself she should be the one to bring it up, but maybe that's a cop-out. Maybe I'm afraid of her answer."

Maddie stood on tiptoe and reached up to brush a piece of blond hair out of Ben's eyes. "I don't think you have to be afraid, Ben, but it is an important thing to know…if you're considering any…future plans."

Ben laughed. "Never one for subtlety, were you, Mad?"

"No, though I try," Maddie said, chuckling. "It's impossible to act delicate with you, Benjamin. So, as long as the subject is open, do you have any future plans?"

"I think that's another something I should ask Rose about first, if you don't mind, Mad."

"Not at all!" Maddie gave him an excited hug. "But I get to know second, all right?"

"Deal. Listen, Maddie, I should go now. Could you tell Rose I'll drop by if it isn't too late tonight?"

"I'll do that." Maddie took his mug from him. "Go on, now, and be careful. I don't like the looks of that lake."

The sky was an overcast mixture of white and gray, and the lake glowered underneath. Ben gave it one more look before moving to the door. "I've got my slicker, so I'll stay dry. Don't worry about me, Maddie. If I'm not home by dark, I'll radio."

"Thanks." Maddie gave him a peck on the cheek and held the door open behind him as he passed out. "Mind the wind, Benjamin."

"I will. Don't forget to give my message to Rose."

Maddie nodded and waved, but the strong figure galloping down the lake path toward the marina never saw it.

When Ben reached the schoolhouse, there were few patients to meet him, although enough trickled in during the day to keep him busy. It wasn't until the sky began turning darker that Benjamin realized Imelda Nightsky had not come in.

After seeing his last patient, a dimpled boy with chicken pox, Ben packed up his bag and headed into the heart of the reservation to make his first house call.

The reservation buildings were like the school: small, rectangular, and weathered. They all looked like the government projects they were. The combination of shadows and weak light made the houses seem less boxy and uniform than they appeared during the day.

After knocking on several doors and being told he had not yet reached the George and Imelda Nightsky residence, Ben found the house of a young boy who offered to guide him.

"They live by themselves at the edge of the woods," he said, grabbing a coat and going ahead of him on the path. "George doesn't like neighbors much, unless they play cards."

The boy left Ben at the steps of a dun house, no better or worse than those he'd seen, but with a beautiful lake mural on its side. He stood on the cement steps and knocked on the screen door. Somewhere inside the house a dog barked, but that was all. He waited several seconds more and rapped again. Nothing.

Ben leaned against the railing and contemplated going home. It had been a long day. Maddie's snacks were only delicious memories. The wind was coming up, and he didn't relish the thought of picking his way home in the dark through rough water.

Maybe the Nightskys were already in town. Maybe that's why Dr. Algers hadn't come today: He was delivering the baby and somewhere along the line that part of the message got lost. With so many relays from town to reach Singing Pines, odds were that something got left out or mixed up in transmission.

Ben gave one more knock, waited, descended the steps, then stopped in mid-stride. Had he heard something? He turned uncertainly. The dog yapped, and Ben thought he could hear the quiet chatter of a television. Impulsively, Ben opened the screen door and stuck his head inside. "Imelda? George? Anyone home?"

The tan linoleum floor was worn and dingy, even in the dim light coming through the windows. Ben was halfway in when he again heard a faint cry. He closed the door behind him and reached for the light switch, moving just in time to avoid the small dog who shot out of a hallway. Ben raised his bag threateningly, and the dog cowered.

"It's okay, boy," Ben said, trying to sound friendly, but holding his bag above the dog's head nonetheless. "Just want to see if your mistress is home."

Ben moved past the dog through the kitchen and connected dining room. The dog growled unconvincingly from his post under the scarred chip-wood table. Ben stuck his head around the corner and into the littered living room, but no one was on the sway-backed couch or the tilted easy chair in front of a lighted TV. The screen showed to its nonexistent audience a scene from Canadian parliament.

After making sure the room was empty, Ben called again, received no answer, and switched off the TV set. A thin cry, now clear without the masking noise of the television, seemed to emanate from the hallway. Ben stepped quietly, opening doors until he came to the last closed one. There lay Mrs. Nightsky in a double bed, barely visible in the bedroom's dimness.

"Imelda?" Ben asked, switching on the light. The woman flinched, and he adjusted the lamp shade to soften the rays. "Where's your husband?"

"Gone. At his brother's place, probably, playing cards. Said we'd be going to town this noon, but he never came back. I sent the kids to my sister's this morning—" Her sentence was interrupted by another low moan.

"Try to relax. I'll be right back." Ben went to wash up in the bathroom. Every available surface was strewn with tiny paintings, as was the entire house, and one whole side of the wall was another mural. As he sterilized his hands and equipment, the thought crossed his mind that Rose would love to see this house.

Imelda had ceased groaning when he re-entered the room. Ben spoke reassuringly to her while he made a preliminary examination.

"Dr. Algers with you, Ben?"

"No, he's not. He couldn't come today. I thought you were in town with him. I wouldn't have come here at all, but I wanted to make sure you were okay. If I hadn't heard you moaning—"

Imelda's face looked even more pinched. "I been trying to keep quiet. The pains aren't so bad—" Another moan parted her lips.

"How long have you been feeling the pains?"

Through a slow conversation halted by more moans and contortions, Ben learned that labor had been setting in for some time. His examination confirmed that, but he had hoped she would contradict what he was discovering from her own body.

"This will be uncomfortable, Imelda, but I need to do it. Go ahead and moan. There's no shame in moaning. All women do when they're about to bring life into the world."

Imelda nodded and twisted the wet bedclothes until Ben had completed his check and prepped the birth site.

"Imelda, you're going to be a mother again soon."

Ben's tone and words made Imelda smile weakly. "Thought so. Wish George was here."

I wish Rob were here, Ben thought, *or anyone but me.* Imelda was experiencing what she at last confessed were strong, regular contractions, and she was dilated to approximately six centimeters, four short of the ten needed for second-stage labor. Though calm and breathing well, Imelda was approaching transition. Birth was probably imminent, and no matter how badly Ben yearned for assistance, he didn't dare leave Imelda long. He had one chance, and after weighing his options, decided to take it.

"Imelda, would you like your sister to be here?" Ben knew

that Linda Ketchinon had some emergency medical training, and she had assisted Rob with difficult cases before Ben had come on the scene. Besides that, she had a cool head, a trait very appealing to Ben in his present situation.

When Imelda grunted yes, Ben flew out of the house, returning in seconds to ask directions to Linda's. Once out again, he charged past the dog, down the steps, and slowed only as darkness impeded his progress.

Ben banged violently on Linda's door until a sleepy, long-haired Chippewa woman appeared. "Yes?"

"Linda, Imelda's almost ready to give birth. I just left her."

"In town? George brought her in this afternoon."

"No, she's at home. Alone. I need your help, Linda!"

Linda took Ben inside and roused her husband. After Ben suggested he try to relay to Warroad and get Dr. Algers to come, Quincey disagreed.

"I'll radio for local help, Ben, but there's a small-craft warning out for the big lake. No one would risk it."

"Call for the float plane, then—"

"Ben," Linda said, "I think it's you and me on this one. Ned shouldn't fly from town with the weather as uncertain as it is. We can manage. You go on ahead, and I'll come as soon as I grab some supplies Dr. Algers left with me."

Ben stood as if deciding what to do.

"Go on. Quince will stay and try to contact George." Linda paused and shook his hand. "Well, Ben, looks like you're a doctor now—ready or not!" Linda grinned and shoved him out the door.

"So he's not home yet?" Maddie asked.

"No, he's not home. His cabin is empty. He told you he'd call if he was going to be late. What's gone wrong?" Rose hung up her slicker on the peg near the door. "It's beginning to rain hard, Auntie. Do you think he's lost on the lake somewhere?"

"Rose, like Ben always says, 'Don't worry; just pray.' It's what I've been doing since nightfall, in fact. Ben's probably just taking his time getting back. The small craft warning is for the big lake, not this part. The storm isn't expected to be too bad here; windy, but nothing near what you and Eric went through. Nothing really dangerous. There's a lot of sheltered water between here and the reserve. Ben's probably chosen a safer route to take advantage of the islands and will be home any time."

Maddie's words didn't ring true, and even when she smiled, the worried crease between her brows did not fade. Ben had told Aunt Maddie he would call if he was going to be late, and never had Rose known him to break a promise. Something was wrong.

Rose sat at the kitchen table as Maddie bustled to make her a mug of hot chocolate.

"I've had a feeling all day," Rose said, following her aunt with her eyes.

Maddie shut the fridge door, nearly catching the milk container in it. "What do you mean?" she asked, filling a pot with several cups of milk and setting it on the gas burner.

"I don't know." Rose slumped in her chair. "I should've gone with Ben today, Auntie. We weren't very busy. I wish he had come to tell me he was leaving."

"Didn't you know it yourself? He goes every two weeks."

"Yes, and I was thinking of going with him this time. In fact, I was all ready, but I wanted him to ask me."

Rose twirled her finger in her hair until it was well tangled. "Then he left without me. And then I ran into Eric! I had an awful time with him. I finally told him how I felt about Ben. He got furious and left in his boat. I haven't seen him since. Have you?"

"Not since before supper time. He and his parents went out to eat at Flag Island, I believe. I hope they don't try to make it back tonight. Especially if they took Eric's boat."

"Me, too. I wish Eric had a safer boat. And I wish I was with Ben. How could he go without me? He probably needs me right now!"

"I don't think he had any idea you wanted to go, Rose, and I don't think he's any worse off for his lack of you—although I'm sure he would've liked having you with him."

Maddie dipped a spoon into the pot and held it up, a piece of milk skin hanging from it. She turned off the heat and soon brought three steaming mugs to the table. "Mark," she called into the living room. "I've got some hot chocolate here for you."

"In a minute, eh? I'm trying to hear the radio."

Maddie set down the mugs. Rose stirred hers until it was nearly cold and Mark walked in.

"Somebody's trying to transmit something," he said, sitting down and eating a spoonful of melted marshmallow foam, "but I can't tell what it is. The static's too bad." He took a gulp of chocolate and stared into his mug after he set it on the table.

"Now I'm not in for an all-night vigil with you two, am I?" Maddie asked, her hands slipping authoritatively to her waist.

Rose looked at her uncle. His face was as bleak-looking as hers probably was.

"Well, all right then," Maddie conceded. "Anyone for a game of Scrabble?"

Mark's face grew darker. Rose shifted in her chair.

"You two really are worried, aren't you? Well, then, let's pray." Maddie knelt down.

"Right here on the kitchen floor? I just read in the Bible that prayers are supposed to be done in your closet—outside of church, I mean."

"That passage is about pride, not location, Rose," Mark said. "The Lord wants simple, sincere prayer, not showy public speeches. Ben's on my mind tonight, too, and if he or anyone else is in trouble, we should petition God for them. We'll be a circle of three, and where two or three are gathered, the Lord is there in the midst of them. The Bible says that, too, eh? Let's pray."

Rose got to her knees, and the three bowed their heads and joined hands. Uncle Mark and Aunt Maddie prayed aloud, the Spirit of God presiding and translating the sweet aroma of their prayers to the Father.

As Rose heard their heart pleadings, she sensed the Holy Spirit in their words, felt an invisible, holy Power in the room. She opened her mouth, stuttered, closed it again, then sent up an unspoken prayer to God asking him to work in her words, in her heart. And then she ceased thinking about herself and became one with the prayers around her.

Though Uncle Mark always led prayers at their regular Sunday church meetings in the living room, tonight Rose could feel the Spirit upon her, around and within. A loving Power stirred her heart, awakening it to an answering love, and she spoke softly, tears choking her words: "Dear Lord Jesus, please bless and protect...Ben, wherever he is...right now. And Eric...God...please protect Eric and his parents, too."

Her heart grew stronger and the fear left, replaced by peace. She listened to her aunt and uncle's prayers, gaining comfort from their shared concerns and the tangible presence of God. It was like their usual Sunday church service, but somehow very different to Rose—somehow very real.

When Mark gave the final "Amen," he strode into the living room, flipped on the radio, and listened intently to a static-filled message. Rose remained kneeling a moment longer, then walked to the door and began putting on her slicker.

"Rose," Maddie intoned, "you're not thinking of—"

"Maddie! Rose!" Mark burst into the room. "I finally got the message, I think. A baby is being born on the reserve: Imelda Nightsky's! They're looking for her husband, George, and anyone else who can help. There's no lightning anymore and I haven't heard a thunderboomer for a good hour. Either of you up for a rough boat ride to the reserve?"

"I am! Ben's got to be there. Let's go!" Rose exploded into action, helping her aunt gather supplies and jackets, and then she led the way out into the darkness.

Twenty

❧

Mark tied his wave-jarred boat to the reserve school's dock near Benjamin's boat and helped his shaky wife and niece climb to stable ground. "Sorry the trip took so long, but I had to go the most sheltered way. Bad enough as it was, eh?"

He, Maddie, and Rose stood bent-limbed, experimenting with trying to straighten their bodies, which, along with the boat they rode in, had been knocked every which way in the waves.

"You did fine, Mark." Maddie staggered forward and reached for her husband's steadying hand. "Let's get to Imelda—and to Ben! I'll hold the flashlight and lead. I know the way. The path is tricky, but no worse than the trail to our cabin."

As the storm gathered its strength and issued forth vigorous blasts of rain and wind, Maddie held her niece's hand tightly and tried to keep Rose's mind off any residue fears about Ben. "Do you suppose we'll arrive in time to see the baby being born?"

"What?" Mark yelled. "Maddie, can't you wait until we're inside to talk?"

"I said, 'Do you think we'll see the baby's birth?'"

"I hope so, Auntie!"

"What do you think, Mark?"

"I don't know. Probably already born. How far's the house, eh?"

"Not far now." Maddie squeezed Rose's hand. "I can see the lights just ahead, I believe. We'll be there in minutes, and then the fun will begin!"

Imelda's groans crescendoed, and one look told Ben that after an agonizing prolonged active phase, she was at last in transition. He signaled Linda to prop up her sister with pillows so gravity would help move the baby down and out.

"I can't do it, Ben. I can't do it!" Imelda was giving way to the natural feelings accompanying the hard labor of transition, the hardest labor in all the birth process. She was irritable, panting, and shaking wildly.

Linda murmured comforting words and caressed her sister's forehead and cheeks. "Yes, you can, Melda. You're doing fine, the baby's fine. Soon we'll see him—or her. I can't wait, can you?"

"Keep it up, Imelda," Ben encouraged from his post as Linda slipped away to freshen her sister's washcloth. "This is the worst it's going to get. You're going to begin pushing soon, and Linda and Rose will help you. Maddie and Mark are in the living room praying, and before you know it, the newest member of the Nightsky family will be in your arms."

Imelda shrieked and shook, then looked at Ben with wide brown eyes. "Yes, yes," she said, straining and twisting.

Ben ran his hand over the prepared birth site, grateful that Linda had cleaned up the mess from Imelda's broken water. The sheets that replaced the soiled ones were white and clean. He was thankful as well that Mark had been able to find some boards and insert them under the mattress, or the surface would have been too unsteady to work with now. Ben examined Imelda and waited for the women to reappear so he could move her to a better birth position.

Linda entered the bedroom with another cool washcloth. Rose followed with a tray of freshly sterilized equipment.

"Well, Sis," Linda said airily, helping Rose and Ben to move Imelda to a left-side position. "Looks like I'll be an aunt again soon!" Linda stroked Imelda's hand and wiped her forehead as Rose assisted by holding up Imelda's leg.

"Glad you're here, Lin. You, too, Ben, and Rose—" Imelda's words dissolved into a sharp cry. She flailed the air with her arms. Linda soothed her until she stilled, moaning weakly.

"Rose, I have presentation." Ben gestured for her to come nearer. "It's breech," he said softly. "She hasn't dilated fully, and we've got breech. Oh, Lord—" Ben's sentence continued as a prayer in his heart.

Rose passed on the message to Linda under her sister's rising cries. The Chippewa woman looked at Rose vacantly. "Ben," Linda said, leaning close, "I've never even seen a breech—"

"I have," Rose said. "I was a volunteer in a hospital for a while. We had a breech. It was successful. You can do it, Ben." Rose didn't add that she had only observed, and that the baby had to be delivered by cesarean section, but Ben knew it as well as she did. And they both knew that under these conditions, cesarean would be deadly.

"I can hardly believe it. I'm sure the baby was in a normal position before," Ben said. "Maybe it'll slip back into place, but we'd better prepare in case it doesn't. Help me get her onto her hands and knees, Rose; Linda, you can relax for the time being and help your sister to do the same. Imelda," Ben raised his voice so the tormented woman could hear. "You're doing fine; you're almost through. We're moving you to a better position now. Can you help us?"

Imelda's cries lessened as she concentrated on moving. Ben aided, watching as Rose worked with the greatest care and Linda stood by, steadying her sister with a hand and voice full of love.

"Good, good." Ben kept close to the birth canal as Imelda turned over. "You're doing fine, Imelda. Keep breathing. Good."

Ben motioned to Rose. "Praise God, Rose, she's dilating. But the baby's definitely in breech. I'll keep working here until the navel appears. Then we have to work fast. We'll have a few minutes. If we don't get the baby delivered to the point where its mouth and nose can get air—"

"I know, Ben. It won't have any oxygen." Rose's lips were tight, and her eyes were hard as jade.

She exhaled slowly, looking at the floor, then straightened her shoulders and faced him. "Just tell us what to do, Ben, and when to do it. Linda and I won't fail. And you won't either."

"Not with God with us." Ben readied himself for the final stage and prayed. Clanging warnings about a strangling cervix melted away under the assurance of a still, small voice. Rose prayed beside him, and he felt God's strength sharpening his mind and body for the ordeal ahead.

Ben held a hushed conference with Linda, telling her only as much as she needed to know to do the most good. Linda nodded and took her place.

"What...wh-at," Imelda puffed. "Is everything...okay?"

214

"Yes, yes," Ben said. He looked at Linda, then Rose, and was heartened by their composed faces. "Imelda, God will help us deliver this baby."

More contractions, more heavy breathing, more screaming and writhing, but Rose kept her station. Linda mopped Imelda's face desperately.

"You're doing great, everyone," Ben called out. "Keep it up!"

"No more!" Imelda cried. "No more—"

"I see the navel, Imelda! Your baby is coming! Rose and Linda, stay close!" Ben's excited voice held no dread, in spite of the fact that the time clock had now been activated.

"Good woman, Imelda. Now bear down!" Ben held the lower part of the baby firmly in one large hand and continued to monitor Imelda. Dilation was complete. It was now or never.

"Bear down, Imelda. With all your concentration, bear down!"

Imelda groaned with the effort as Linda looked at Ben worriedly.

"One, two, keep bearing down, Imelda! That's it!"

With his mother's contractions, the baby's navel emerged. Ben rejoiced in the sight, but knew that the umbilical cord's blood supply was now shut off, and with it, the baby's oxygen. "Way to go, Imelda! Steady, Linda, Rose."

Ben waited for two contractions, then exerted downward pressure on the baby's legs, calling out encouragement to Imelda. He held the wriggling baby securely, careful to keep the child's back toward his mother's belly as he assisted in the delivery. Rose stayed close, but kept her hands out of his way.

Imelda screamed and panted. Ben was about to grab his

forceps when he saw the baby's armpit appearing.

"Praise God!" he said under his breath, and carefully, gently, used one finger to push on the baby's shoulder. The child's arm dropped down. "Just like clockwork."

"Don't mention clocks." Rose flashed him a smile. "It's going to work, Ben. I know it is!"

Ben looked at the burden he held in his hand. Half a baby. If only a whole child were cradled there! Ben's arms throbbed; his shoulders were cramped from his awkward position near Imelda, but he ignored his own sensations and devoted his attention to the mother and child.

So far, so good; Lord, Benjamin prayed. *Let this baby live. Please, God, help me to remember what the treatise said, help me remember everything I've ever heard about breeches. And please, my God and my Savior, let this baby live!*

The infant's second arm dropped down, and Ben held him steadily, rejoicing that yet a bit more of the baby was safely in his hand.

"Keep going. A little more, young fellah," Ben urged, and inserted a finger in the baby's mouth.

"What is he doing?" Linda whispered, coming close.

"The baby's chin must be bent to his chest," Rose answered softly, "otherwise his head will get caught. It won't be long before he's out now."

She looked at the wriggling baby in Ben's hand. "Want me to help hold him?"

"No. You're doing fine." Ben tried not to think how much time had passed. "Just be ready for when I need you—and keep praying!"

Imelda's screaming intensified.

Ben felt the baby's chin flatten to his chest. "Now, Rose! Push down on Imelda's abdomen, just like we read. Push!"

As Ben watched, the baby's head emerged, and the whole, tiny body was at last in his palms.

"You did it, Ben! Imelda, Linda, you did it!" Rose helped Imelda into a comfortable supinated position and looked, enthralled, at the little cheese-covered human in Ben's capable hands.

Ben cleared out the baby's mouth and nose, and the child's wail soon filled the air. Ben wiped the baby and evaluated him with quivering hands before transferring him to a clean blanket and then to his mother.

"My baby! My baby!" Imelda held out her hands for the infant who was crying himself into a healthy pink. She cooed over him as Ben clamped and cut the umbilical cord, a process which Imelda appeared not to feel at all. He and Rose were busy with third-stage labor, but for Imelda, the trial was over.

After a good first nursing, Imelda held her new son to her cheek. The infant returned her gaze with blurry blue eyes almost too big to be real. Imelda laughed and kissed him as he tried unsuccessfully to focus on her. "Oh, Ben, Lin, Rose, thank you! Thank you!"

"Thank God," Ben said quietly, and moved away to sit on the bed near Rose. His hands shook, and tears dimmed the sight of maternal bonding before him. He looked from Imelda, who was oblivious now to anything but her child, to Linda, who stood above the mother and son with a tear-streaked face, but Ben's gaze rested on Rose. She reached toward him and buried herself in the folds of his sweat-stained shirt, wetting it even more.

"It's all right, Rose; everything is all right." Ben smoothed the shining black hair and kissed the top of her head. "Praise the Lord, it's all right!" He bent and rested his cheek on hers, neither knowing nor caring which of their tears trickled down his face.

"Hey, you two!" Linda said. "Quit your crying and come see the new baby!"

"I think I've already had the pleasure," Ben replied, helping Rose up. They held hands and stood before Imelda, whose brown eyes looked soft as a doe's.

"Doctor, Nurse," Imelda said, dipping her head to Ben and Rose in turn, "I have four children, now five, thanks to you. And since I already have one Linda, I want to name this baby after you."

They looked at her quizzically.

"Both of us?" Rose asked.

"Yes," Imelda nodded firmly. "Benjamin, Rose, I want you to meet Benjamin Rose Nightsky."

Standing near the doorway where she and Mark had crept, Maddie gave her blessing. "A fine choice, Imelda, if a bit colorful. And you could always just use the middle initial: Benjamin R. Nightsky."

Imelda shrugged. "My baby will be Benjamin Rose. And he and I will never forget you or this night. And George," she said, scowling briefly, "I will never let him forget it either. He's a good man, but in a card game or when he paints, he forgets everything."

"I don't doubt it," said Rose. "He's a serious painter. I even have one of his paintings. Magnificent."

Imelda shrugged. "Serious painter, forgetful husband."

218

Imelda shrugged again. "But all is well. I thank you for coming, Doctor."

Doctor. The name finally seemed to fit him, and Ben bowed his head, afraid that his eyes would become moist again. "Thank you, Imelda. I'm very glad to have been here." He blinked hard and raised his face. "And thank you, Linda and Rose, Maddie and Mark. Without your help and prayers—well, who knows what would have happened?"

"God knows," Maddie said. "And I think God's the only one who needs to know."

Imelda ordered Maddie and Mark to come near so she could show off her baby. In the midst of congratulations and compliments, and after making his last evaluation, Ben slipped out of the room.

In the hall, he turned and saw Rose looking after him. He smiled but didn't invite her to follow. Rose smiled back and nodded as he continued down the hall.

The living room was dark and quiet. Ben sat heavily on the couch and stared straight ahead until his weariness lessened. He rubbed his throbbing temples, lowered his head, and covered his face with his hands.

As soon as his breathing was normal and his mind was clearer, he slid from the couch to his knees, folded his hands, and closed his eyes.

Thank you, Lord God, for the miracle of life, for how you give meaning and purpose and direction to your children. Thank you for helping me save that baby and for providing help for Imelda. I know now what I am supposed to be. Now, I know.

Ben spent more time in prayer, then straightened and headed back to the bedroom to check on his first of many patients.

Twenty-One

Maddie and the bunch from Singing Pines were in high spirits as they tripped down the path to the boats. The sun was beginning to shed its rays through the thick mist, and the morning was soft and still, so unlike the windy night before.

"Watch out!" Rose cried. "You're going too fast, Auntie. How can you see where you're going in this fog? All we need are some broken skulls!"

"Nothing bad can happen now, Rose," Maddie called, keeping her quick pace. "I feel about as invulnerable as you did after your rescue. Praise God for the birth of that precious child!"

Ben dropped back and kept Rose with him. After only a few seconds, Maddie and Mark were invisible in the fog.

"Rose! Rose, are you coming?" a voice called.

"Tell her yes," Ben whispered, "and challenge her and Mark to a race home. I'm feeling pretty good myself. Tired, but very good."

Rose relayed the message and soon they heard a kicker start up and buzz away. She pulled on Ben's hand. "That's enough of a head start. Let's go! They'll beat us."

"No, they won't." Ben carefully wound his way down the path, holding Rose's hand. "No need for rashness. I know a shortcut."

"I can still hear them, but I can't see them. I think the mist is even thicker now."

"Sometimes it does that, gets thickest just before it fades away. The sun's rising. The fog can't last too long." Ben halted. "Easy, now. Here's the first board of the dock. And is the wood ever slick!" He held her close and together they slid to his boat.

"It's another miracle that Auntie didn't fall. She sure is full of pep."

"Yes, she is," Ben agreed, helping Rose in. "And I wouldn't want her any other way. That's Maddie."

"I'm not criticizing. I wish I were more like her—more like Jesse. Lilla's been telling me how energetic she was, and the times you two had."

"Lilla?" Ben was about to start the motor. He paused. "How would she know?"

"She said you told her."

"I guess I did, once. But that was a few years ago. I didn't expect a featherbrain like her to remember."

"Ben! Lilla isn't a featherbrain."

"No, you're right. I'm sorry. She isn't a featherbrain, she just acts like one."

"Ben!"

He fended off the light blows Rose rained on his outstretched arm. "Okay, okay," he said, laughing. "I really am sorry this time. I'm just running on adrenaline."

Rose pursed her lips. "That's no excuse."

"Really, Rose, I'm sorry. I didn't mean to insult your friend—my friend, too, for that matter. Lilla is just a little thoughtless sometimes. I didn't expect her to take anything I said to heart, especially something I said so long ago. You're right, though—that doesn't excuse my choice of words. I guess I'm thoughtless, too. I'm riding high, Rose. Please forgive me. Lilla would, don't you think?"

Rose didn't answer. She wondered if she should tell Ben about Lilla's former feelings for him. Maybe then he'd be more considerate of her.

Ben pulled the starter rope and untied the stern line. "Get the bow, will you?"

Rose did, deciding not to reveal Lilla's crush on him. It was a thing of the past, anyway. Ben's place in Lilla's heart was usurped by a lanky, freckled young man from Flag Island called Nick, who matched Lilla perfectly. And though Rose couldn't imagine her friend considering such a serious step as marriage, Nick seemed too suited to Lilla to be anything but a lifetime mate. Rose suspected she'd hear about it the instant it happened; Lilla wouldn't be able to keep a secret like that for very long.

Benjamin started the boat and guided it slowly from the dock. The visibility was extremely low.

Rose grew nervous. "Ben, how can you see to drive? I feel like we're at sea."

He steered a little more to the port side. "Don't worry. We'll skirt the reserve, then cross the channel until we hit a narrow waterway, a favorite shortcut of mine. We'll be able to see land on one side at all times; that'll give us our bearings. It's pretty rock infested, but I know it well. I think it's less risky than Mark's way, down the wide main channel. They'll probably get turned around and have to wait for the sun to burn off the mist. We'll be home in time to have breakfast ready for them."

The boat edged by open water and then a shoreline came into view. "See? No problem. We'll steer by the shore. We'll probably be done eating breakfast before those two get back."

Ben gave the boat more gas, and the engine grew louder. "As long as we stick near the right edge, we'll be fine. This opens up a few miles from Singing Pines, at almost a perfect diagonal." He illustrated with his hand. "I'll keep close to the shoreline, and then go at an angle. Can't miss."

Ben twisted the motor's handle and the boat moved faster. The rocky shore swerved to the right and Ben followed.

"Aren't we going too fast, Ben? I'm getting dizzy watching the shore, and the fog's getting thicker."

"Often does in these little passages. But it's quicker this way. Safer, too. I'd hate to meet a boat out there. Too hard to hear it until you're close. I've heard of crashes in the fog and in the dark, even by experienced guides. You turn a corner and—"

"Ben, I think I hear a boat!"

"You do? How can you hear anything above this motor?"

"Slow the motor and you'll hear it. It's just ahead."

"Rose, this is my private passage. Nobody goes down here. I'm in complete contro—"

As they turned a sharp corner, another boat was in the passage, bearing down on them from the left. Ben spun the throttle to idle and squeezed as close to the shore as he could, but whether his boat hit a submerged rock, or whether the other boat glanced off the bow, Rose never knew. Ben's boat took a blow, and Rose was airborne.

The water was dark, cold. Behind and ahead of her, Rose heard boat motors, one shrill and receding, one sputtering and near. The other driver was leaving them!

"Ben?" Rose turned a circle in the water. She saw the shore through the fog, but nothing more.

"Ben!" She took a few strokes forward. Nothing. "Ben! Ben!" Rose swam and prayed, moving closer to what she estimated was the area of impact, where Ben probably went in. "Ben! Where are—"

Ahead she could make out the orange of a life jacket. Rose swam toward it and saw him, his arms floating limp at his sides, a bloody gash above his temple.

Rose pulled him toward what she hoped was shore. Her legs hit several rocks, and then weeds, a sign that she was heading in the right direction. By the time she dragged him on shore as far as she could, her own body was sore and bleeding.

"Oh, Ben!" Blood flowed from his wound. In an attempt to lessen the bleeding, Rose laid a piece of driftwood under his head to raise it higher than his heart. She tore the sleeves of her shirt and made a bandage to staunch the flow and tried to pull him farther on shore. Then she sat shivering in the fog.

Somewhere in the channel a boat kept on cruising, Ben's boat, Rose was sure. But though the fog was lifting and the air was much lighter, she couldn't see Ben's kicker anywhere. She checked his pulse and felt brief assurance until looking at his bandaged head. A concussion. If only she'd studied concussions with him!

Rose pulled her knees together and laid her head on them. *Dear Lord, I need help! I don't know what else to do, and I don't know how much blood he can lose without harm. Dear God, please help me!*

"Rose?"

She started and turned toward Ben. Could prayers be answered so quickly? "Yes, I'm here. Can't you see me, Ben?"

"I can, but you're spinning. I feel so light-headed...."

"Ben, listen to me. I think you've got a concussion. You've got to tell me what to do!"

He tried to focus. "Rose? You're swirling! And you've got so many faces...every one of them with deep, green eyes ...going round and round and round...." The image must have struck him as funny.

"Ben! Quit laughing! What am I supposed to do?"

"I don't feel like a concussion," Ben giggled. "Feel fine. What happened?"

"We hit something, or maybe that boat hit us. We both went flying. You must've hit a rock on your way in. Now tell me, Ben, what do I do?"

"I'm fine. Feel fine," Ben repeated dully. "Just want to sleep...."

The word sparked a memory: sleep. Concussion victims must not, under any circumstances, sleep. Why Rose did not remember, nor did she remember where she had learned this fact, but she was sure it was right. "Ben! Ben!"

"Hmm?" He squinted at her. "What? Want to sleep...."

"Ben, you can't sleep! You have a concussion. Come on!" Rose lifted his heavy hand and began rubbing, then slapping it.

"Hey!" Ben's eyes opened like shades snapping up, and for a moment he looked angry. Then weariness reasserted itself. His lids drooped.

"Stay awake, Ben! Stay awake!" Rose slapped him harder.

"Hey! Stop! What are you doing?" The blue eyes flew open again, and Rose was relieved to see they were not dilated yet, a sign of heavy concussion.

"I'll stop only if you stay awake," Rose threatened.

"I'm awake!" His speech was less slurred. "Take it easy, Rose!"

"Ben," Rose said patiently, rubbing his red hand, "we had an accident. You hit your head and lost consciousness. You're bleeding. Now what do I do?"

Ben tried to sit up but slumped back down. He groaned. "My whole head feels like its got a pulse!" He touched the bandage and brought his finger before his eyes. "Blood. A concussion?" His words were clear.

"Yes!" Rose could have cried with relief. "I got you to shore. Your boat's still out there somewhere. I can hear it."

Ben tried to sit up again, and again failed. "Guess I'm better off keeping still. Where is the boat? Can you see it?"

"I don't know." Rose turned her head in the motor's direction. "I can see the sun now, but no, I can't see the boat. It's barely moving, from the sound of it. You pulled back hard on the throttle before we crashed. Should I try to get it, Ben?"

"What? The boat or the throttle?" Ben grinned.

"The boat, smart guy." Her spirits rose and she curbed an impulse to kiss him. "Oh, Ben, I'm so glad you're all right!"

"Me, too. But I am sleepy. And you're right, I shouldn't lose consciousness. Brain damage can occur, and I need every ounce of smarts I have for the MCAT. Do you think you can get the boat?"

"I don't know. The mist is lifting fast—Ben, I think I can see the boat!"

"I can't. Rose, I'm having trouble sitting."

She bent down to him, alarm in her eyes. "Ben! What—"

"Don't worry. I shouldn't sit anyway. Listen, I'm fine for now, but it would be good if you could catch the boat and bring back help." He looked around dazedly. "We're not far from Singing Pines…I think. It's just around the corner then out at a diagonal from there, a few miles or so."

"I know, Ben. You told me before the crash. Don't you remember?"

He changed the subject. "Go catch the boat, Rose, if you can. The fog is lighter?"

"Yes, it's just hanging over the water now. I can see the boat clearly. The motor stopped. It looks like it got hung up in the weeds near the other shore. It didn't make the corner."

"It wasn't the only one. Rose, when you reach the boat, paddle out into the channel, clear the weeds with your hand, and then start the motor. Gun it, slam it in reverse, then in forward with plenty of gas, but only for a second. That'll cut any remaining weeds, and you won't move too much ahead."

"What about the rocks? You said this passage was full of them."

"If I said that, I was wrong." His voice sounded harsh. "Listen, once you get past the turn and go at about a forty-five degree angle, it's clear. No rocks. If the fog lifts, you'll be able to see Singing Pines before long."

"What should I do when I get there?"

"Stay and radio for the plane. Mark can come and get me, and I'll worry less if I know you're there. Promise me, okay?"

"Yes." Rose bent down to kiss him. "I love you, Benjamin.

You know that, don't you?"

"Yes, I do. And I love you, too. Now, please go. And be careful. Don't give the motor too much gas until you're past the corner. There are still plenty of rocks until you get there."

"I'll go slowly until I'm past the corner. And Benjamin—I was very proud of you last night. Even with all the blood and pain, I was glad to be with you. It was a privilege."

"Yeah. Uh, thanks, Rose. I was…glad, too."

"Last night made me think of your plans in a new way. Maybe being the wife of a missionary doctor wouldn't be so bad if I could help you. I was thinking that—Ben? Ben!"

"Yeah?"

"You scared me! Your eyes were closed again. I thought you were losing consciousness." She touched his face.

"Maybe I was. I thought I heard you talking about being my wife. Wait, don't say anything. If I didn't hear right, I don't want to know. Leave me with that thought. God go with you, Rose."

She touched his bandage. The crimson was still seeping, and the sight made her rush to the water.

"Don't dive! Remember the rocks!"

"All right!" Rose waded into the water and advanced more slowly, but still she hit several sharp edges. "It's getting deeper, Ben! Here I go!"

Ben held up his hand in a wave and dropped it when he thought she could no longer see it. The weak feelings were returning, and the earth spun, even when Ben closed his eyes.

As Rose made her way toward the entangled boat, the mist was almost gone from the water, but a deeper fog was settling upon the brain of the young man she had left onshore.

Twenty-Two

❧

The float plane didn't stop with its passenger at Singing Pines, but Rose thought one wing tipped toward her as it flew over. "He's in there, Lilla," Rose said, her face lifted to the sky. "He's got to be all right."

"Ned just radioed from the plane," Maddie announced, walking into the porch. "They'll be in Warroad in no time. Dr. Algers is standing by. Praise God the accident happened this morning and not last night!"

"Auntie, did they say whether or not Ben was awake when they got there?"

"They didn't say, but we'll know soon. Here comes Mark."

Rose shook free of Lilla's hand and ran toward her uncle. "Is Ben all right? How was he when you found him?"

"He was—he looked—" Mark turned to his wife for help.

"Rose knows you're not a doctor. She just wants to know if Ben was conscious when you found him, Mark."

Mark's gray eyes were full of compassion. "No, Rose, he wasn't. He didn't come to even when I got him into the boat and drove him to the plane. Ned and I loaded him up, and then they were gone. I'm sure by now, they—"

Rose lowered her face. Mark stepped closer and laid his hand on her shoulder. "I'm sorry, Rosie. Wish I had better news."

He patted his niece's back, but Rose didn't respond. "I'll go inside and listen to the radio, eh? If I hear anything, I'll let you know immediately."

"Rose," Maddie said, standing in the doorway. "The God who helped you and Ben save a child last night is still in control. He's still hearing prayers, still caring for his children, even the adult ones. Do you and Lilla want to come inside, and we'll talk to him about Ben together? We haven't had church yet today."

"Sure," Lilla said, but Rose turned away. "Um, we'll be inside in a minute, Maddie…I guess."

Lilla shuffled toward her friend. "Rose, do you want to talk about it? Sure you do. Come on, let's sit in the swinging chair."

Rose allowed herself to be led and sat mechanically near Lilla, hardly feeling the concerned pressure of her friend's arm around her shoulders or the rocking motion of the swinging chair. The swinging chair…site of so many talks between her and Maddie, her and Lilla, her and Ben. After meals and before them, always talking and swinging, Rose remembered. If she had known those times would come to an end so abruptly, she would have cherished them more then, not now, when they were over.

"What are you thinking, Rose?" Lilla ventured.

Rose answered in a monotone. "About swinging and talking. So many words here, with you, Auntie…Ben." Her mouth clamped closed.

"Ben." Lilla pounced on the name like a drowning person on a ring buoy. "Ben's going to be okay, Rose."

"How do you know, Lilla? Are you a doctor?" The words were slivers of fire and ice, and Rose repented of them immediately. "I'm sorry, Lilla, I—"

"No, you're right. You're totally right. I don't know if Ben's going to be okay. Neither do you. Probably the only one who does know right now is Dr. Algers...and God."

And I think God's the only one who needs to know, came Aunt Maddie's words. Rose remembered her saying them after little Benjamin Rose's birth. The phrase was Aunt Maddie's answer to the battle of the what-ifs, her final answer: All that humans could never even hope to know, God knew. The thought comforted Rose some, but not enough. Not nearly.

"He knows," Rose murmured. "God knows. But does he care? Will he do something about it? Will he save Benjamin?"

Lilla squirmed. "I'm not Maddie, Rose. I don't know how to answer that. He cares, I guess. And he's already done something. You and Ben survived getting hit by a boat or rock or whatever it was in the fog, right? And you found him and brought him to shore. And then the boat got stuck in the weeds so you could get it and come back for help. That's all something, isn't it? What if the fog hadn't lifted or you never found Ben at all? Oh, don't cry, Rose! I'm no good at this! Oh, why can't I keep my mouth shut!"

Lilla started to stand and Rose stopped her. "No, Lilla, don't go. You're right. I know God has spared us from so much already. But if Ben dies...I..."

"It's okay, Rose. It's okay." Lilla patted her awkwardly. "I mean, I don't know if it's okay, but...Oh, Rose, never mind!" Lilla sobbed into her friend's hair. The two young women cried and leaned on each other for support.

Rose recovered first and shifted Lilla to her shoulder. "It's okay, Lilla. Now you've got me saying it! What I mean is, I'm doing better now, so you can stop crying."

"I'm not!" Lilla wailed.

Rose held her and rocked the swing gently. She thought about the afternoons she and Ben had spent on the lake: their first sunrise together on her first fishing trip, the day he'd taught her to water ski, stargazing at Eagle Rock, the night of the fireworks…all lovely memories, gifts from God already. She didn't want the tears that gathered in her eyes, and shook her head to banish them.

Lilla looked up, wiping her cheeks. "What are you doing?"

"I'm sorry. Go on with your cry. I was just thinking.…"

Lilla snatched a tissue from the table near the swinging chair and blew her nose loudly. "I'm done crying. Sorry I got eye juice on your shoulder." She took another tissue and dabbed at Rose ineffectively. "What were you thinking about?"

"Ben, of course. I was remembering times we've had together. Do you know, Lilla, I've sat by him and pretended to paint, all the while dreaming of being his wife? And I never admitted it, except when he was almost delirious. Fear, or pride, stopped me; I'm not sure which. But if he comes out of this all right, I'm going to tell him straight out. See if I don't!"

"I believe you, I believe you, Rose!" Lilla's eyes were wide. "What—what else did you remember?"

"Oh, many things. But you know what? I don't think now is the time for memories. I think Auntie's right. Now is the time for prayer!" Rose stood decidedly and hauled a sniffling Lilla behind her, and soon they were kneeling with Mark and Maddie on the floor, their hands joined and their voices and hearts raised in a circle of prayer.

Dr. Algers kept his hand tantalizingly on the doorknob but did not turn it. "You all have to realize that Ben sustained quite an injury and lost a substantial amount of blood. And he did lose consciousness for a short time."

"But Dr. Algers, didn't you say that Ben had no long-term damage done? He'll be fine, won't he?" Maddie asked.

"That's what I told you, and that's what I told his parents when they called and asked the same question. I don't believe he will suffer from any serious long-term effects. However, he has some short-term memory loss, and even now he shows some confusion. I just wanted to prepare you all before I open this door. Ben may not seem exactly like the Ben we know. Be patient, don't draw attention to his difficulties, and I think he'll become more and more clearheaded as the days progress."

"Doctor," Rose said, clutching a vase of wildflowers and a portrait she'd done for Ben as a get-well gift, "how far back does the memory loss extend? Ben is taking the MCAT in a few weeks now. He'll be able to remember all he's studied, won't he?"

Dr. Algers pulled on his beard. "It's hard to say. He'll probably remember what he did several weeks ago, but the events of this week and even those of last week might be completely erased. We'll have to wait and see."

"He'll know all of us, won't he?" Lilla asked. "I mean, um, I won't know what to say if he doesn't know who I am. You know? Oh, I hate hospitals! Wish Nick could've come."

"This isn't amnesia," Dr. Algers said. "Everything Ben has known for more than the short time surrounding his accident, he will still know. As I said, someday he may recall even those events. I've seen it go both ways. Now, are you all prepared?"

The four comrades from Singing Pines nodded and murmured their readiness.

"There's no time limit on visiting, except Ben's own. If you see him becoming drowsy, it would be best if you left."

"It's safe if he sleeps now?" Rose asked anxiously. She bent too far over, and water from her vase dribbled down the front of her green dress. She wiped it away impatiently.

"Yes, perfectly safe. Should I open the door now?"

Rose nodded and stepped back.

Ben, clothed in white, lay in a bed of white, surrounded by a room of white. He raised his hand in greeting. Rose was relieved to see no bandage on his head, only a neat track of stitches.

"This place is creepy!" Lilla whispered to Mark. "Ben looks like he's all laid out for a funeral."

"Well, I'm not," Ben replied, sitting up and punching his pillow. "I'm back from the dead. And I don't plan to visit again— for a while."

Rose placed her flowers and portrait on the bedside table.

"What, no hug? Then what's the point of getting hurt?" Ben wanted to know.

Rose bent down gingerly, careful to avoid putting any of her weight on him.

Ben cocked his head. "Hm. I've had better hugs from you, my love, if my memory serves me correctly. Rose, I'm not in critical care. If everything checks out, they're actually releasing me today, you know."

"No, we didn't. Dr. Algers didn't say anything about it," Maddie said. "I'm certainly glad we could come in today. We would have loved to come yesterday, but the water was too rough, the resort was swamped, and Dr. Algers didn't want you disturbed."

"Yeah, he's been observing me very closely. I've had enough observation. Usually they only keep you overnight for minor head injuries like mine, but being the Doc's favorite..." Ben shrugged. "So, what do you think of his needlework?"

"Nifty, eh?" Mark said. "Wonder if he ties a good lure."

Ben laughed. "Maybe we should try him out next summer. I did tell you about my plans to guide for you next summer, didn't I?"

"Yes, Ben, just a few days ago."

"Oh, yes," Ben answered vaguely. "Well, I'll be coming home soon. Sure will be good to get out of here. Did the Doc tell you he's releasing me today?"

"Um, no, *you* did, Ben," Lilla said. "Don't you remem—"

Rose dug her in the ribs. "I'm so glad, Ben. I've been sitting on our spot and drawing, but it isn't the same without you. Nothing is the same." She placed her hand in his.

"Thanks, my love. I can hardly wait to get out of here. Seems like a long, long time since I was at the island. The last thing I remember is leaving it to go to the reserve. Things get fuzzy after that. Oh, well, soon I'll be home; then I'll remember. I'm being released today, as soon as I get the okay. Won't that be great?"

Rose nodded miserably.

"Well, you all don't look too happy about it! What's wrong? Did you forget me in two days?"

"Not at all," Maddie soothed. "We've been thinking of nothing but you since the accident, Ben, and we're so glad to see you now that conversation doesn't come easily. I'm sure most of us are giving thanks to the Lord right now just for being able to see you again." She smoothed the hair on his head, being careful to stay clear of his gash. "Quite a nasty cut you have there. It's a good thing you had Rose to take care of you."

Rose saw the blank look on Ben's face and his struggle to remember. "That's not what you said when I told you what happened, Auntie, remember?" With her eyes, Rose cued her aunt to answer the question.

"Yes," Maddie answered, understanding. "I said, 'It was God who allowed you to find Ben so easily in the fog, and God who kept the boat close at hand.' I wonder, though. Was it the other boat or a rock that caused you two to fly into the water?"

"It happened so fast. Your guess is as good as mine. What do you think, Uncle Mark?" Rose saw Ben listening carefully, recording in his mind the events that plagued him by their absence. Getting the story at last was a mental relief for him. She could see the tension draining from his face.

"No telling, eh? But I had no trouble finding Ben on shore," Mark supplied, evidently comprehending the game. "And Ned flew up right away. We got you here as quickly as we could, and Dr. Algers was ready on the spot. Praise God, Ben, we're so happy to see you!"

Ben settled into his pillows. "So that's how it went," he said softly, and closed his eyes. "Well, it's over. I'm coming home."

"Just in time to get in a few weeks of study for the MCAT," Rose said.

"The MCAT?" Ben asked, his eyes blue with wonder. "What's that?"

Rose's mouth dropped open. She looked to her aunt for help.

"Just kidding!" Ben squeezed Rose's hand. "As if I could ever forget that, even if I tried. Rob—Dr. Algers, that is—says I should take it easy for awhile and only study when I feel up to it. I have to confess, my head is still a little sore." He raised his hand to the black stitches and winced.

"Of course it is, Ben," Maddie said. "Now I think you should have some rest. Dr. Algers warned us not to tire you out. We'll all go eat and come back as soon as he says we can take you home. Are you certain you're up to a ride in the boat?"

"Doc's arranged my passage on the *Wanderer* tomorrow morning but says I can't go unless the lake is calm. I'll be released from here later today if everything checks out."

"Well, we can all stay at your sister's place tonight, don't you think, Mark?"

"Sure. Mardella's always asking us to come stay with her. She won't mind a few more. She's told me so often enough."

"And then when the *Wanderer* leaves in the morning, we'll escort you home, Ben," Maddie said. "Or maybe Rose can be your traveling nurse, and we'll meet you at Singing Pines for the end-all welcome home feast! Right, Ben? Ben?"

"What? Uh, that'd be great, Maddie," Ben replied, continuing to gaze at Rose.

Lilla, Maddie, and Mark said their farewells and left discreetly. Rose didn't turn her head when the door closed.

"Ben," she began, holding his hand to her cheek, "there's so much I want to tell you; but not here—" She looked around the sterile atmosphere and back to the man she loved: a prisoner in white. His robust body did not belong in a hospital bed; his sharp mind did not deserve to be bruised and muddied.

Even as she felt these things, Rose knew they were wrong, a selfish manifestation of the old nature she thought she'd shed for good the night she and Aunt Maddie and Uncle Mark knelt on the kitchen floor in prayer.

She had felt God's presence then, experienced his love in a way she hadn't since the day she was born again, when she realized the man who had hung on the cross was the Son of God, suffering and dying to pay for her sins. Rose had immediately repented and given her life and allegiance to him, but the days following had choked the seed that sprung up in her heart, making it weak, crowding it out with worldly worries and riches. Her good breeding taught her to keep God and everything about him inside, separated from life. The night she, Aunt Maddie, and Uncle Mark had prayed, the weeds had been uprooted and flung aside, and Rose began to grow again. That night she knew God wasn't merely part of life: God was life. And he cherished her.

Ben sat up and took her hands in his. "Rose, it doesn't matter where we are or where we will be. I love you. And I want to thank you for your courage. I owe my life to you."

"Ben!" Rose's voice was sharp with dismay. "One of the things I learned through all this is that God is in control—not me. I prayed to him, Ben, and felt him answering me, comforting me, like he did the night Imelda gave birth. Jesus is alive and working! He's the one who saved you, not me."

She turned her head as a nurse entered the room and began reading Benjamin's chart. "I guess I'd better leave. Ben, what's wrong?"

"Nothing, nothing." Tears lined his lower lids. "I was just thinking how much you sound like a missionary."

Rose lifted her head in surprise, then smiled. "Maybe I do at that." She remembered her dreams of being Ben's wife. Maybe God was preparing her for that role after all. Rose bent down and placed her hand on his cheek, then turned to leave the room. "Remind me to tell you more about that subject some-time," she said, and threw Ben a kiss from the threshold.

He pretended to catch it. "Got it!" He waved his closed hand over his head as the nurse strapped a blood-pressure sleeve on his other arm and began filling it with air. "I got it, Rose. And I'll never let it go."

Twenty-Three

A s the hot, lazy days of August progressed, Ben gradually regained his memory about everything but the accident itself. He and Rose spent time among the islands, searching for plump blueberries to fill their stomachs and supply Maddie with the makings for pie, jam, and juice.

Many afternoons would find them in some fern fen, sitting in a bed of springy moss, heaping buckets of blue within a hand's reach, ready to serve as refreshment. Ben would study and Rose would sit at his side, sketching or singing. Oftentimes she would do both.

The summer was ending, though the weather was the most pleasant and calm of the season. Highs were in the eighties and nineties, and the skies were consistently clear and blue. The leaves, which had been so full and verdant not long ago, began showing the faintest yellows of autumn, and purple aster and goldenrod replaced the wildflowers of middle summer. Algae invaded the lake, turning the water to green, and now when Benjamin made his sprays while skiing, the rainbow did not appear.

After many false starts, dunkings, and wipe outs, Rose had finally mastered slalom skiing, and though her sprays were much lower than Ben's, she jumped the wake well, and skied with a grace and abandon that surpassed his own. She loved to be on the water, near the lake, or on an island. In one of their final forays together, Rose told Ben that she had found her niche.

"Really?" Ben stopped gleaning the last of the season's blueberry crop from a thick bush. "So you're not going home this fall?"

Rose adjusted her back against a moss-covered stump. "I don't think so, even though Mother's expecting me. I'd like to be completely reconciled with her, the way you and your parents are becoming now, but a letter won't do it. I'd have to go home, and I want to see autumn here...and winter...and the early spring. I think if I lived on the lake for one year, observing and drawing the seasons, my art would improve so much that I might be able to sell it. There's a place in Lakeshore City that I think might take some. Imelda's husband, George, sells there. The last time I helped you and Rob at the reserve, I talked to George and he said he might be able to arrange it. I want to get better before I try that, though."

Ben tilted the canvas of her latest work, a picture she'd done from memory of a pink lady's slipper. Though the sketch was in black and white, the flower and foliage were accurate as a photograph, and as beautiful and delicate as the real thing.

"I'd say you could sell your work now," Ben said.

"Maybe, but I want to get better, do more finished work and less sketching. I have a dozen or so sketches that could be good acrylics, I think. Maybe when the resort closes this fall I'll have the time to do them."

"You want to be an artist, then?"

Rose balanced the tip of her pencil on her lip and studied her sketch. "No. I *am* an artist, and I'll never give it up. But I want to be a doctor."

"Rose! When did you decide that?"

"Medicine has always interested me; you know that. But when I told Frederick and my parents I wanted to be a surgeon, I was doing it to impress them. I wasn't deciding it for myself. After Frederick and I broke up, I had my art, and that was enough. But ever since the storm, I started wondering why I was still alive, what meaning and purpose my life had—or was supposed to have. I didn't know, but after your accident, I realized how much I wanted to be a doctor. A family practitioner, not a surgeon. I want to help people, Ben. I want to heal them, with God's help."

"So you're ready to try again?"

Rose rested her hand on Ben's knee. "When I first came up here, I was looking for an escape, a place to hide from pain. There is no such place, I realize now. Unless you live a life without risk, without feeling, there will be pain—and pleasure." Her smile expressed the change in her soul, an awakening, like a flower's unfolding, full of blooming, rustling beauty.

"I've found God here, and I've found you. Ben, when I had to leave you on that island, it tore me apart. I didn't know if you would live or die, but I knew I had to get help or you would die for sure. I wished I knew more about medicine then, more than I ever had before. I spent the day praying for you, thinking of you and all the things we'd shared. I realized I'd been holding a part of myself back, letting you get just so close before I'd pull away and shut you out again, just like you said. Remember the day you asked me if I could ever be the wife of a missionary doctor?"

"Yes." Ben hadn't shifted his gaze from her since she'd begun speaking, and he'd hardly moved. Now he inched closer and tucked her near him so she rested in his arms. "I remember, Rose. You think you could now?"

"I'm still not completely ready to answer that, but I want you to know I've considered it. I've dreamed about it. While you were in the hospital, I wished with everything inside me that someday it could be true, that someday I could be your wife, maybe even your peer—a doctor, too, and we could do missionary work up here together. But before that happens, if it ever does, I have some searching of my own to do. I've learned a lot from helping you study. I learned so much the night we helped Imelda have her baby. That night helped me overcome my failure at the emergency room." She smiled. "Can you remember delivering Benjamin Rose yet?"

"Parts of it. Emotions more than events. That was the night I really felt God calling me to be a doctor. I've been sure of it ever since."

She nodded. "If you do well on the MCAT."

"Rose, I feel prepared. I've studied hard. I don't want to sound overconfident, but I know I'll do well on the MCAT, at least well enough for some medical school to accept me next fall. I'll probably never darken the halls of Harvard or any other Ivy League school, but somewhere there's a program for me. And a couple years after that, there'll be an internship available with my name on it, and then an opportunity to do my residency. Then, at last, I'll come back here."

He tucked a lock of hair behind her ear. "Rose, where will you be?"

She looked at the mossy ground. "I don't know. I can't ask you to wait."

"I will, though. And meanwhile I'll be doing what I love. It won't seem long to me. Rose, can I dare believe, can I dare hope that...someday you'll be my wife?"

Her hands had been picking at the moss. She stopped and flung them around his middle, leaning hard against him. "Maybe someday." She raised her eyes, but he wasn't looking at her.

"My future seems...like smoke, without you, Rose, like grayness, loneliness. If I can't even hope for someday—"

"Ben, I know that's a horrible answer! I wish it could be better, but you have your calling; I have to make sure of mine. I can support myself now, through my art, maybe, or at least through housecleaning. I plan to spend the winter working on my art, and then enroll in a pre-med program next fall, if I've earned enough money. Aunt Maddie said I can have a job here next summer, and with that and a few pieces sold, I could make it half a year. Then I could start school and get work study. Completing my courses will probably take a little less than two years, so I'm already that far behind you."

He touched her cheek. "Are you telling me I only have to wait two years after I'm done with my own studies, or are you saying I have to wait that long before you'll tell me whether or not I have a chance?"

"Do you really think you'll still want to marry me in two years? Or four? Or six? That's a long time. So much could happen before then. I want to be sure. I want you to be sure!"

"I am sure, Rose. I'd marry you today if you'd let me, and I'm not going to change my mind, no matter how many days go by. I'll be working, going to school, and finally setting up my own practice here; but every day I'll be marking time until you join me—if you ever choose to join me."

"Ben—" Rose groped for the right words. "I love you, you know I love you; but if I did marry you, how could I do everything I want to do? We couldn't be married with both of us going to school!"

"I don't know about that. You make a great study partner. And I could use a little help with the rent and cooking—"

"Benjamin!" Rose laughed and swatted him. "But I never did think of it that way. Do you think we could end up going to the same school? It might happen. Wouldn't that be something? I mean, even if we weren't married."

"Yes, it would. I know who would be my study partner, even if she wouldn't do the dishes." Ben sighed and rubbed his shoulders against the stump. He waited for Rose to get settled comfortably before he continued. "Rose, after Jesse died, I was bitter. Bitter even against God, and I didn't know it. You have changed me. This summer has changed me. God has changed me."

"And me," Rose was glad to say. She turned her cheek so it rested against him. "Where do you think we'll be this time next year?"

He nuzzled her ear. "No telling. Didn't you say you'd be starting school?"

She craned her neck and gave him an impish grin. "Maybe. Or maybe I'll be selling my art from home while my husband is in medical school."

"I don't dare think about that." Ben kissed his way across her cheek to her lips, then pulled back reluctantly. "Rose, do you ever worry we'll get carried away so many miles from the nearest chaperon?"

"God is our chaperon. It's never just you and me, Ben. No matter where we are. God is everywhere, and I know you take your orders from him. I want to, too. I was just reading this morning about how there's no place on earth where God is not. Psalm 139—I've been memorizing it: 'If I take the wings of the dawn, If I dwell in the remotest part of the sea, Even there Thy hand will lead me.'" She kissed him. "But we really should get back."

"I hate to leave, but you're right. I should master the last chapter in my inorganic chemistry book. Can you believe I'll be taking the MCAT in less than two weeks?"

"No." She held him tighter. "So soon?"

"I'll be catching the *Wanderer* out of here on her last voyage."

"Her last? You mean for the season?"

"I mean forever. Didn't Maddie tell you? The coast guard issued a directive last summer about freighters. More regulations, and the *Wanderer* will never meet them, Cap says. She barely made the regulation for steel hulls in the seventies that took every other freighter off the lake. The deadline falls the first part of September. Cap figures he'll make the last run about the time I need to go, then he'll have her pulled out and grounded in Warroad."

Rose shook her head. "That beautiful old boat."

"She's not so beautiful, but I love her, too. Can't imagine what it'll do to old Cap."

Rose recalled her first voyage. It seemed so long ago. Her life had been empty of Ben, of Aunt Maddie, Uncle Mark, and Lilla, of wildflowers, and islands, and waterskiing, and God. Her life had been empty.

Could I ever stand to leave this place? And is it the lake I've fallen in love with, too, or only the man who's helped me come to know it? Truthfully, she didn't know.

"The lake will seem so different to me when you leave, Ben, as it was when you were in the hospital."

She arranged the hairs on his forearm with her fingertip. "I can't imagine saying goodbye to you."

"Then don't." Ben took her hand urgently. "Come with me, Rose! We wouldn't have to get married right away, not until you're sure; you could live with your parents, finish your sketches, find work or save money—maybe take your math and science courses. After the MCAT, I'm staying in the cities and working until I get into a program next fall. Hey! I could wait until you finish your pre-med courses and take the MCAT, and we could start med school together! What do you say?"

Rose laughed. "I say you are off and running, my love. It is tempting, though.... Don't get me started, Benjamin," she finished. "Let's just play this one by ear, all right?"

"Okay, Sweetheart," Ben drawled. "We'll play it by ear. Or by nose. By cheek—" he kissed each as he named it.

"Come on, Romeo." Rose brushed him away and stood. "We've picked this place clean. Are you in the mood to study?"

"Study what?" Ben deadpanned.

"That answers my question. Then let's go skiing. One last run before you leave me."

"I'm not leaving for days."

"But the days will fly. We'll be trying to do everything we've already done in order to store up memories to last until you come back. That means fishing, swimming, having shore lunches and going on walks, watching sunsets and sunrises, not to mention reviewing everything you've studied this summer. Before

247

you know it, Benjamin Haralson, the *Wanderer* will be docked at Singing Pines, and you'll be climbing on board."

"You may be right," Ben returned, taking her hand and leading her through the woods to the boat, "but until then, let's pretend I'm not going. Let's dispense with a countdown and live as if our time together will never end."

"Agreed," Rose said, but in her mind she saw him leaving even as he walked in front of her. She saw his hand raised in farewell, saw herself and Aunt Maddie waving from the dock. They could pretend all they wanted that their time was not running out, but it was, and the *Wanderer's* whistle was only moments away.

Twenty-Four

❧

The small cabin on the point was swept clean and ready to be closed up for the season. Its bookshelves, drawers, and closets were empty, and the books and clothes which had sat in them all summer were now packed in the two suitcases and one huge duffel bag at Ben's feet.

Rose stood beside it, her hands now thrust deep into the pockets of her jeans, now reaching around Ben for another good-bye hug. Though they had been waiting together on the dock for more than a half hour, few words had passed between them.

Sunlight splashed on their backs and the shadow cast by Ben's duffel bag looked like a gargoyle. The rays were hot; the lake was still. It would have been a perfect afternoon for one more ski run, but neither said so. The skis were hanging in the shed, and when Rose handed them to Ben to put up in the rafters, she promised herself she wouldn't take them down again until he returned.

As if reading her mind, Ben said, "I shouldn't have put the skis so high. You and Lilla will have a hard time reaching them. Go on a run for me this evening, will you? Just as the sunset is the brightest. Run your fingers across the reflections like you always do. I'd like to know that's what you're doing tonight."

"What will you be doing?"

"Probably reading or telling stories to the kids. Mark's sister loves it when I do that, and I owe her one for staying there last time when you all came to visit me at the hospital. I'm sure the kids have my whole evening planned."

"That's good." Rose motioned him to sit as she just had. "It will get the yarns out of your system before you return to civilization."

"Civilization? I never think of the cities as that. Unnatural, impersonal, out of whack, yes. But civilized? Lake of the Woods is a lot more civilized than any city I've ever been in, Minneapolis included." Ben sat behind Rose, and their feet dangled above the water.

"If you feel that way, why go?" Rose's voice sounded spiteful, and she dropped her head forward so that her long hair hung over her face and hid it.

Ben's voice was soft and low. "I go so I can come back, my love. So that someday we can live here forever—work and play and live and love here always, you, me…and our kids."

He looked into the water. "I can see them now, the little scamps. Can't you? Running around, causing trouble, into everything—each one with the flashing green eyes of their mother and towheaded like me. Can you imagine our children, Rose?"

"Yes, I can." Her head came up as she thought about it. But in her vision, their children were all tiny replicas of Ben; even the girls, with their long, blonde braids, had a shadow of his strength and all the mutable blueness of his eyes. Eyes the color of periwinkle blossoms, she had decided the instant she allowed herself to really look at them. How much time had she wasted before then? How much time was she about to waste?

"I suppose Eric will be trying to cut in on me now, won't he?" Ben asked, drawing his arms tighter around Rose's waist.

She glanced at him. "Didn't Auntie tell you?"

"What?"

It was too late to withdraw her words. He was looking at her intently, and Rose knew that she had to break the news herself. "He was taken away after the accident, Ben. He's in treatment for alcoholism. The Ontario Provincial Police stopped him the morning of our accident. He was driving a stolen boat like a maniac. It was filled with beer cans, empty and full. He'd been tossing some overboard as he went. They think Eric might be the one who drove us into the rock or hit us himself, though there's no proof. They never found his boat, but he could've sunk it. I thought the boat that turned into us was flat and black, like his. It was going so fast, and the fog was so thick that I'll never be sure, but it could've been."

Ben shook his head. "I don't think so. Eric couldn't have known about that passage. And even if he did, he could never have maneuvered it, drunk and in fog and going wide open. And if he did hit us, why didn't he go flying, too?"

"Maybe he was strapped in. Maybe he wasn't drunk yet. Maybe he was just coming into the passage when we met him, or maybe he slowed down after that, or followed your wake trail."

"Maybe," Ben conceded. "It really doesn't matter. I'm okay, you're okay. As you say, we might have hit him or someone else or even a rock. No use blaming him for something we're not sure about. Sounds as if he's got enough problems of his own."

251

"I'm glad you feel that way, Ben, because there's more: Eric snapped. Part of the reason the OPP took him in was because he wouldn't stop when they flagged him down. He led them on a chase and didn't stop until they boxed him in. When they brought him to the resort, he was out of control, rambling on and on about Jesse. Ben, he said that *it had happened again and he didn't mean it.* He begged Aunt Maddie and Uncle Mark to forgive him. He seemed to think I was dead, too, although I was standing right in front of him."

Now it was Rose who used the mirror at their feet to read Ben's expression. "Ben," she said gently, "it doesn't mean that's what happened. Eric was nearly crazy. Ben, are you all right?"

His face had gone pale except for the shadows under his eyes, and he seemed focused on something far away.

"Ben?" Rose wondered if this news would have been better told in a letter or on a future visit instead of the afternoon of his departure. But his first words assured her that she had done right.

"I think Eric loved Jesse, too. They were going out before I came on the scene. Maybe I shouldn't have cut in on him. Anyway, Jesse warned me about him. She said he'd never let her go. I didn't pay much attention. When she died, he was the one who found her."

Ben paused to pass his hand over his eyes and rub his temples. "I guess I blamed him for killing her at first, not that I had any reason. From all indications, he had been trying to save her when the others got there. It was no use. He said...He said she died in his arms." Ben choked a little, but managed to keep speaking. "That must have given him a lot of trauma...a lot of guilt."

Rose reached for him and Ben took her hand, holding it between his own. "I had my own trouble with guilt, too. After I realized it wasn't Eric's fault, I took all the blame for Jesse's death. That wasn't much more logical, I know, but I was almost crazy myself for awhile."

A long sigh welled up from within him, leaving his shoulders deflated. "Even if Eric...did have something to do with Jesse's accident...even if he ran into us, I refuse to get into a war of hate again." His voice picked up speed and conviction. "No matter what the circumstances of Jesse's death and our accident, God allowed it all to happen. For some reason, he let it occur. If I'm going to blame anyone, it has to be God, and I know that's wrong." Ben straightened and Rose nestled against him.

"He's given you to me, Rose—not as a replacement for Jesse, but as a new beginning for me. I loved Jesse and couldn't let her go. Now I love you, and I have to let you go. God is teaching me through you that 'love is patient' and 'kind....' It 'believes all things, hopes all things, endures all things. Love never fails.' That was in my morning reading today, and I thought of you the second I read it. That's how God's love is. It's how I want my love for you to be. By God's grace, in six more years or so, I won't have to let you go again. Until then, I trust you to my Father's care."

Their kiss was long and chaste, a pledge of patience rather than passion, though that, too, was in its powerful undercurrents. How long it lasted Rose didn't know, and she wondered how long it might have gone on if not for a faraway whistle blast that made her release Ben and look past his shoulder.

In the distance, a slow-moving vessel of white and gray cut the water, creating a line of silver that extended from its bow and trailed behind it; it was a line that caught the sun's rays and burned almost as brightly as that heavenly body itself. It looked to Rose like a lifeline, but this time, she held onto Ben tightly and prayed to her Father above.

"Well, I guess that's it. Mark, Maddie, thanks for everything." Ben shook hands with Mark and pretended to do the same with Maddie.

"Ohh, you!" the short woman said, and pushed his hand aside, wrapping her arms around him, standing on tiptoe to plant a motherly kiss on his cheek. "We'll be praying for you, Ben. You'll do just fine on your test. Let us know as soon as you can, will you? Maybe this Christmas we can all come for a visit."

"Not me," Lilla chimed in. "I'll be in Iowa."

"Iowa?" All four people looked at her.

"Nick and I are getting married this Christmas! I don't have a ring yet, but I, um, wanted to announce it before you left, Ben."

Rose threw her arms around her friend and scolded her for waiting so long to tell. Maddie and Mark wished Lilla well, and Ben gave her a hug that lifted her off the ground.

"Congratulations, Lilla. I'm happy for you, I really am," Ben said.

"Whew!" Lilla said, when she was on terra firma again. "No more of that, Ben, or I might tell Nick he's out of luck!" Her smile was wide. "Maybe you'll have an announcement of your own to make this Christmas!" Lilla threw Rose a sidelong glance.

"None of your matchmaking, Lilla," Maddie cautioned. "If there's any to do around here, I'll do it." She looked past Benjamin to the *Wanderer's* deck. "Done with the pie, Cap?"

"Yep. Thanks, Maddie," the thin man responded. "Good as always. Better finish up your good-byes now. I've got a schedule to keep! May be the last time ever that this ol' girl feels the water beneath her hull, but I plan to pull into Warroad on time. We're leaving in five minutes."

Mark took Ben's suitcases. "Wow! Heavy, eh?" He set one back on the dock. "Guess I'll make three separate trips!"

As Mark toiled up the gangplank, Maddie tugged on Lilla's sleeve, and they prudently moved away. Ben turned Rose so that she faced him. His broad back was toward the boat passengers.

"Rose, I'm trying to be calm about all this, but it's ripping me inside out." He enfolded her in his arms and rested his cheek on her head. "You won't forget me, will you? Minneapolis is so far away, hundreds of miles, and it'll be so long before—"

"Benjamin, don't you worry about me. There's not a chance in the world that I could ever forget you or change my mind about you. 'Love never fails,' remember? Always, always know and trust that I love you." She tilted her head and gazed at him. "I have you drawn more clearly on my heart than all the sketches I've ever done or ever will do. Benjamin Haralson, I cherish you!"

"I know you do, I know." His eyes were on the rough boards at his feet. "It's hard for me to believe sometimes. Oh, Rose, if only I didn't have to leave so soon! We've only known each other three months. You won't change your mind, will you? I mean, I know you won't, but there isn't anything that could—"

"There isn't anything," Rose said firmly. "I am bound to you, Ben, not by chains or cords, but by heartstrings. No matter where you go, no matter how long we're apart—" Her voice cracked. "Oh, Benjamin, I can't stand this! I'm trying so hard! I want to be strong for you!" Her voice was watery with tears. "I don't want this to be any harder for you than it is, but Ben—"

Her own weakness awakened the strength in him, and he laid his forefinger on her lips. "Rose, Rose, my love. I'm sorry. I won't doubt you again. You just seemed so cold, it shook me up. I'm sorry for losing faith. If this is love, and I believe it is with all my heart, it will never, never fail." He kissed her damp cheek and turned his head as Cap gave the all aboard and the cabin boy blew the whistle, five short blasts.

"That's the boarding signal. I'd better go. Maddie," he said, transferring Rose from his arms to her aunt's, "take care of her. Take care of my love."

Rose huddled miserably with Maddie's arms around her while Ben ascended the gangplank, carrying on his back the heavy duffel bag Mark had been unable to heave. When Ben reached the halfway point, he turned and threw Rose a kiss. She straightened and pretended to catch it, waving it over her head. "I got it, Ben! I got it." Her voice grew soft. "And I'll never let it go."

When Ben reached the deck, he tossed his bag into the hold and made sure his suitcases were safely stowed. He turned around to wave to Rose, but she was nowhere to be seen. Maddie and Lilla raised their hands to him, and Mark skipped up the plank.

"Where's Rose?" Ben asked, but Mark rushed past and went directly to Cap, who was adjusting the controls and preparing to give his boy the order to cast off.

"Looks like we'll be late after all, eh, Mark?" Cap said. "Well, if ol' Wanda gets a little extra time on her farewell voyage, I won't grudge it to her."

"Mark, where's Rose and what—"

"Goodbye, Ben. And God bless." Mark shook Ben's hand briefly before he was gone.

"Cap? What's going on?"

"Don't just stand there, young man!" Cap said violently. "Give the lady a hand with her bag!"

Ben turned to see Rose flying down Singing Pines's humped back, a small blue bag in her hand and several canvases under her arm.

Maddie pecked Rose on the cheek and hustled her up the gangplank after Rose hugged Mark and Lilla. "Don't worry! We'll send everything else along later. And don't forget to greet your folks for me!" Maddie waved as Ben met Rose.

"You're coming?"

"I'm coming."

He stared at her as if frozen.

"It's all right with you, isn't it?" Rose asked, a mustard seed of doubt creeping into her heart.

Ben threw back his head and uttered a shout of pure joy. He scooped up Rose and carried her and all she held to the main cabin. The gangplank shook under his bounds.

"All right Ben!" Lilla cried, jumping up and down on the dock. "Hey, Rose, maybe we'll make it a double wedding!"

"Maybe we will," Rose called back to her, still in Ben's arms though they had reached the main cabin door. "Goodbye, everyone. Thank you so much! I love you all!"

"Cast off!" Cap cried, and slowly the *Wanderer* pulled away from Singing Pines.

"Hey, Ben, kiss the bride!" Lilla yelled over the freighter's engines, and as the lumbering vessel turned and headed out toward the big lake, the future doctor kissed his future peer and wife so soundly that the cabin boy's eyes were as large as the *Wanderer's* gold steering wheel.

"Well!" Cap chuckled under his breath. "I do believe they'll keep it up all the way to Warroad! Going to be a warm cruise, Wanda ol' girl," he said, patting the steering wheel and guiding the *Wanderer* to her final rest. "Not a bad way to end."

Dear Reader:

I began writing *Cherish* a month before my husband, Mark, and I found out I was pregnant with our first child. I wrote the bulk of the manuscript in between dreaming and choosing names, with time out to return to the lake to visit my family and do "research." I finished the final chapters at home while dealing with the grief of a miscarriage.

The novel's main theme had always been how God heals and gives us the strength to try again, but I defined and expanded that theme as I went through my own healing process. For a while, I was stuck with guilt: Had painting the house before I knew I was pregnant hurt the baby? Had radiation leaked from my old computer? Had I roughhoused too much? What if, despite what the doctors said, it really was my fault?

With the Lord's help, I am moving through the pain. I guess Maddie speaks for me when she gives her answer to the what-ifs: All we can never even hope to know, God knows—and he's the only one who needs to know. *Cherish* is the Lord's gift to me, the first fruits of a dream I've had since childhood and, in part, consolation for the dreams I cherished about our child, who was to have been born in March.

I believe this story may also be a gift for some of you who have been hurt. Whatever your wound, I pray you will be encouraged to open yourself to the Lord Jesus' healing. He can comfort when no one else can. He can heal the deepest pain. He can provide the courage to try again. And he cherishes you.

Constance Colson

Constance Colson
c/o Palisades
P.O. Box 1720
Sisters, Oregon 97759

Palisades…Pure Romance

Titles and dates are subject to change.